P9-DYY-393

The WAR I Finally WON

The WAR I Finally WON

Kimberly Brubaker Bradley

DIAL BOOKS FOR YOUNG READERS

Dial Books for Young Readers
Penguin Young Readers Group
An imprint of Penguin Random House LLC
375 Hudson Street
New York, NY 10014

Copyright © 2017 by Kimberly Brubaker Bradley
Penguin supports copyright. Copyright fuels creativity, encourages diverse voices,
promotes free speech, and creates a vibrant culture. Thank you for buying
an authorized edition of this book and for complying with copyright laws by not
reproducing, scanning, or distributing any part of it in any form without permission.
You are supporting writers and allowing Penguin to
continue to publish books for every reader.

Printed in the United States of America
ISBN 9780525429203

1 3 5 7 9 10 8 6 4 2

Design by Cerise Steel
Text set in Imprint MT Std

This is a work of fiction. Names, characters, places, and incidents
either are the product of the author's imagination or are used fictitiously,
and any resemblance to actual persons, living or dead, businesses,
companies, events, or locales is entirely coincidental.

To Jessica Dandino Garrison

The WAR I Finally WON

Chapter 1

You can know things all you like, but that doesn't mean you believe them.

"Ada! You need to drink something!" Susan's voice, scolding. Susan's hands, pushing a cup of cold tea into mine.

"I don't want to," I said. "Really I don't."

Susan curled my fingers around the teacup. "I understand," she said, "but please try. It's the last thing they're going to let you have. You'll be thirsty in the morning."

My right foot was twisted sideways at the ankle. It had been all my life. My ankle bones grew curled, so my toenails scraped the ground and what should have been the bottom of my foot faced the sky. Walking hurt like anything. Despite the calluses, the skin on my foot tore and bled.

This night in the hospital—nearly three years ago now—was September 16, 1940. A Monday. It was a little over a year into the war between Hitler and most of the rest of the world. Eleven years into the war between the rest of the world and me.

The very next day surgeons were going to chop my curled ankle bones up and rearrange them. Maybe into something like a functional foot.

I put the teacup Susan gave me to my lips. I forced myself to sip. My throat closed. I choked. Tea splattered across the bedcovers and my tray.

Susan sighed. She mopped up the spilled tea, then motioned for one of the nurses that was putting up the blackout to come take away my tray.

Since the start of the war, we covered our windows with blackout screens every night, so that German bombers wouldn't be able to aim at our lights. My hospital wasn't in London, which was getting bombed every night right now, but that didn't mean it wouldn't be hit. You never could tell what Germans would do.

"Letter for you, Mum," the nurse said, handing Susan an envelope as she scooped up the tray.

"Delivered to the hospital? How odd." Susan opened it. "It's from Lady Thorton." She unfolded the letter inside. "She must have sent it before she got my note with the boardinghouse's address. Ada, are you quite sure you don't want something to eat? Toast?"

I shook my head. The mouthful of tea I'd swallowed swirled in my stomach. "I think I'm going to be sick."

Susan gasped. She looked up at me, snatched a basin from the bottom shelf of my bedside table, and thrust it beneath my chin. I clenched my teeth and held everything in.

Susan's hand shook. The basin shook too. I looked at her face. She'd gone pale, her eyes dark and wide.

"What's wrong?" I asked. "What does that letter say?"

"Nothing," she said. "Breathe deep. That's it." She put the basin down, folded Lady Thorton's letter, and tucked it into her handbag.

Something was wrong. I could see it on her face. "Is it Butter?" I asked.

"What?"

"Has something happened to Butter?" Butter was Susan's pony. I loved him. He was staying in Lady Thorton's stables while I was in hospital.

"Oh," Susan said. "No. That is, Lady Thorton didn't mention Butter, but she would have if anything were wrong."

"Maggie?" Maggie was Lady Thorton's daughter, my best friend.

"Maggie's fine," Susan said. Her hands still shook

very slightly. Her eyes didn't look right. "Everyone's fine in the village."

"And Jamie's fine," I said. It was a statement, not a question, because it had to be true. My brother Jamie wasn't in the village—he was here with us. Susan and Jamie and Bovril, Jamie's cat, were staying in a rented room in a boardinghouse near the hospital. Jamie was there with the landlady now.

Jamie was six years old. We'd guessed he was seven, but we had his birth certificate now and he wasn't, not quite.

I was eleven. I had my birth certificate too. I'd known my real birthday for just over a week.

Susan nodded. "Jamie's fine."

I took a deep breath. "Is something stopping my surgery?" Before last week, when Mam tried to snatch us away from her, Susan had said she couldn't give permission for me to have surgery. She still couldn't give permission, but she didn't care anymore. She said that what was right and what was permitted were sometimes different things. I needed surgery and I was going to have it.

I didn't ask questions.

Susan smoothed my hair back from my forehead. I pulled away. "I won't let anything stop your surgery," she said.

There was still something off about her voice and expression. I knew it had to do with Lady Thorton's letter. Lady Thorton could upset just about anyone. When I'd first met her, before I knew her name, I called her the iron-faced woman. She was sharp like an ax.

Lady Thorton couldn't meddle with us here. We'd lost everything inside Susan's house, but I still had Jamie, Susan, Bovril, and Butter. And surgery tomorrow. It was more than enough.

You can know things all you like, but that doesn't mean you believe them.

A little over a year ago, I'd taught myself to walk in Mam's one-room London flat. I kept it secret, wiping up the blood before Mam came home every day. I'd only wanted to be able to leave the flat, not the city, but learning to walk saved me. When Mam sent Jamie away from London with all the other kids, because of Hitler's bombs, I snuck out too. We ended up with Susan and Butter in a seaside village, in Kent.

Susan didn't want us then. We didn't want her either, but I wanted her pony, and Jamie and I both liked her food and eventually we all three wanted to stay with each other. Of course that was when Mam showed up to take us back. Only a week ago, that was. Susan decided to fight for us. She followed us to London, which meant we were all away from Susan's house the night German bombers destroyed it entirely. So the worst thing—Mam's return—became the best thing—not dying from the bombs.

Now everyone was acting like my surgery tomorrow would be the best thing ever, which made me worry it might turn out bad. Susan said it couldn't be bad. She said she hoped my foot would work properly after the surgery, but if it didn't I would be fine. I was fine now and I would be fine afterward, no matter what.

Maybe.

Depended entirely on what you meant by *fine*.

We were still in a war. The nurses claimed they'd be able to get all the patients into the basement quickly enough if the air raid sirens went off. They hadn't had to do it yet, so who knew if they really could.

Susan leaned forward. She hugged me. It was awkward for us both. I let out my breath. My stomach still churned. "Don't worry," Susan said. "I'll see you in the morning. Go to sleep."

I couldn't sleep but the night passed anyhow. In the morning Susan held my hand while a nurse wheeled my bed down the hall. We stopped outside a heavy white door. The nurse said to Susan, "This is as far as you can go."

I hadn't realized Susan would have to leave me. I clung to her. "What if it doesn't work?"

For a moment her fingers tightened around mine. "Courage," she said, and let go.

In the operating theater a man in a long gown held a mask in front of my face. "When I put this over your mouth," he said, "I want you to very slowly count to ten."

I only made it to four before I fell asleep.

Coming out of the ether was harder. My right leg was pinned, trapped. I couldn't move. I broke into a sweat struggling to pull myself free. I'd been caught in a bombing, buried in rubble. I couldn't move my leg. Then somehow I was trapped again in the dank cabinet beneath the sink, in our old flat in London. Mam had locked me inside. The cockroaches—

"Shh." Susan's voice, soft in my ear. "Settle down. It's over. You're fine."

I was not fine. Not in the cabinet, not with Mam—

Someone pinned my arms. Threw a blanket over

me, tucked it tightly around my sides. "Open your eyes," Susan's voice said, still gentle. "The surgery's over."

I opened my eyes. Susan's face swam blurrily in front of me. "You're safe," she said.

I swallowed hard. I said, "You're lying."

"I'm not."

"I can't move my leg. My right leg. My clubfoot leg—"

"You haven't got a clubfoot," Susan said. "Not anymore."

I woke properly in the middle of the night. Screens surrounded my bed. A dim light shone behind them. "Susan?" I whispered.

One of the night nurses came to my bedside. "Thirsty?" she asked. I nodded. She poured me water and I drank. "How badly does it hurt?"

I couldn't move my right leg because the doctors had put a cast on it after the surgery. I remembered that now. Beneath the plaster, a strong dull ache centered around my right ankle and pulsed toward my knee. "I don't know," I said. "It always hurts."

"More than you can bear?"

I shook my head. I could bear almost anything.

The nurse smiled. "That's right," she said. "Your

mother said you were a tough one." She handed me a pill. "Swallow this."

I said, "Susan's not my mother." Thank God for that. I swallowed the pill and fell back asleep.

When I opened my eyes again Jamie's face was inches from mine. His hair looked like it hadn't been brushed in weeks. His eyes were red and swollen. He was crying. I pushed myself up in a panic. "What's wrong?"

Jamie launched himself onto the bed. He banged into my cast. I winced.

"Easy," Susan said, pulling him back.

Jamie burrowed against me.

I put my arms around him and looked over his head to Susan. "Tell me what's wrong," I said.

"It was in Lady Thorton's letter," Susan answered.

I nodded. I knew that.

Jamie said, "Our mam's dead."

You can know things all you like, but that doesn't mean you believe them.

Chapter 2

I knew my mother—Mam—worked nights in a munitions factory in London. I knew bombs were falling on London now, every single night in fierce, horrendous waves. I knew the Germans targeted factories, especially munitions ones. I'd been caught in a bombing raid myself. Brick walls exploded above my head. Afterward shattered glass drifted across the streets like snow.

So I knew Mam could die. I just didn't believe it. Even despite all the bombs. I thought Mam would live forever.

I thought Jamie and I would never be free.

I hugged Jamie. He sobbed. He thunked my cast again. I managed not to scream.

Susan tucked a pillow between Jamie and my cast. She eased herself onto the corner of the bed. She rubbed Jamie's back.

"Is it real?" I asked.

"It's real," she said.

"Really real?"

"I'm sorry," Susan said.

I said, *"Are* you sorry?"

Was *I* sorry? I supposed I was. Maybe? My mother hated me.

You'll never see us again, I'd said to her, a week ago in London. She'd said back, *Is that a promise?*

Now it was.

"This isn't a happy ending," Susan said. "It's not the worst possible ending, but it isn't happy, and I'm sorry for that. I am grateful to have an ending, though. Your mother can't hurt you anymore."

"No." I don't know whether Mam and I could have had a happy ending. I always hoped so—of course I did, she was my mother—but it was another thing I didn't fully believe. I turned to Jamie. "Why are you sad? Mam hated us. She said so."

Jamie sobbed harder. "I loved her," he said.

Jamie was nicer than me. He probably did love Mam. I didn't. I wished I did. I wished like anything she loved me.

I looked at Susan again. "How am I supposed to feel?" A good daughter would feel sad, I supposed. But if Mam was dead, then I was no longer anyone's daughter.

I wasn't sad. I wasn't happy. Or angry. Or anything.

Susan's hand clasped mine over Jamie's narrow back. "However you feel is fine."

"Is there a word for feeling nothing?"

"Yes," Susan said. "Stunned. I felt stunned when I first heard my mother died."

I looked at her. "When did your mam die?"

"A few years ago. Several months before Becky."

Becky, Susan's very best friend, died of pneumonia three years before the war. I knew that. They had lived together; Susan's bombed house had belonged to Becky first, and it was Becky who gave Susan Butter.

"Both deaths were hard," Susan said. "My feelings about my mother's were more complicated."

I let go of Susan's hand. "How did Lady Thorton know about Mam?" Before last week, we'd heard nothing from Mam for an entire year, not one word despite all the letters Susan and I wrote her, until she showed up in person to drag me and Jamie back to London.

"I'd given the WVS your mother's new address," Susan said. "One of the WVS groups in London contacted Lady Thorton. I suppose they're monitoring casualty lists."

The WVS was the Women's Volunteer Service.

They did war work. Susan was part of our village's WVS. Lady Thorton was its head, which made her in charge of evacuees like Jamie and me.

Susan reached for my hand again. I pulled it away. Jamie kept crying. I wanted to comfort him, but my insides felt hollow. I didn't know what Jamie and I were, if Mam was dead. Could we still stay with Susan? Were we still evacuees?

"What happens next?" I asked.

Susan paused. "I don't know," she said. "I'll ask Lady Thorton about the arrangements."

I blinked.

My heart stuttered.

It wasn't the answer I expected.

It wasn't the answer I wanted.

Arrangements.

The word came ringed with worry. It arrived on a wave of panic. It fell to the pit of my stomach. Where had I heard that word before?

Susan didn't say, *Don't worry.* She didn't say, *Of course you'll live with me.* She didn't say, *I'll make sure you're taken care of.*

She had said all those things the day she rescued us from Mam for the second time, the day her house was bombed. She said we'd stay together always.

I'd believed her.

Had she been lying? Or did everything change because Mam died?

"Is there a word that means children with dead parents?" I asked.

Susan swallowed. She said, "Orphans."

Orphans. Jamie and I were orphans now, not evacuees. We wouldn't stay under Lady Thorton's protection. Susan wouldn't be able to keep us. Something different happened to orphans.

Pain gripped my gut. It hurt worse than my foot ever had. I tightened my arms around Jamie. I would hang on to him no matter what. I would never let us be separated.

"I'll be walking soon," I said. "I'll be very useful then."

Susan blinked. "Your recovery will take a few months," she said. "You know that."

I said, "I'm very hardworking."

"Yes, you are," Susan said. "But you won't heal faster because of it. I don't know if you'll be allowed to leave the hospital, whatever else happens."

"Do I have to leave right away?" This day grew worse and worse.

"No, no, of course not." Susan sounded distracted.

"I only mean for the funeral. If we have one. Whatever we do."

Funeral. Another word I didn't understand. Even after a year of living with Susan there were so many things I didn't understand. Mam hadn't been much for words, and there was a limit to how much I could teach myself, looking out the one window of our flat.

Arrangements. "Line up against that wall," Lady Thorton had said last September, in her crisp head-of-the-WVS voice. "We're going to make arrangements."

We'd just come off the train that had evacuated us to the village from London. A whole herd of dirty, shabby children, and Jamie and me the most wretched-looking of all. I was nearly done in from the effort of getting away, my clubfoot oozing blood and hurting so badly my knees shook. The villagers filed past us, looking us up and down.

No one wanted Jamie and me.

I was back to that place now, only cleaner and with my right foot in plaster.

"You'd better go," I said, turning my back on Susan. "You'll need to start making arrangements."

Chapter 3

At least when Mam locked me up I'd been able to move around the room. Now I was trapped in a hospital bed, helpless, immobile, away from Jamie and Butter.

I wouldn't have Butter if I had to leave Susan.

Susan didn't love Butter, not the way I did. He was left over from Becky. Maybe Susan would let me borrow Butter, if I ended up somewhere I could keep a pony. I was the one who took care of him.

I put my hands over my face. Tears soaked my pillow. I tried not to make any noise.

Probably Jamie could keep his cat. Bovril was a good mouser. Even Mam might have let Jamie have a cat.

"I'm that sorry about your mother," one of the younger nurses whispered. She pulled my blankets over my shoulders.

I didn't reply. Susan had tried to teach me manners,

but I didn't know the manners for when people said they were sorry your horrible mother died.

"Is your father in the army?" the nurse asked.

I shook my head. "He's dead," I whispered. "A long time ago. Nothing to do with the war." I said, "We're orphans now."

The nurse looked stricken. "You poor dear!"

I rolled over to face the wall. "What happens to orphans?" I asked her. "Where do orphans live?"

"In orphanages, I suppose," the nurse said. "But surely your aunt—"

"She isn't our aunt," I said.

When Susan returned that afternoon, I pretended to be asleep. When she came back after teatime, she brought Jamie. She brought our book too, *The Swiss Family Robinson,* the only book we had left. It had been inside our Anderson shelter when the bomb fell on our house. Nice to know the shelter saved something.

Susan opened to the beginning. "'For many days,'" she read, "'we had been tempest-tossed—'"

"No!" I covered my ears with my hands. "Please—I don't want—"

The Swiss Family Robinson got shipwrecked onto a beautiful island where everything turned out splendid for them. Jamie loved the story. I had always disliked it. I hated it now.

Jamie and I were shipwrecked, but we hadn't been rescued after all. We hadn't reached an island. We were still struggling not to drown in the storm-tossed sea.

Susan closed the book. I held on to Jamie and wept.

Days passed without arrangements. I asked the young nurse about orphanages. "Oh," she said, her face clouding, "I'm sure some of them are nice places nowadays. Nothing like how they used to be. I mean, you get enough to eat and all. Nobody starves."

"Could I keep a pony?" I asked.

"I wouldn't know about that," she said, which meant no.

Every day doctors poked and prodded my leg. They changed my cast for another cast that looked exactly the same as the first one. They wouldn't let me have crutches. They refused to let me out of bed.

Susan visited every morning, her face gentle and sympathetic. She brought Jamie to see me every afternoon, as soon as he got out of school.

When we came to live with Susan, she gave me crutches. When Mam came back for us, she threw them away. That's how Jamie and I got caught outside in the London air raid. I couldn't move fast enough to find a shelter before the bombs came. We'd been on the street, cowering under the hail of bricks and glass.

A night nurse shook me awake. "You're screaming," she said. "Stop."

I was shaking and drenched in sweat. "Bombs," I said. "A wall fell on my leg. I couldn't move."

"It was a nightmare," she said. "Pull yourself together. You're frightening the younger ones."

The nurse walked away. I stared at the ceiling. My heart raced. I had to pee, which meant calling a nurse and using a bedpan, which reminded me of Mam making me use the bucket in our old flat. I knew where a toilet was—I'd used it before my surgery. The ward was dark, but some light shone from the nurses' station in the hall.

I sat up. I pulled the blankets and sheets away. I tapped the hard plaster of my cast. My foot scarcely hurt at all. I swung my legs to the ground.

It would have been easier with crutches, but there were beds every few feet along the room. I steadied myself on the bedrails and dragged my cast along the floor. It was hard work but I was so glad to be moving. I slid into the bathroom, used the toilet, and came out. I was halfway back down the darkened ward when a voice behind me barked, "What on *earth* are you doing?"

I jumped, startled. I lost my balance. I waved my arms in the air, fell against the nearest bed, and whacked its sleeping occupant, a small girl with a broken leg in traction. She screamed. I pushed myself sideways and fell. My right knee twisted. Pain shot through my ankle. I screamed too.

The whole ward woke. Someone flung on the lights. A pair of nurses hoisted me back into my own bed. Others calmed and comforted the little girl.

"As if you weren't old enough to know better!" the head nurse hissed. "Waking everyone up with your ruckus, and taking such ridiculous risks! You'll be lucky if you haven't hurt your recovery. Wait until your mother hears!"

"She's not my mother!"

The head nurse didn't care.

In the morning the doctor said I didn't seem to have done myself harm. The nurse told Susan anyway. Susan wasn't happy. "I don't know what got into her," the nurse said.

"I do," Susan replied. To me she said more softly,

"I know it's difficult, but you must rest until you heal. If you get up again, they'll tie you to the bed."

I shuddered. Then I saw what Susan was carrying. "You've another letter. From Lady Thorton." My stomach lurched. Here came the arrangements.

Susan waited until the nurse walked away. Then she sat down on my bed. She looked unhappy. "I'm afraid it's hard news," she said. "I've been trying to think of a way to say this gently, but I haven't found one." She reached for my hand. I pulled it back.

I thought I might stop breathing.

I had to stay with Jamie.

Had to.

"Your mother was cremated," Susan said. "It was because of the war, because there were so many victims at the factory and because we didn't hear about her death in time to claim her body. Her ashes were put into a mass grave. We won't be able to have a funeral. We won't be able to bury her, in London or in our village. I am so sorry."

I had absolutely no idea what she was talking about.

"Ada?" Susan asked. "Are you okay?"

I didn't know where to begin. The word *funeral*. Cremated. Her ashes—someone was cleaning out Mam's grate? What did any of it mean?

"But I do have a bit of good news," Susan continued. "Lady Thorton's offered us the use of a cottage on her estate. To live in. She says it's quite small, but mostly furnished."

I couldn't speak.

"I didn't know what we were going to do," Susan said. "The government will pay me damages for Becky's house, but they say it might take years. I haven't been able to find anything for rent in the village." She looked at me. "You're so quiet. I know it's a shock. What are you thinking?"

When things were very bad I could go away in my head, to a place where no one could touch me. I went away to Butter's pasture, to galloping through the green fields on Butter—

"Ada," Susan said. She tapped my arm to bring me back.

I took a deep breath. "When do we go to the orphanage?"

"*What?*"

"When do Jamie and I"—Oh God, please. Please let me stay with Jamie—"when do we go to the orphanage?"

"Orphanage?" Susan looked as shocked as if I'd slapped her. "Ada! Why on earth would you go to an orphanage?"

I glared at her. "Where are we going, then?"

"Nowhere!" Susan said. "Nothing's changed. How could you possibly think—it's your mother that's dead. I'm still here!"

"You said you had to make arrangements!"

"Funeral arrangements!"

"I don't know what that means!"

Susan went perfectly still. "Oh," she said. "Oh, for heaven's sake. You poor dear. You must have been in agony. Why didn't you say something?"

"You never wanted children," I said. "You said so." She had, over and over, when we first came. "And we aren't evacuees anymore. We're orphans. Lady Thorton's not in charge of us and neither are you and the orphanage won't let me keep Butter."

"Oh, Ada." Susan leaned forward and wrapped her arms around me. I tried to push her away but she held tight. She was stronger than she looked. "You misunderstood," she said gently. "You are orphans, technically at least, but of course you're staying with me. In some ways it's simpler now that your mother's dead. I shouldn't have any trouble becoming your legal guardian. When I said arrangements, I meant for your mother. For her remains."

I didn't know what *remains* meant. I could guess, but I was afraid to.

"For her body," Susan said. "Only that. You and Jamie stay with me."

I tried to speak but no words came. I choked and then I was sobbing, and Susan rocked me back and forth, back and forth as if I was a little baby, as if she loved me, as if she always had.

Chapter 4

The next fine Saturday, Susan convinced the nurses to let her take me out in a wheelchair. It was October now, the air brisk and chill, the sky a bright, bright blue. There was a hint of wood smoke in the air. No airplanes in sight. No bombers. No invasion, at least not yet.

I wore a cardigan and a dress Susan found for me at a jumble sale. I had a blanket tucked over my cast and bare left leg. Susan pushed the wheelchair. Jamie skipped alongside. "We'll go up the high street and have tea," Susan said, "but first I want to show you something." She stopped the chair outside a church. It was larger than our village church, but otherwise much the same, brown and rectangular, with a tall steeple and a graveyard filled with upright stones.

"Keep your voices down," Susan whispered. "And don't point, but look over there. See the people, and the empty grave—that's the hole in the ground—and the wooden box? The box is called a coffin. This is the final part of a funeral. The first part happens inside the church. Now they're going to bury the deceased."

"Deceased?" asked Jamie.

"The dead person," said Susan.

"In the ground?" His voice squeaked.

"Well, yes," Susan said. "Where would you want to put them?"

I'd noticed that the stones in our village church's graveyard had names on them, but I hadn't known it meant people's bodies were buried there. I said, "I never thought about it before."

"I had hoped we could bury your mother in our village," said Susan.

"Why?" asked Jamie.

"So you would have a memorial. A place to go and think about her. To think about the good memories."

I would have to think hard to find any good memories.

"But she was cremated," I said. I could remember words. I just didn't always understand them.

"Yes," Susan said. "That means her body was burned to ashes."

I turned to her. "You're joking."

She looked slightly uncomfortable. "No," she said.

"It's actually a perfectly respectful way to treat the dead. And useful in wartime."

I said, "If we don't have her body, how do we know she's really dead?"

"You'll get a death certificate," Susan said. "In the mail. Like your birth certificate, only the opposite."

"Oh," I said. I kept my birth certificate in a special box.

"When it comes I'll give it to you," Susan said. "You can keep it safe for us."

I nodded. That would be good.

Jamie said, "Can we have tea now?"

She squeezed his hand. "Of course."

In the tea shop I scowled at the prices on the menu. "If we aren't evacuees anymore," I said, "the government isn't going to keep paying you to take care of us. You won't be able to afford it." Susan's bombed house had been fancy, but she always said she didn't have much money, and she didn't have a job.

"I'll take care of it," Susan said. "I told you, I've started the paperwork. I'm going to become your legal guardian."

I liked the sound of that. *Guardian* was a strong word. "As soon as I'm out of the hospital, I'll find work," I said.

Susan smiled. "Oh, Ada," she said. "Please relax. You don't need to worry about money."

"Who paid for my surgery?" I asked. "And the hospital and the boardinghouse and all our new things?"

Susan shook her head. "I'm not sure you need to know."

"I do," I said.

She sighed. "I bought your clothes," she said. "The WVS took up a collection to help with our living expenses." She took a deep breath. "Lord and Lady Thorton paid for your surgery."

"*Lady Thorton?*" I said.

Jamie took a sip of tea. "They've got gobs of money."

They did, but it didn't mean I wanted them spending it on me. "So now I have to be grateful," I said. "To Lady Thorton." I'd never met Lord Thorton. He was away working for the war.

"I hope you're already grateful to her," Susan said. "All the things she's done for you—getting you help with Butter, giving you Maggie's old clothes—not to mention the cottage we're going to be living in."

Jamie looked up at Susan. "She gave us you."

That was true. In the end, Lady Thorton's arrangements for Jamie and me had been to sling us into her automobile and dump us at Susan's house. It had been the best possible thing, though it didn't seem so at the time.

"I don't want to have to feel grateful," I said.

Susan smiled. "I understand," she said. "Do it anyhow."

Grateful to the iron-faced woman. Grateful for each new cast on my leg. Grateful to be tied into the bed when I got caught trying to use the bathroom again. Grateful that nurses woke me when my nightmares had me screaming.

"Keep going," Susan said. "The only way out of this is straight through." She brought me books from the library, wool from the shops and new knitting needles, pencils and paper to pass the time. Letters from Maggie, away at boarding school. A game of draughts I could play with Jamie in the afternoons. "Courage," she said.

"Is that the same as being grateful?" I said. I felt rebellious.

Susan nodded. "Sometimes."

November twenty-ninth was Jamie's seventh birthday. Susan and I gave him a tiny cake and a tin toy

airplane—a Spitfire, the kind of fighter plane Maggie's
brother Jonathan flew.

Three days later the doctor cut off my latest cast.
Then, instead of getting my leg ready for a new cast,
the way he usually did, he said, "Right. Let's have
a bit of gravity." He put his hands on my waist and
lifted me off the table.

Onto my feet.

So that I was standing.

Susan was smiling. The doctor said, "Go on, put a
bit of weight on it."

I held the edge of the table and pushed my right
leg down. I felt my right ankle move the smallest bit.
It hurt, but I expected that. I shifted more weight to
my right leg. My legs trembled. I hadn't used them
in so long.

I was standing. Standing. On both feet. I pulled
my nightgown aside to look down. Two feet. Ten toes,
all pointed forward; ten toenails, all facing up. My
right foot was smaller, and scarred, and the skin on it
still had a callus from how the top used to be the bottom, but it looked like a foot, not a monstrosity.

Mam might not have screamed at me for having a
foot like this.

The surgery had worked.

I *didn't* have a clubfoot anymore.

As I stared, my feet grew blurry, then cleared, then grew blurry again. Great blobbing tears fell out of my eyes. My shoulders started to shake, and I might have crumpled except that Susan threw her arms around me. She hugged me the way she'd hugged me the morning she found me in London, after the bombing, still alive. "I don't know about you, but I'm getting used to this hugging business," she whispered into my ear. It made me laugh even though I was sobbing. I stood and sobbed and stood and sobbed and stood and stood and stood.

Jamie ran into the ward that afternoon carrying a cardboard box. "Show me your foot!" he said.

I was lying on top of my blankets with my two bare feet stretched in front of me. "Go on," I told him. I'd been admiring my foot all afternoon.

Jamie climbed onto the bed. His fingers traced the thick scar around my right ankle. "Cor," he said. "It's like a real foot now."

I wouldn't have guessed my foot could change so much. My ankle would never bend correctly, the doctor said, and the insides of it weren't normal, but I would be able to walk with the bottom of my foot against the ground, and I would be able to wear real shoes on both feet. That was more than enough.

"Here," Susan said, handing Jamie's box to me. "In celebration."

I lifted the lid. It was a pair of shoes. Leather shoes with a strap around the ankle, like the ones Maggie wore. Good new shoes that were almost impossible to find in the shops anymore.

Jamie said, "We bought them weeks ago. The day before your surgery."

I slid the left shoe on first. Then I reached down to my new right foot. Stuck the toes inside the shoe. Pushed the heel down. Buckled the strap. The right shoe was a little loose. Both shoes had room at the toes. Room to grow. I could wear the shoes a long time.

In shoes my feet looked identical. You couldn't even see the scar.

Nobbut a monster, with that ugly foot. That's what Mam had said. Over and over, until it took everything I had not to believe her.

I would never have to hear that again.

I felt a wave of sudden, overwhelming despair. "This was all it took?" I said, looking up at Susan. "A couple of months in hospital fixed it?" All my life I'd been miserable because of that foot.

Tears came to Susan's eyes. "Your mother didn't know," she said.

"She did," I said. "She wanted a reason to hate me."

Jamie looked from me to Susan and back to me again. He whispered, "I thought you'd be happy."

"Oh, Jamie." I took a deep breath. "I am happy." I swung my legs to the floor. "Help me walk."

"Careful," Susan said. "Your legs aren't yet strong."

"Jamie'll take care of me." I held my hands out and let him balance me. We started to walk down the room. One step, then another. Left foot. Right foot.

Before, when I walked on my bad foot, the bones crunched. The skin tore and bled. Every step hurt more. Now every step hurt less. My legs were weak and shaky, but I was walking.

"You're doing it!" Jamie said.

I could scarcely believe it. "Pretty soon," I said, "I'll be running. Faster than *you*."

Jamie grinned. "I'll still be faster," he said. "I'll always be faster."

"Will not."

"Will too!"

I wanted to sleep in my shoes, but the nurses made me sleep with my right foot in a brace instead. Only for a little while, they said. I spent another few weeks in hospital, doing exercises and strengthening my legs, and then, in the third week of December, we said good-bye to the nurses and the doctors and the ankle brace and the crutches and everything. I put my new shoes on over thick winter stockings, and we went home.

Chapter 5

"Draw me a map," I said to Susan as we climbed aboard the train. I walked to the station like a regular girl. Right foot, left foot. No crutches. Barely even limping. Not like the day I'd been evacuated, when my neighbor Stephen White ended up carrying me. "Are we going to travel through London? Show me where we are and where we're going." Susan sometimes drew me maps of our village, so I didn't get lost when I was out on Butter.

"Not through London, no," Susan said. Soldiers moved aside to give us seats together. Susan stowed our bags in the luggage rack and tucked Bovril's basket beneath the seat. She found a pencil and a piece of paper in her handbag. She drew. "This is England. Here's where we are. Here's London. Here's home." She added a squiggly line to show the train route to Kent.

Jamie pointed at the blank space on the side of the paper. "What's over there?"

"Dragons," said Susan.

We stared at her. She laughed. "It's a joke," she explained. "People used to draw dragons on the edges of old maps. When the world hadn't been fully explored, mapmakers imagined dragons living at the far ends."

We still stared. "What're dragons?" asked Jamie. I didn't know either.

"Enormous, mythical, fire-breathing creatures, like giant lizards," said Susan. "Sometimes they can fly."

Jamie's eyes widened. I frowned. Was Susan serious? I couldn't tell. "I don't want dragons," Jamie said.

"All right," Susan said. "We'll keep them off our map."

She drew the English Channel instead, south of England, and a line for the coast of France on its far side. She wrote *Occupied by Germany* across France. "Worse than dragons," she said.

I doubted that. Worse than giant, fire-breathing lizards that could fly? Sounded like we should send dragons after Hitler.

It was night before we reached our village station. We took the taxi to our new cottage. Jamie pressed his forehead against the taxi's window. "We used to live in a tree house," he said, "but now we're going to go live in a cave." This was, of course, from *The Swiss Family Robinson*.

"That's right," Susan said. "It'll be spartan at first, but we'll make it cozy. It will be much warmer and drier than living in that tree."

I rolled my eyes. "Why do you encourage him?"

She grinned. "Can you suggest an alternative?"

Well, no. I really couldn't.

The cottage was set in a gloomy woods, bare now in winter and somber and gray. Its pale stone walls glimmered in the moonlight. "I thought it was supposed to be little," I said. The cottage was twice the size of Susan and Becky's old house.

Susan blinked. "I expected it to be little. Lady Thorton described it as little."

Little compared to Thorton House, which was the size of a train station, but not little compared to anything else.

Susan paid the cabdriver, took an enormous iron

37

key from beneath a flowerpot on the front step, and slid the key into the lock on the door. Inside, the cottage was entirely dark. Blackout screens covered the windows. Susan fumbled for a light switch, and a single electric bulb, hung from the middle of the ceiling, flickered on, barely illuminating a large, nearly empty room. In the corner something skittered out of sight. I hoped it was a mouse, not a cockroach or a rat. Jamie pulled the lid off Bovril's basket. Bovril growled and streaked toward the noise.

For the first time ever, I loved Jamie's cat.

The air smelled fresh, not dank, but the plaster walls radiated cold. I followed Susan as she inspected the ground floor, clicking on lights as she went. On one side of the big room was a kitchen, with a rickety table and a set of chairs. Behind that was a small back room, empty, and a sort of scullery with a washboiler and a bin full of coal. "Thank heavens," Susan said when she saw the coal.

As we approached the stairs Jamie ran down them. "Five bedrooms!" he said.

"Oh, good," I said. "Bovril can have his own."

Jamie shot me a look. "Bovril and I are sharing. You can have *your* own."

"Even better," I said.

I went upstairs. Five bedrooms and a bath. Two

bedrooms were empty. Three contained beds already made up with pillows, blankets, and sheets.

It was kind of Lady Thorton to furnish our beds. Generous, like the full coal bin.

Like my surgery.

I went back down the stairs. This is how I did it: Right foot, left foot. Right foot, left foot. Just normal. Just walking.

It felt fantastic.

Jamie was hauling a full coal scuttle into the sitting room and Susan was making up the fire. I said, "We don't need this much space."

"I know," Susan said. "I appreciate it, I truly do, but I'd have preferred something smaller. This will cost the earth to heat."

Jamie looked up at her through a fringe of tousled hair. "We want a big cave," he said. "When the storms come, we'll need room for everyone."

Susan gave me the bedroom at the top of the stairs. A whole bedroom all my own. It was large and spare, with a single window, yellow wallpaper, and a cold, bare wood floor. It had a bed, a table with a lamp on it, a bookshelf, and a small dresser for my clothes. Everything I could possibly need.

I took off my shoes and put them on the bookshelf,

where I could see them if I woke in the night. I unpacked my bag, taking out my nightclothes and my extra socks and underwear. From the very bottom I pulled out the box I kept my birth certificate in. I put that on the shelf beside my shoes. I took off my sweater and dress and put on my nightgown. I shivered, and put on my hospital dressing gown. I turned off the light, took down the blackout screen, and looked through the window into the garden behind the house. An Anderson shelter lay half-buried near the scullery door, and a large, empty square pen enclosed a patch of grass farther back.

I heaved the window open and thrust my head into the night air. "Butter," I said. At Susan's old house, Butter lived in the back pasture. Whenever I called him he'd come galloping, ears and tail alert. He would slide to a stop just in front of me and gently lower his head. He never once knocked me down, not even in the beginning when I was weak and afraid. "Butter," I whispered, choking back tears. I missed him so much.

Susan came in carrying another blanket. She stood beside me at the window. Tears were rolling down my face now, but Susan didn't comment on them. "It's a lovely garden," she said instead.

"I miss Butter."

Susan pulled the window shut. "You'll see him tomorrow," she said. "First thing." She hugged my shoulders. "To bed now. You're worn out."

I was. I hadn't realized it, but I was suddenly so tired I could barely stand. I slid between the cold sheets of the bed. Susan tucked the extra blanket around me. Her lips touched the top of my forehead as I fell asleep.

Chapter 6

"Bovril caught a mouse!" Jamie yelled from down the hall.

I jerked awake. It was morning. I was glad my bedroom door was closed.

Though mice were better than roaches or rats.

I dressed quickly. *Butter.* Downstairs, Susan was fiddling with the unfamiliar stove. "Oatmeal?" she asked.

"No, no, no," I said, stuffing my arms into my coat. Susan laughed. She told me the path to take to the stables, and handed me a piece of bread to eat on the way.

It was cold and the sun barely lit the gray woods. The air smelled like home—like hay and grass and salt from the sea. I breathed deep. I'd missed it so.

After a few turns, the path opened onto the side road that went from Thorton House to the stables. I could see the stable cupola. I knew where I was. "Fred!" I yelled, and then I *ran*.

I hadn't run much yet. I lurched and stumbled and felt out of breath, but I was running, actually running, and it was so much fun I laughed aloud. I turned the corner into the stable yard and there was Fred, Lady Thorton's groom, lifting his cap to scratch his bald head like always.

His face lit up. He held out his arms. That was good, because I couldn't make my legs stop. I smashed straight into him. Fred laughed and swung me up in the air in a circle, and when he set me down firm on both feet he kissed my cheek. We had always been friends—he taught me how to ride and I helped him with chores—but he'd never kissed me before. "Ah, lass!" he said, taking out his handkerchief and wiping his eyes. "I didn't think I'd see you so spry. I didn't think they could."

"You never said that!"

"I thought you'd be some better," he said. "Running, now, running I didn't expect."

I grinned at him. "Running," I said.

"Running," he repeated. "Eh, I've missed you. It's good you're back." He took a deep breath. "We've plenty of work to do."

I turned toward the row of stalls. *"Butter!"*

Butter tossed his yellow head over one of the open half-doors. His ears flew forward. He whickered low in his throat. His eyes shone.

"He missed you," said Fred. "We all missed you."

I'd never been missed before.

I swallowed hard. I went to Butter and rubbed his forehead. He sniffed my hands. I said, "I was afraid he'd forget me. I was afraid you both would."

"Not a chance," said Fred. "We need you, don't we? We're that glad you're back."

Needed. I was needed. "Is Maggie home?" Her boarding school was a long way away.

"Soon," Fred said. "She'll be happy to see you too."

Not more than I'd be happy to see her. I ran my fingers through Butter's mane. "Can I ride first, before I start work?"

Fred took down my old sidesaddle. I shook my head. "I'm going to ride astride, like Maggie," I said. "I've got two useful feet now."

He hesitated, grinning at me. "Posh ladies ride aside."

I laughed. "I'm not a posh lady," I said. "I'm a regular girl."

"Eh, you could be," Fred said.

"Could be a regular girl?" I said. "Yes, please."

Fred laughed and dug Butter's old straight saddle out of the Thortons' tack room. Our tack hadn't been bombed; it had all been in the stable beside Susan's house. Fred had it now.

It was a joy to settle the saddle onto Butter's back, to tighten the girth around him, to slide the bit into his mouth and buckle the bridle around his head. A joy to hoist myself into the saddle and slide both feet into stirrups. Fred helped me lengthen the leathers. I'd grown while I was in hospital.

Fred patted Butter's neck. "Not too much now," he said. "You'll not have your balance back nor your strength, and I'm counting on your help with the chores."

I knew he was right. I wasn't strong yet. I wouldn't ride up my lookout hill or far into the fields. I'd ride into the village and find my friend from London, Stephen White. He'd want to see my new foot.

Butter's hooves clopped against the paving stones. The winter air nipped my nose. Butter's strides made my hips sway. I breathed deep and felt myself relax. My right ankle was stiff in the stirrup. It would always be stiff, no matter what, but it didn't hurt. I nudged Butter into a trot. I'd never had much practice posting—you didn't post the trot in a sidesaddle—but I understood how it should work and after a few bounces I found a soft rhythm. My right foot was fine as long as I didn't force my ankle down. I steadied my shoulders and worked to keep my hips even. I'd always been lopsided before.

Butter blew out a long breath. I scratched his shoulder. If I could stay in the saddle forever, I'd never be afraid.

Stephen White lived with a very old man named Colonel McPherson in a small house on the near side of the village. I hadn't heard from Stephen while I was in hospital, but I hadn't expected to. Sometimes I wrote to Maggie, because she was away so much at school, but writing letters was still hard for me. I hadn't been reading or writing for very long.

Stephen White was the first friend I ever had. When we evacuated London he helped me escape. He was the only person besides Jamie who really understood what my old life with Mam had been. I knew he'd be as happy as Fred to see me walking well.

I drew rein in front of the colonel's cottage. Stephen always kept it neat but now it looked forlorn, abandoned. Dried leaves blanketed the front stoop. Blackout curtains covered the windows and I couldn't see smoke coming from the chimney. The colonel chilled easily; he always kept a good fire.

I dismounted and dragged Butter up the front walk. I knocked.

Behind me, a flat, emotionless voice said, "Ada. I

didn't expect to see you. I didn't know when you were coming back."

I turned. "Stephen?"

Stephen White stood in front of me holding the handles of a bicycle. He looked awful. His face was gray and thin, and dark circles ringed his eyes. His bony wrists stuck out from his shirt cuffs. He wore a wide black armband on one sleeve. "What's happened?" I asked.

Stephen swallowed. "Lots," he said. "It's good to see you. I'm leaving in the morning. I've got something for you—for Susan, really."

"Leaving?"

"My dad joined the merchant marines. His ship signed me on as a cabin boy. Pay Hitler back, we will."

"What about the colonel?" I said. "Besides, you're not old enough to fight!"

Stephen shrugged. "Thirteen's old enough for a cabin boy. I didn't have to lie. Dad and I are spending Christmas with my aunts in London, then we're off."

I didn't know what to think. "That's dangerous," I said. Hitler blew up supply ships all the time.

"I suppose." Stephen looked me up and down. He still didn't smile. He'd always been cheerful before. "You look good," he said. "The surgery went well?"

"Yes," I said. I couldn't understand the flatness of his expression. "What's wrong?"

"I've got something for Susan," he repeated. "I'm staying at the vicar's overnight. You're in the Thortons' old gamekeeper's cottage, right? Can I come around after tea?"

I nodded. Butter nudged my arm. I reached up to pat him. Stephen mounted his bicycle and started away. "Wait—come back!" I called.

He said over his shoulder, "After tea."

When I asked Fred about it he shook his head. "Ah, Stephen, that's a bad business," he said. "Reckon I'll let him tell you. Seems that's what he wants."

"Why was the colonel's house shut up?"

"The colonel died," Fred said. "Back weeks ago, just after you went away. Died in his sleep. He were eighty-eight years old."

"Why didn't you tell me?" I'd quite liked the colonel.

Fred looked uncomfortable. "Ah, well—I didn't think of it right off. It wasn't a tragedy, an old man passing. Then the other came right on the heels." Fred paused. "Stephen said he's coming to see you tonight?" I nodded. "That's good," Fred said. "He'll tell you himself."

I couldn't get any more out of him. I untacked Butter, rubbed him down, and put him back in his stall with fresh water and hay. Then I went down the row of stalls—Maggie's pony, Ivy; Jonathan's beautiful horse, Oban; Lord and Lady Thorton's hunters—checking water buckets and giving out hay. I got out a wheelbarrow and pitchfork—I could use a wheelbarrow now I had two good feet—but Fred took them away from me. "That's enough for your first day," he said.

"I'll be back tomorrow," I said, "unless you need me tonight. I'm ready to work hard." If I learned everything Fred could teach me, perhaps I could get a paying job in a stable when I was a little older. It wasn't impossible.

"You'll not push yourself," Fred said.

"Fred." I grinned at him. "I have to."

Susan thought we should have our tea with Stephen. She and Jamie had gone shopping. She made fish paste sandwiches and brewed a fresh pot of tea, and we set the little table for four. When Stephen came in he was carrying a paper bag. He looked at the table, not smiling. He sat down.

Jamie plopped into the chair beside him. "How's Billy?" Billy, Stephen's little brother, was Jamie's best friend.

Stephen swallowed. He started to speak. He choked, swallowed, and tried again. He tried two or three times before his mouth would make words. Then he said, "Dead."

Chapter 7

Susan caught her breath. Jamie made a sound half-way between a sob and a scream. I was sure I'd heard Stephen wrong. Billy White was the same age as Jamie. Billy White couldn't be dead.

Stephen said, "The Nazis bombed London fifty-seven straight nights."

I knew that. I'd been in London for the first night of it. Mam's factory had been hit the next week.

Stephen said, "They're all gone."

Jamie said, "Not Billy—"

"Gone where?" I asked, stupidly, before I realized what he meant. "Oh. Oh, Stephen. Not—not all of them?"

Stephen's little brother and three little sisters had all been evacuated, same as Jamie and Stephen and me. But when there weren't any bombs at the start of the war, lots of parents, including Stephen's, took their evacuated children home. Stephen only stayed because the colonel had become so frail he needed Stephen's help.

"All except my dad," Stephen said. "He was at work. If only I'd—"

"You don't know that," Susan said quickly. "War is terrible."

Tears streaked down Jamie's face, and Susan's. I could feel them starting to roll down mine. Stephen didn't cry. He looked like he might never cry again.

"Dad and me, we're going to stick close now," he said. "Pay the Germans back, we will."

I couldn't picture Stephen's father. I knew he worked at the docks. Where we grew up, nearly all the men did.

"Anyhow," Stephen said, "I brought you something. Found it in the wreckage of your house. I had a look around, after you left but before the bulldozers came."

The airfield near our old house had used the rubble from our home to fill bomb blasts in their runways. I knew that. Now Stephen reached into his bag. "It isn't much—"

I didn't expect much. We'd rummaged through the wreckage ourselves the day after the bombing, and not found anything worth saving beyond a few pots and pans.

"It's this." Stephen set a battered metal frame in front of Susan.

Susan gasped. She grabbed the frame. Then she threw her arms around Stephen.

It was Susan's photograph of her friend Becky, the one that had stood on her bedside table. The glass in the frame was broken, but the photograph was fine.

Stephen said, "I thought it might be important."

Susan used her handkerchief to wipe her eyes. "I couldn't replace it," she said.

He nodded. "I know. I wish I had a photograph of my family."

I didn't have a photo of Mam. Or Jamie, or myself, or my father. Mam's flat had been hit the night Jamie and I were in it; we'd barely escaped. We hadn't had photographs anyhow. No one did, on our lane.

"Have some tea," Susan said to Stephen, very gently.

"I can't stay," Stephen said. "The vicar's expecting me. I only came back to the village in the first place to fetch the things I'd left here. I'm leaving tomorrow, early train."

"Visit when you can," Susan said. "You're always welcome here. Send us your address. We'll write."

"I don't think they get much mail on ships," Stephen said.

"They do," Susan said. "We'll write you. We're so sorry."

Stephen stood. At the doorway he turned. "I'm glad your operation worked, Ada," he said. "You're walking grand."

"Our mam died too," I said.

A cloud passed over his face. "I didn't know that," he said. "I suppose I'm sorry. I'll say I'm sorry."

I nodded. "I say I'm sorry too."

"All right, then." The door closed and he was gone.

Chapter 8

Thorton House stood in front of the stables, square and grand like a palace. I never went there. I never even walked around to the front side. Now I fidgeted in the stable yard, staring at the house's empty windows. "Why isn't Maggie home?"

"Another day or two," Fred said. "She'll be here before Christmas."

You'd think I'd have learned patience in the hospital, but I hadn't. I wanted Maggie and galloping and sunshine and summer and all I had was cold rain and miserable footing to ride in. I wore a pair of Maggie's cast-off paddock boots to do the morning chores, and by the time I got back to the cottage they were soaked through. Susan fussed at me. She fussed about everything. The cottage was furnished, but it wasn't well-equipped, and we needed scads of things we'd never be able to buy. The stores were mostly empty, because of the war.

Susan said, "I don't know what we'll eat for Christmas dinner. The butcher wasn't expecting us back." You had to register your ration cards with specific shops in order to buy rationed food, and of course that took some time. Meat was rationed. So was bacon, butter, cooking fat, tea. Jam, sweets, everything you'd actually want to eat. Fortunately, Jamie and I grew up hungry enough that we weren't picky.

Jamie said, "No GOOSE?"

So maybe Jamie was picky. Living with Susan spoiled him. I wasn't. We'd had roast goose last Christmas, my first goose and my first real Christmas. We'd invited three pilots from the airfield to share our dinner. They were all dead now.

Dead pilots. Dead Mam. Dead colonel. Dead Stephen's family.

I counted them off on my fingers. Ten people. They took up every finger I had.

I could hardly breathe.

"I'll make lunch," I said. "Jamie, get up. There's still dishes left from breakfast. Go wash them." Jamie was rolling with Bovril on the rug. "Get busy."

"Jamie's fine," Susan said. "The dishes can wait."

I poked Jamie. "Get to work—now!" I went to the kitchen. "What do we need from town? I'll go get it."

Susan raised her eyebrows. "Not in this rain. Not now. We can make do."

"I want to be useful."

"Sit and work some fractions for me. That's useful."

I'd never been to school. I'd hoped to go after my surgery, but the village school was closed because most of the village children got evacuated north during the Battle of Britain. Susan was teaching me at home, same as always.

Fractions made me feel stupid. When the bottom number got bigger, the real number got smaller, which was the opposite of how I thought it should be. Five was larger than three—but one-third was larger than one-fifth. Then Susan expected me to add them, $\frac{1}{5} + \frac{1}{3}$, even though five had nothing to do with three.

I looked out the window at the rain.

Susan set a weak cup of tea in front of me. Tea was rationed strictly enough that we never could brew it as strongly as I'd like. "Take your time," Susan said. "Draw it out." She'd taught me to draw pictures for fractions, half a pie, a third of a pie, a fifth of a pie. The drawings were like a different kind of map.

"Too many dragons," I said. I stabbed my pencil against the paper. The point snapped.

"Yes," said Susan. She handed me her penknife to

resharpen the pencil. "Maths dragons are the worst."

"I thought you loved maths." She'd studied it at university, at a place called Oxford.

"I do. But its dragons are fierce."

Suddenly the front door flung wide. Maggie swooped into the room. "Ada!" she yelled. "Happy Christmas! I'm finally home!"

"Maggie!" I jumped up and threw my arms around her. "Finally!"

She laughed. "Finally! Look at you! Look at you! No crutches!"

"Shoes!" I said.

"Does it hurt?"

"Hardly at all. Want to see?"

"Please!"

I stripped my foot bare and stood on it. My ankle could bend almost half an inch now. More than ever. Maggie ran her fingers over my scar. "That's amazing," she said. "Tell me everything."

I laughed. "There's so much."

Susan brought in three more mugs of bad tea. "You'll stay for lunch, Maggie?"

Maggie pulled a face. "Can't," she said. "I promised Mum I'd go shopping. The housekeeper has a cold, so Mum said we'd do it. But I've got excellent news. We want you all to come to Christmas dinner at our house. Father's home for almost a week, and Jonathan's got four days starting tomorrow—"

"Then it will be a family party," Susan said, "and we shouldn't interfere."

"No, no, please interfere!" Maggie said. "The last thing we want is just family. We want to have fun. And Ada, guess what? On Boxing Day, we're going to host a paper chase! Jonathan wrote and said so."

Boxing Day was the day after Christmas. I didn't know what a paper chase was. "Like a fox hunt," Maggie explained, "only without foxes, or hunting, or hounds. It'll be brilliant. You'll see."

Suddenly Maggie's eyes went wide, as though I'd frightened her.

"What?" I asked.

She touched the black cloth on my sleeve. "Your armband."

"Oh." I touched it too, and for a moment our fingertips met. "Susan made it for me." She'd made us all armbands, like the one Stephen wore, out of an extra piece of blackout material she'd found in the scullery. Jamie had asked her for one, and then I did too. "They're a symbol of mourning," I said. "*Mourning* spelled with a *u,* not *morning* like early in the day. You wear one when you're sad because some-one died."

Maggie nodded. "I know. I'm so sorry about your mother. I should have said that first thing."

"It's not for Mam," Jamie said. "It's for Billy White."

"It's for Mam too," I said quickly. It wasn't really— I hadn't even known about armbands when Mam died. But I didn't want Maggie to think me uncaring. What sort of girl didn't mourn her own mother?

Maggie said, "Who's Billy White? I only know Stephen."

We explained. "That's awful," Maggie said. "That's worse than awful."

"And the colonel," I added. And the dead pilots, though I no longer remembered their names.

"My mother wrote me about the colonel," Maggie said. "She didn't say anything about Stephen's fam-ily." Maggie shook her head. "I think she thinks that if she doesn't tell me about sad things, I won't find out about them, and then I won't be sad." Maggie sighed. "In the middle of a war."

It didn't make sense. Perhaps Lady Thorton just forgot. She was the sort of person who might forget important things.

Bovril stalked into the room. Jamie scooped him

up. "I made Bovril an armband," Jamie said, scratching behind the cat's ears. "He chewed it."

"Cats don't mourn," I said.

Jamie cut his eyes at me. "They feel very sad," he said. "They just don't like armbands."

Maggie stayed half an hour. At the end of her visit, she looked around the room and said, "This place is so gloomy. How do you stand it? Even without the blackouts up, it's like living in a cave."

"It is a cave," Jamie said. "It's our cave, we moved here because it's drier than inside the tree."

"*Swiss Family Robinson,*" I murmured.

"Yes, but didn't the Swiss Family Robinson have carpets or curtains? Or pictures or anything?"

"Susan says she'll make curtains as soon as she can," I said.

Jamie added, "Her sewing machine died in the bombing."

Maggie nodded. "That's right. I suppose your rugs and curtains died too."

Everything was dying, but I wasn't going to say it. Maggie knew we were fighting a war.

I walked Maggie back to Thorton House. The rain had stopped, but the sky was dark and the wind blew hard. "I don't know what to think about your mother," Maggie said. "I know you were afraid of her. I know she was awful."

I turned my collar up against the cold. Susan had found a winter coat for me at another jumble sale, but it was already a bit too small. Susan was going to try to let it out. "Don't say you're happy she died," I said to Maggie. "I don't want to hear that."

"Of course not!" Maggie looked shocked. "But don't you have any family left? Grandparents? Aunts or uncles?"

I shrugged. "I don't think so."

"So I suppose Susan's your mother now."

I said, "No. She's our legal guardian." The papers had come. I had them in my box.

"Is that better than a mother?" Maggie asked.

"Of course."

I hugged Maggie good-bye at the stables, gave Butter a pat, and headed home along the sodden path. I was nearly back to the cottage when I heard Jamie scream.

Chapter 9

One scream, cut short by a thud. Then silence. I ran.

The invasion. All spring and summer we'd been preparing for the German army to land in England. Our village was right on the sea, directly across the Channel from Occupied France.

I hadn't heard gunshots. Would the Germans shoot Jamie? Would they kidnap him? My breath came in ragged bursts. My feet squelched through the cold mud. I ran faster.

A final bend in the path, and there was the cottage. Jamie lay sprawled, alone, unmoving, beneath the tree in the front yard.

Dead. Oh, God. *Jamie.*

I ran to him. He lay with his hair flopped against his forehead, motionless on the cold, wet ground. One arm fell across his body, but the other bent unnaturally at his side. Bent where it should be straight. I knelt beside him, sobbing. I grabbed his shoulders.

"Don't touch him!" Susan ran out of the house. I froze. "He might have hurt his neck," she said. "Don't move him."

I couldn't bear it. I would die without Jamie.

"He's not dead," Susan said. She put her hand on my shoulder. "He's breathing, see? Watch his chest." Beneath his coat I could see Jamie's shirt moving very slightly, in and out. "He must have hit his head. He's knocked himself out." She looked at me. "Can you go to the stables? Ask Fred to phone for help?"

I shook my head. I couldn't leave Jamie on the ground.

"All right," Susan said. "I'll go. But don't move him, understand? If he wakes up, make him lie still."

I nodded. I touched Jamie's hand.

"Promise," Susan said.

I nodded again. Tears poured down my face.

Susan ran. I couldn't remember seeing her run before. The wind rattled through the tree branches and ruffled Jamie's hair. He looked so cold. If I covered him with a blanket, would that count as touching him? But I'd have to go into the house for a blanket. I couldn't leave him. But what if he got too cold?

Much sooner than I expected, I heard a car come up the drive. I looked. It wasn't Susan or Fred or Dr.

Graham. It was Lady Thorton, tall and thin in an elegant wool coat. She drew herself up and smiled and waved. "Is Margaret still here?" she asked. Then she saw Jamie and her smile froze. She hurried over.

"I think he was climbing the tree," I said. "He fell. Susan's gone to get help."

"We can use my car," Lady Thorton said.

"Susan said not to move him."

"Yes. I suppose that's right. I'll go, then, and find Susan. Unless you'd rather I stayed with you?"

I shook my head, hard. Lady Thorton shrugged herself out of her coat. She draped it over Jamie. "Tuck yourself under the edge of that," she said. Rain began to fall again. "I'll be back as quickly as I can."

I bent over Jamie, shielding him from the rain. His chest rose and fell. The wind blew harder. I shivered. Jamie's eyelids fluttered. With a sigh, he turned his head to one side.

"Don't move!" I said.

His eyes opened. Relief flooded me. I nearly collapsed.

"My arm hurts," he said. "It really hurts. And my head."

"Don't move," I said.

Jamie scowled at me. "Where's Mum?"

It had always been me that comforted Jamie, not Mam. "It's me, Ada," I said. "I'm right here. Don't move. Help's coming. You're going to be okay."

"I want Mum," he whispered. Tears pooled in the corners of his eyes.

Susan and Lady Thorton came back in Lady Thorton's car. "Mum," Jamie said. He tried to get up. Susan held him down. She let his head rest against her legs and stroked his hair. Minutes later, Dr. Graham pulled up in his own car. By then Jamie could tell us that he could feel and move his hands and feet. Susan said that was good. It meant he probably hadn't broken his neck.

He'd broken his arm. It was bent because he'd broken his arm bones.

He'd end up with a crippled arm, like my foot used to be.

Dr. Graham wrapped sticks and bandages around Jamie's arm. He helped Jamie stand and walked him toward the car. Jamie looked back, eyes fearful. "Mummy?" he said.

"She's not your mummy," I said.

Susan put her arm around me. "Come. We'll all go."

In his office Dr. Graham straightened Jamie's broken arm. Jamie howled. I covered my ears. My stomach hurt. Dr. Graham put Jamie's arm in a plaster cast like the casts I had in hospital. He said Jamie had a concussion, a bad knock on the head. We would have to wake him up all through the night to make sure his brain wasn't injured.

"I can do that," I said. I would sleep in Jamie's room.

"You need your rest," Susan said.

"I want Mummy," said Jamie.

"Stop calling her that!"

"It's all right, Ada," Susan said. "What a mess we've had. But everything's going to be all right."

It was not all right. Jamie would be crippled. He would be unlovable. Just like me.

Back at the cottage, Lady Thorton and Maggie were waiting for us in the kitchen. They cooed and fussed over Jamie. "My son Jonathan broke his arm once in just the same way," Lady Thorton said. "When you fall from a height, never try to catch yourself. Pull your arms in, take it on your shoulder, and roll."

Jamie stared at her. Lady Thorton said, "I'm sure you'll remember next time."

I said, "He can't climb trees if he's going to fall."

"Nonsense," said Lady Thorton. "All boys climb trees."

The Thortons had brought over some stew their housekeeper had made, and brewed tea, a whole strong fresh pot.

"I had to boil the water in a tin pan," Lady Thorton said. "I couldn't find a kettle. I thought this place was better stocked."

"It's very nice," Susan said. "Believe me, we're grateful."

Lady Thorton shrugged. "Silly to have it sit empty when you needed shelter."

Jamie wasn't hungry. Susan took him upstairs. I sat down beside Maggie at the table. "This wasn't the day any of us were expecting," Lady Thorton said. "Ada, I'd originally come to see your foot."

I'd been happy to show it to Maggie, but not Lady Thorton.

"No, thank you," I said.

Her smile stiffened. "Don't be silly."

I wasn't being silly. I'd hidden that foot my entire life.

Lady Thorton didn't like being refused. Her whole face said so. "Mum—" said Maggie.

"Come now." Lady Thorton tapped her fingers on the table. "I've taken an interest in you, Ada. I want to see how you're progressing. Show me."

Taken an interest sounded a lot like *paid for your*

surgery. I knew I didn't have a choice. I unbuckled my shoe and removed it. I took hold of my stocking. My breath felt tight. My fingers trembled. I peeled off my stocking, pushed my foot forward, and looked at the floor.

"Hmm." Lady Thorton leaned close. She stretched out her hand as though she might touch me. I scooted my foot away. "They seem to have made a good job of it," Lady Thorton said. "How does it feel?"

"Fine." I could barely force out the word.

"Wonderful," Lady Thorton said. "I'm very happy for you."

I was not happy. Mam's voice echoed inside my head. *Nice people hate that ugly foot.*

Lady Thorton wasn't nice. She was fierce. She was nosy. She always got her way.

She had brought us dinner and put her own coat over Jamie. *She had paid for my surgery.* I knew I had to be grateful, but I didn't have to like it.

Chapter 10

Susan insisted I lie down in my own bed. She set her alarm clock so she could check on Jamie throughout the night.

I couldn't sleep. My muscles twitched. Pictures flashed through my head, of Jamie sprawled on the ground, of Stephen's pale anguished face, of Mam, of Mam, of Mam.

Mam was dead. She couldn't hurt us.

I couldn't forget her.

Eventually I took my pillow and a blanket and crept into Jamie's room. He was sleeping with his head propped on two pillows, his mouth open, snoring slightly. Bovril snored beside him, tucked under the covers too.

I wrapped myself in the blanket and lay down on the floor. I couldn't see Jamie, but I could listen to him breathe.

I was still awake when Susan tripped over me in the dark. "Ada, go back to bed," she said. "I told you. I'll take care of him."

"It's my job to take care of him. Not yours."

"Not actually," Susan said. "Not anymore. Go to bed." She tried to hoist me up, but I made myself boneless and limp and slithered back to the ground. "Oh, very well," she said. "Stay where you are. But go to sleep. I'll take care of him."

I slept some. I woke each time Susan's alarm went off. I watched each time Susan shook Jamie awake and talked to him to be sure his brain was working.

She kissed his forehead.

He called her Mummy.

The next morning Jamie was tired and grouchy but definitely still alive. He stepped on me when he climbed out of bed. "Why're you on my floor?" he asked, scowling.

"I was taking care of you."

"No, you weren't." He stalked off to the bathroom.

"Yesterday I thought it was the Germans," I said to Susan downstairs. "When Jamie screamed. I thought the Germans had invaded."

She nodded. "I understand. But I think the

invasion's off, at least for the winter. That's what people are saying. Because of the Battle of Britain— because we won."

The Battle of Britain was when all the pilots died. It was when the village children went away.

Susan looked into the teapot. She sighed. "Quite a bit left over from yesterday," she said. "Can't waste it." She drained the tea off the leaves into a pan and set it to warm on the stove. I shuddered. I hated warmed-over tea. "Oatmeal?" Susan asked.

I nodded. I could hear Jamie singing to himself as he walked down the stairs. He sounded fine. Not frightened. Not even hurt very much.

Susan came up beside me. "Ada, what you said, last night—"

I knew instantly what she meant. "It is too my job to take care of Jamie," I said. "It will *always* be my job to take care of him."

Susan sat down at the table. She patted the chair beside her until I sat too.

"You will always be Jamie's big sister," she said. "You've done a very good job taking care of him. But now it's my job to take care of both of you. It will always be my job. Let me do it. I'm the grown-up. You get to be the child."

As though Susan could just take over, manage everything—

"What would you have done," Susan continued, "if when you woke Jamie up, he sounded confused?"

"I'd have shaken him," I said. "I'd have yelled at him until he made sense."

"What if that didn't work?" Susan shook her head at me. "Would you really have gotten angry at Jamie because of something he couldn't do? That doesn't sound like you."

"Not angry—"

"So what would you do?"

I didn't know. I hadn't listened to everything Dr. Graham said about Jamie's concussion. I'd been too worried about his arm. I'd always known how to take care of Jamie before.

"I knew what to do," Susan said. "I made sure I woke him up as often as I needed to. If he needed it, I would have gotten him proper care." She looked at me steadily. "The same as I get you proper care."

I hadn't put my shoes on yet. I flexed the toes on my right foot. My toes that faced forward, after all this time.

"Breathe," Susan said.

I breathed. In. Out. I said, "Will Jamie end up— will he—you know—"

She waited.

I said, "Will his arm be crippled?"

"No," Susan said.

I swallowed.

She said, "In a few weeks he'll be completely fine." Susan touched my shoulder, lightly, the way she did when she was trying to make me come back from in my head far away. "Just as you would have been fine, if you'd had proper medical care when you were a baby."

Of all the things I hated my mother for, that was the worst. That I could have had a regular foot all along.

Susan got up to pour us some tea. I sipped it. Horrible bitter stuff. I said, "I have so much to learn."

"We all do," Susan said. "We never stop learning."

It was nice of her to say that. I knew it wasn't true.

Jamie came into the kitchen. "I'm hungry," he said. "Can I have double oatmeal?"

"Yes," said Susan. "Just a minute now." She got up and gave the oatmeal a stir.

"Can I have lots of sugar on it?" asked Jamie.

"No," said Susan.

"But I'm very hurt and very hungry." Jamie looked up at her through his long eyelashes. "I banged my head and broke my arm."

Even I could see he looked perfectly normal.

"You can have all the oatmeal you want," Susan said, "and no sugar at all. I have plans for the sugar." She bent down and gave him a kiss.

A kiss just out of nowhere.

These things were so easy for Jamie.

"You'll spend today being quiet and still," Susan told him. "You will take naps. If you feel well enough we'll still go to church tomorrow night." Tomorrow was Christmas Eve.

"I thought you were dead," I said. Jamie stared at me. "When you were laying there. I thought you were dead and I'd die too."

Jamie said, "Why would you die? You didn't fall."

I swallowed. Couldn't speak.

"It was very scary," Susan said. "But everything's fine."

I shook my head. Bombs fell from the sky. Boys fell from trees. Anything might happen. Anytime.

Susan made Jamie a nest of blankets and pillows on the cottage's dingy sofa. She read eight chapters of *Swiss Family Robinson*. I sat in front of the fire and practiced breathing, in and out, to keep myself calm. "Are there any books with dragons in them?" I asked when Susan paused.

"There are," she said. "St. George, the patron saint of England, is said to have killed a dragon. I'm sure there must be stories written about him. I'll see if I can find us some."

In the afternoon while Jamie slept, I went out alone and cut down a tiny scraggily fir tree with an ax Fred lent me. I dragged it into the house and propped it near the fireplace. It looked pathetic. Susan's old lights and ornaments had blown up, and there weren't any new ones to buy. We couldn't even find colored paper to make our own decorations.

"It's a war tree," Susan said. She hung a few bright buttons on it, and a feather I found in the yard. "A wartime Christmas."

Last Christmas I'd been so flooded by bad memories. I said, "Jamie and I don't need Christmas. We're used to not having Christmas."

"I know," Susan said. "But I love Christmas. I want a happy one, and I want to share it with you."

I didn't want Susan to expect me to feel happy. I didn't want to disappoint her. I didn't want to embarrass myself at the Thortons' house. The closer it got to Christmas, the more I just wanted to forget the whole thing.

On Christmas Eve, at night, we went to church, the way we'd planned to the year before. I didn't have a fancy dress. Susan couldn't make me one this year, not without a sewing machine, and the dresses she'd bought me while I was in hospital were ordinary. So that was good. Susan insisted on tying a ribbon in my hair. When she wasn't looking I pulled it out.

"It's just church," Susan said. "You'll be fine."

Inside, the church smelled like spice and candle wax and wet wool. Near the altar, a set of wooden dolls sat inside a little pretend stable, with statues of sheep and cows. "It's called a Nativity set," Susan said. "Mary, Joseph, and baby Jesus."

"No horses," I said.

"Not in Bethlehem," said Susan. "Donkeys."

Why not horses? I felt cranky, but then Susan opened a hymnal and passed it to me, and I could read the hymn! I could read the words quickly enough that for the first time I could actually sing along. The tune wasn't hard either.

I was standing on two feet, without crutches, wearing two shoes. I could read and I could sing. I had walked to church even though it was a long way. I needed to remember that. I tried to force myself to feel happy, but underneath the happiness I felt prickly, like my skin was stretched too tight all over. I might not be a cripple, but I didn't know who I was.

At home Susan made us hang our stockings and chivvied us off to bed. In the morning my stocking bulged with something I never expected, or wanted at all.

Chapter 11

It was a doll. A soft, squishy rag doll with embroidered eyes and a permanent smile. It had long brown hair tied back in plaits, like mine, and little green ribbons like the one Susan had given me. It wore a green dress and tiny cloth shoes.

I stared at it. I said, "I'm not a baby."

Susan replied, very quietly, "I made it for you."

I knew that was nice of her. I knew I should say thank you. But I really, really didn't want a doll. "Stephen White's sisters had dolls," I said. I could hear my voice rising. "All the girls on our lane had dolls." I used to watch them out my window playing on the stoop.

I thrust the doll back at Susan. "Not me."

"We can make up for that," Susan said.

"No." What would I do with a doll? Dress it and talk to it and pretend I'd been like the little girls on our lane? The girls who grew up with friends and kind mothers and two good feet?

I'd told myself over and over that I was not going to lose control this Christmas. I was not going to thrash and scream. Now I could feel anger and panic building. I didn't know what to do. I stared at Susan.

She stuffed the doll into the pocket of her dressing gown. "Go outdoors," she said, grabbing my shoulders and pushing me toward the door. "Run around the house a few times. Fast as you can. Go."

Jamie said, "Mummy made me a stuffed cat. Look!"

Susan moved him aside. "Ada needs to blow off steam."

I went out without putting on my coat. I ran through the frozen grass, the frosty air burning my lungs, until I started to sweat despite the cold. My right foot ached, but Susan was right. I felt better.

I'd knitted Christmas presents while I was in hospital. For both Susan and Jamie, I'd made mittens out of bright red yarn. I was proud of them—they didn't have any holes, and you could tell the right mittens from the left ones—but when we got ready to go to Thorton House, I could see how their garish color clashed with Susan's dark green winter coat and navy wool hat. "You don't have to wear those," I said.

"I like them," Susan said. "They're pretty, and they'll keep my hands warm."

Before her house got bombed Susan had nice leather gloves.

I might have chosen a better color for my mittens, if I'd been able to choose the yarn myself, if there'd been lots of yarn to choose from in the shops, which probably there wasn't.

I scowled.

The closer we got to Thorton House the harder it was to breathe. "Relax," Susan said. "They're our friends." She held a small cake she'd made as our gift to the Thortons. It had taken most of our remaining sugar ration for the month. We climbed the stone steps to the massive front door.

"Ada, if you need to calm down," Susan said, "just say 'excuse me,' and you and Maggie can take a walk. Go down to the stables and visit Butter."

I nodded.

The door swung open before we could knock. Lord Thorton, dressed in some sort of fancy war uniform, stood in front of us holding out his hand.

I'd seen him once at a distance, but never up close.

He was enormous—not fat but so tall and broad he filled the doorway. "Welcome," he said in a deep, solemn voice.

"Welcome," I echoed. I bobbed my head at him, afraid to touch his outstretched hand.

Lord Thorton blinked. I hoped I hadn't done something wrong.

"Happy Christmas," Susan said. She shifted the cake to one hand and shook Lord Thorton's hand with the other.

Jamie bounced past me into the enormous front hall. "Cor!" he said. "You could fly an airplane in here! A real one! A Spitfire!"

Maybe not a Spitfire, but a kite, for sure.

"Jamie," Susan said, "get back here and wish Lord Thorton happy Christmas."

"Whee!" yelled Jamie, running the length of the hall.

"Hey there, sport!" A tall, thin man—very like Lord Thorton but much younger and not nearly as intimidating—grabbed Jamie around the waist. He tossed Jamie over his shoulder and brought him back to Lord Thorton. "Shake hands like a gentleman," he said. Jamie, upside down and giggling, shook Lord Thorton's hand with his left hand, the one that wasn't in plaster.

The man shifted Jamie higher onto his shoulder and smiled at me. "I'm Jonathan Thorton," he said. "You must be my sister's friend."

I shook his hand. "Ada Smith," I said. My manners came back to me. "Pleased to meet you, Lieutenant Thorton." Susan had told me to say that.

He bent forward. "Call me Jonathan," he said. "In the RAF we're not much for rank. And I'll call you Ada, shall I? Happy Christmas."

Maggie ran in just as Lord Thorton was offering Susan something called an aperitif. "Happy Christmas!" she said. "I'm so glad you're here!" She whispered in my ear, "Dinner's going to be inedible. I just came from the kitchen. Mum's having kittens."

I whispered back, "We brought cake."

Lord Thorton led us into an impossibly grand room with glossy furniture, carpet woven in flowered patterns, and bookcases that reached from wall to wall and floor to ceiling. Thorton House was miles fancier than Susan's old house, which had been the nicest place I'd ever seen.

I grabbed Maggie's arm. "I'm glad I already know you," I said. "Otherwise I'd be afraid of all this."

Maggie rolled her eyes. "Pish," she said. "As if you're ever afraid."

Maggie's house had an entire room just for eating in. The table was so big that twenty chairs could fit around it, and they *had twenty chairs in the room.* I counted. The extras stood against the walls.

Lady Thorton came from wherever the kitchen was, looking harassed, and we all sat down. Each place at the table had a plate surrounded by three glasses, two knives, three spoons, and two forks. I froze. What were we supposed to do with all that?

"Hey," Jamie called out, "why've I got so many forks and things?"

Lord Thorton grimaced, as though he'd spilled his aperitif down his trousers. Susan leaned forward, but Jonathan spoke first. "They're extras," he said, "in case you fling some onto the floor." His smile lit the table. "Isn't that right, Mater?"

Mater must have meant Lady Thorton, because she smiled back. "We're having three courses," she told Jamie.

I didn't know what *courses* were, and I didn't think Jamie did either.

"Three courses!" said Jonathan. "It must be Christmas. We don't get three courses in the air force."

Jamie leaned over. "It *is* Christmas," he whispered.

"Right," Jonathan whispered back. "You having a good one? Presents and all that?"

"Candy," Jamie said. "And a cat. And Bovril got a mouse."

"Excellent."

"Bovril's our cat," I explained. "A real one, not a toy."

"So the boy got a toy cat, and the cat got a toy mouse? Or a real one?"

"A toy mouse," Jamie said, wide-eyed. "Bovril would crunch a real one."

"Ah, good," Jonathan said.

I knew that the Thortons' housekeeper, the only servant remaining out of bunches they'd had before the war, was cooking the dinner. Maggie said she was a terrible cook, but I didn't believe it until the food started coming out. I can cook. Susan teaches me. It isn't hard.

Christmas dinner started with bowls of greasy, salty soup, slices of crumbly gray war bread, and celery sticks. Apparently that was the first course.

I ate everything. I'd had plenty worse. It made me feel calmer that the food was so bad.

Jamie nibbled his bread, ignored his soup, crossed two pieces of celery in his left hand and flew them in circles over his plate.

"Knock it off," Jonathan said quietly. "They'll banish you to the nursery even if it *is* Christmas."

Jamie blinked and put his celery airplane in his lap.

Meanwhile, Susan and Lady Thorton were discussing fire-watching. It was something they were going to be doing with the WVS. The phrase itself— *fire-watching*—seemed unsettling. "Whose fires will you watch?" I asked. *And why do they need watching?*

"No one's, I hope," Lady Thorton said. "We'll be keeping a lookout for bombs or incendiaries. From the church steeple."

Incendiaries were small bombs designed to start fires. I said, "From the steeple? You'll need a really long ladder to get up there."

Maggie grinned at me. "There's stairs."

I grinned back. When Maggie knew things I didn't, I didn't mind.

The joint—a big piece of roasted beef—came in, along with a platter of vegetables and a massive Yorkshire pudding. It smelled fantastic, but it tasted awful, dry as sawdust, as though it had finished cooking sometime the day before and then sat shriveling in the hot oven overnight.

Jamie murmured something under his breath. I thought it was probably a quote from *Swiss Family Robinson,* and hoped he wouldn't repeat it. Susan took a bite, and chewed, and chewed, and chewed.

"Mmmph," said Lord Thorton. "I thought you said she could cook." He lifted an eyebrow at Lady Thorton.

Lady Thorton shook her head. "I didn't think anyone could butcher roast beef."

It was funny. *Butcher* roast beef. Without thinking, I laughed.

Maggie jumped, startled. Jonathan grinned. I looked at Susan, anxious, but then Lord Thorton let out a rough sort of guffaw. "Quite," he said. "Butcher roast beef. Quite." He put his napkin up to his eyes and started to chuckle. Then he laughed. Lady Thorton laughed. Susan and Jonathan and Maggie laughed. After a moment I felt safe enough to laugh again too.

"Why aren't there Christmas crackers?" Lord Thorton asked. "None in the shops, I suppose."

Lady Thorton shook her head.

"Pity. I think this whole day would go more smoothly if we all had silly hats on our heads." He passed the gravy boat to Susan. "Drown your meat, my dear, it can only help."

Halfway through the dried beef course, Susan turned to Lord Thorton and said, "I wonder if you might be able to help me find a job."

I looked up, surprised. Lord Thorton raised his eyebrows. "A job?" he said. "What sort of job?"

"Something I could do from here so I could stay with the children," Susan said. "Lady Thorton thought you might know of a project I could help with. Analytics, say—"

"*Analytics?*" said Lord Thorton.

"Well, yes," said Susan. "Or some other type of computational work. There must be war projects or industrial things that aren't classified." Susan's face was turning pink. She persisted. "I'm sure I'm rusty, but with a bit of time to bone up—"

"Come," Lady Thorton cut in, "don't look so astonished. Don't you know her credentials?"

"*Credentials?*" Lord Thorton wiped his mustache. He said to Susan, "I know you as the spinster who was Becky Montgomery's friend. The quiet one."

"She's got a first from Oxford in maths," Lady Thorton said.

"*A first from Oxford?*" It was becoming amusing, how Lord Thorton kept repeating things people said to him.

Susan's face was bright pink now, but when she spoke her voice was firm. "My concentration was numerical analysis."

"You're joking," Lord Thorton said.

Susan's eyes flashed. She lifted her chin. She wasn't joking.

"I can find you work immediately," Lord Thorton said. "I know just the department. You'll have to put the children into schools—"

"No," said Susan.

"It'd be easy enough. Ada could go with Margaret, and we'd find a good place for the boy."

"Away from Jamie?" Let alone me at Maggie's posh school. I could never.

"No," Susan said firmly. "The children and I stay here."

A wash of relief squelched my panic at its start.

"But I do need work," Susan said, "and I'd be better off using my education than clerking in a shop in the village, which is the only obvious local opportunity."

"I'm stunned," Lord Thorton said. "Flabbergasted. I had no idea."

"Yes, we can all see you've thoroughly underestimated her," Lady Thorton said. She rolled her eyes at Susan, who responded with a slight smile.

"Well, I apologize for doing so." Lord Thorton poured a bit more gravy over his shards of meat. "And yes, I probably can find you something. Don't know what, but I'll have a poke around. I'll be in touch."

"Thank you," Susan said.

After the third course, Susan's cake, we went into the room next door. The Thortons gave us all Christmas presents. Jamie got a set of toy soldiers that had once been Jonathan's. Susan got a sewing machine. "It's too much," she protested, running her finger over the shiny metal wheel.

Lady Thorton waved her hand. "It was in the housekeeper's room," she said. "No one's used it in years. I hope it works, and if not, I hope you can repair it."

I got a book, a thick, heavy one. "Margaret told me you liked words," Lady Thorton said. "She thought you'd find this useful."

I did like words, but I didn't understand what Lady Thorton meant until I opened the book. It was full of words. All the words in the world, and what they meant.

"It's a dictionary," Lord Thorton said. "Susan can show you how to use it."

I looked at the first page. A. *Aardvark*. What a funny word. A-ard-vark. *"A nocturnal burrowing mammal with long ears, a tubular snout, and a long extensible tongue."* I laughed. A tubular snout and long extensible tongue? Even if I didn't know what the words *tubular* and *extensible* meant, that sounded. fabulous. I looked up at Lord and Lady Thorton. "Thank you!"

Maggie poked her mother. "Told you she'd love it," she said.

Lady Thorton smiled. "I see that now."

I waited until we were putting our coats on to go home to give my gift to Maggie. I'd knitted her a little neck wrap, in a fancy pattern Susan found for me. I showed Maggie how to button it. "For riding," I said. "It'll keep you warm, but it can't get caught in the reins like a scarf might."

"I love it," Maggie said.

"Well done," Susan murmured on the walk home. She held Jamie's hand but didn't try to take mine. "Both of you. Your manners were very nice. I was proud of you."

At home Susan and I put up the blackouts and Jamie swept out the fire. Susan made tea and fresh scones—she'd saved some sugar back for them—and while we ate by the fire, she read us a long funny Christmas story about ghosts and a man who started out mean but turned nice at the end. It was the sort of story you hoped might be true.

"Why did you ask Lord Thorton about a job?" I

said when we were gathering up our cups and saucers and banking the fire for bed.

"He's got a mathematical background himself," Susan said. "Whatever he's doing for the war, I suspect he's using it. Plus, he's the sort of man that has connections. Lady Thorton suggested I ask him."

Whatever Lord Thorton's war work was, it was secret. He wouldn't tell anyone a thing about it.

"If you get a job, will you earn enough to keep us?" I asked.

"Stop," Susan said. "Lady Thorton's in charge of the paperwork for evacuees. She said she'll continue your and Jamie's stipend for the duration of the war. I am merely preparing for the future. That, and I should like to feel useful again."

I thought of all the hundreds of ways Susan was useful. I said, "I should like to feel useful too."

"You're eleven years old," Susan said. "You get to be the child now, Ada, for once in your life. I will be the adult." She paused. "You really don't want that doll, do you?"

I didn't say anything right away. Coals crackled in the grate. Jamie rubbed Bovril's belly, and the cat stretched long, hooking his claws into the rug.

"It's all right if you don't," Susan said.

"I needed a doll a long time ago," I said. "It's too late for me to have one now."

Susan studied me. "I wish that wasn't true," she said. But it was true, and she didn't try to talk me out of thinking it. Susan was good that way. "I'll give you a different present."

"You don't need to." I leaned against Susan's shoulder. I'd survived Christmas. That was gift enough.

Chapter 12

The next morning I woke early, nervous and excited about the paper chase. I dressed and made the fire and started oatmeal and tea.

Jamie woke up cranky. He said his head hurt and so did his arm.

"You must have overdone it," Susan told him. "Too much Christmas. Pop back into bed. I'll read to you after I come home from walking Ada to the stables."

I said, "I can stay home. I'll take care of him." A paper chase was like a fox hunt, without a fox or hounds. Did I want to go on a fox hunt, really?

"Don't be silly," Susan said. "Jamie just needs sleep."

I looked at her.

"Fill the coal hod while I fry you an egg. You'll need it, for staying power. You'll probably be in the saddle for hours." She smiled. "Becky was a great believer in eggs before a hunt."

Eggs weren't rationed yet, but they were scarce. Jamie wanted hens.

I brought in more coal. I straightened the sitting room. I ate my egg with toasted war bread, drank my tea, and started to do the breakfast dishes.

Susan came into the kitchen, pulling on her coat. "Leave that, it's time to go. I'll walk over with you."

"You don't need to," I said. As if I couldn't walk to the Thortons' stables without help.

"I'd like to," Susan said. "I'll probably know everyone there. These were Becky's friends."

"Shouldn't you stay with Jamie?"

"Ada." Susan raised her eyebrows. "He's asleep. Also he's perfectly capable of being left alone for a short time."

He might break his other arm. He might—

"I don't need you," I said.

"I know that," Susan said. "Neither does Jamie just now. Let's go."

The Thortons' stables were crowded with unfamiliar adults wearing posh riding habits and gleaming horses with braided manes. Maggie had lent me a tweed coat, and I had jodhpurs and proper boots, Maggie's hand-me-downs, so I knew I looked all right—I looked just like Maggie—but I felt wildly out of place. I hadn't braided Butter's mane. Couldn't; I didn't know how.

Susan surveyed the people with a slight smile. "Same old crowd." She spoke to a few of them, then followed me into Butter's stall and stood by Butter's head while I brushed him.

"You never rode," I said. She'd sold Becky's hunters after Becky died.

"I gave it a good try," Susan said. "Becky wanted me to. It just wasn't quite my thing. Too frightening, being on top of a thousand-pound animal with a tiny little mind of its own."

I looked up. Susan, afraid?

"But I went to the parties," she continued. "The hunt breakfasts and the teas and once even the hunt ball." She buckled Butter's girth on his off side and passed it under his belly to me.

"Did you like the parties?"

"I did," Susan said.

This surprised me. When we'd first come, Susan had been so sad about Becky's death that she didn't enjoy anything. She never went anywhere.

Susan said, "I have fond memories."

"What's *fond*?" I wrestled the bit into Butter's mouth.

"Happy. Content."

"You're going home now, right?" I slid the reins over Butter's head and led him out of the stall. I looked around for Maggie.

"Butter!" A woman I didn't know clapped her hands in delight. "Look, everyone, Butter's back! And Miss Smith!" She extended her hand to Susan, who shook it firmly. "Are you riding again?" the woman asked.

"No," said Susan. She patted my shoulder. "This is my ward Ada. She's taken over Butter."

The woman shook my hand too. "How lucky for you," she said. "Becky Montgomery trained that pony well."

Susan and the woman kept talking. I saw Maggie across the yard with her pony, Ivy. I walked Butter over to them, tightened my girth, and climbed into the saddle. Someone blew a horn—there was a lot of laughing at that, though I didn't know why. Susan smiled and waved at me through the crowd. I nodded to her and gathered up my reins.

"You're not scared, are you?" Maggie said. "You look scared. I didn't think you were ever scared."

Mam was worse when she knew I was afraid. I had learned never to admit it. "There's so many people," I said instead.

"Before the war it was always like this," Maggie said. "In season the hounds went out thrice a week."

There weren't any hounds now. Instead we chased a trail of scraps of paper, strewn by Fred from horseback a couple of hours beforehand. Lord Thorton led the way. Maggie and I held our ponies until the field cleared. As juniors we had to ride in the rear.

The galloping horses made Butter wild. He wanted to race. I held him tighter while he fought me, snatching at the bit. Sweat streaked his sides. I braced my hands against his neck. "Stop it, stop it," I said to him. "You idiot, behave!"

Butter tossed his head. He danced sideways. He jigged.

"Let him go," Maggie said. "Let him run a little, he'll settle down."

I let him run, but I still had to grip the reins so hard my fingers hurt. I'd never known Butter to misbehave.

"You're winding him up!" Maggie said. "Relax!"

I couldn't relax. I didn't dare. A rabbit darted out from under Butter's hooves, startling me more than it startled Butter. My hands hurt. My breath hurt in my chest. The wind forced tears from my eyes.

We came to a big ditch full of water. Ivy plonked into it and waded through. Butter hesitated, then leaped. I flew with him, up, out of the saddle, miles from the saddle. He landed on the ditch's far side. I kept going.

I dropped the reins, pulled my arms in, and took the fall on my shoulder like Lady Thorton had said. I rolled across the grass, unhurt. Butter pranced in place, his feet tangled in the dangling reins. He'd break the reins next, the wretched pony. I scrambled to my feet.

Jonathan Thorton stopped Oban at Butter's side. "Easy," he said to Butter. To me he said, "Are you all right?"

I nodded. I could feel my face flame. It had been months since I'd last fallen off—since before the hospital.

Jonathan dismounted. He untangled Butter and offered me a leg up.

"I can do it myself," I said.

"Of course you can," he agreed. "I'm just trying to act the gentleman."

I didn't mean to be prickly at him. "I'm sorry." I let him toss me back into Butter's saddle.

"Don't be," he said. "We don't call it the Champagne Ditch for nothing."

I didn't know what he meant.

"That ditch is famous for getting people off. And

if you fall off during a hunt you have to buy a bottle of Champagne for the masters." He grinned. "Don't worry. I don't think the paper chase counts. Besides, you're a little young for Champagne."

I frowned at him. I didn't know the word *Champagne.*

"Fizzy wine," Maggie said helpfully. "French stuff. I've had a sip, it's lovely." Jonathan raised his eyebrows. "A *sip,*" Maggie said.

The other riders had left us far behind. We started after them at an easy canter. Butter quit fighting; either he was finally tired or he was sorry he'd dumped me. Probably tired.

"Where'd you learn to ride?" Jonathan asked.

"Here," I said. "Fred teaches me." Then I laughed, remembering. "I actually started with your horse. Oban. He jumped into our field. I jumped him out again."

Jonathan stared. "That was *you?*"

"That was me," I said. It had been the day I first met Maggie, the day she whacked her head.

"But Mum said that was an evacuee," Jonathan said. "A lame little girl from the slums. She made it sound like an accident you weren't killed."

"It probably was an accident. I didn't know anything." I added, "I'm not lame."

"I see that," Jonathan said.

"I was never lame," I said.

Maggie frowned at me but didn't say anything. Neither did Jonathan.

"Your horse is lovely," I said, to fill the odd silence.

Jonathan grinned. "My sister despises him."

"I know," I said, "but I love him. He didn't dump me when he could have. And he's beautiful." Oban had a grace and elegance Butter could never touch. It was like the difference between the Honorable Margaret Thorton and me.

We cantered on, jumping a stile and then another smaller ditch. Butter had settled, and I felt safer riding between Jonathan and Maggie.

"I have to go back to the airfield tomorrow," Jonathan said, "but next time I'm on leave we'll ride out together. The two of you and me, just us three."

"Do you mean that?" I asked.

His brown eyes looked directly into mine. "Word of honor," he said.

The rest of the riders had paused at the far end of the field. Jonathan trotted toward some of his friends. I said to Maggie, "You never told me he was so nice."

She shook her head at me. "I never knew he was." Then she said, "Why'd you say you were never lame?

He knows all about your clubfoot and your surgery."

I shrugged. I didn't know why. "I'm not lame," I said.

It wasn't entirely true. I knew I still limped some even now. But all those words—*lame, crippled, nobbut a disgrace.* I wanted to forget I'd ever been that girl.

After the chase, the Thortons hosted what they called a breakfast even though we didn't start eating it until midafternoon. "Any meal you have after hunting is called a breakfast," Maggie said. "It doesn't make sense to me either." Maggie said if there wasn't a war on we would be eating steak and kidney pie, but instead we had a variation on Lord Woolton pie, a particularly awful wartime dish of baked vegetables thickened with oatmeal.

It was nearly full dark by the time I got home. Susan had put the blackout up by herself, and she and Jamie were snug by the fire. She smiled when I came in. "Did you enjoy it?"

I took off my filthy boots in the entry. I nodded to Susan, smiling back. She got up and came toward me.

"I've come up with the perfect gift for you," she said. She handed me a slip of paper. "Here. Happy Christmas."

I padded into the room and pushed Jamie over so I could sit on the sofa. I unfolded Susan's paper. In large, clearly printed letters, it read: "Transfer of ownership: the pony named Butter, from Susan Elisabeth Smith to Ada Maria Smith. December 26, 1940."

Chapter 13

Butter.

To Ada Maria Smith.

To *me.*

I swallowed. I said, "If you're joking, it isn't funny."

"Why would I be joking?" asked Susan.

I said, "And no one can take him away?"

"No," Susan said. "No matter what."

I said, "What if something happens and I can't take care of him?"

Susan said, "I'll help you. I'm your guardian. We'll manage."

"What if something happens to *you?*"

"Nothing will happen to me."

She didn't know that.

"We'll manage," Susan said. "We've managed so far."

I closed my fingers around the paper. I whispered,

"Thank you." Then I turned and ran up the stairs.

"Where are you going?" Susan yelled.

"I'm putting this in the box with my birth certificate!"

Susan had shown me how to look up words in my dictionary. I stayed up in bed that night with my light on, reading.

Guardian: one who guards, protects, or preserves; a keeper, defender; sometimes = guardian angel.

Guardian angel: an angel conceived as watching over or protecting a particular person or place.

Angel: A spiritual being believed to act as an attendant, agent, or messenger of God, conventionally represented in human form with wings and a long robe.

Honestly, I had no idea what any of that meant. Guardian was someone who guards, sure. That made sense; it was what I expected. But humans with wings? Messengers of God? Not so much.

Ward. That word was complicated. It meant the rooms of a hospital, like where I'd stayed after my surgery. It meant a division of a city or a town. It meant a minor under care of a guardian—that was me—but then it said, "archaic: to guard."

Archaic: belonging to the past.

The next morning, I asked Susan, "Do you know anyone with a guardian angel?"

She didn't look up from slicing bread. "Maybe," she said. "It's one of those odd religious ideas. Sounds nice but doesn't actually matter."

I wished she'd look at me. "Have you ever seen one?" I asked.

"No," she said. "I'd be rather surprised if I did. Set the table, please. Where's Jamie?"

Once we'd sat down to breakfast I said, "You call Jamie and me your wards. The word *ward* used to mean the thing that did the guarding."

This time Susan gave me her attention. "Have you been reading your dictionary?" she asked.

I nodded.

"Well, the key part of what you just said is *used to mean*. *Ward* used to mean the thing that did the guarding. Now it means the girl who gets to be guarded and who therefore doesn't have to spend quite so much energy worrying."

Jamie said, "Why can't you just be our mum?"

I said, "Because she isn't."

"Ada," Susan said, "I really don't mind Jamie calling me Mum."

I said, "I'd rather be your ward. I want to help you."

Susan paused to sip her tea. She said, "You've been very strong your whole life, Ada. You get to be guarded now. You get to feel safe."

"Huh," I said. "I'm supposed to feel safe?"

"Of course."

I never did. Never once. Anything could happen, anytime—Mam's death proved it. "Do you feel safe?" I asked her.

She looked back in surprise. "I do," she said. "I mean, for a bit there, with the air raids, and when we thought the invasion was coming, and that night in London—but mostly, yes."

"But Becky died," I said. "She left you all alone."

"That made me sad," she said. "It still makes me sad. But not unsafe."

I said, "Can I go fire-watching?" Susan had done a shift already. She'd stood in the church steeple for two hours in the dead of the night. She'd watched for fires and protected the village.

Susan looked me up and down. She said, "I think that's an excellent idea."

Chapter 14

The WVS was pleased to let me help fire-watch, but they said it would take a few weeks to get me onto the rota. On Saturday, in daylight, Susan took Jamie and me up the church steeple so I'd know where to go and what to do. Right inside the church was a small door near the vestibule that I'd never noticed before. Behind it rose a narrow, ancient staircase made of chipped, uneven stone.

Susan led. Jamie followed. I went last, slowly and carefully, picking my way. I could never have climbed stairs like these before my surgery—my crutches wouldn't have been able to find steady purchase. I would have fallen for sure. I clutched the handrail. My heart pounded and my mouth went dry.

The stairs opened into a space like a balcony, high up, looking down on the rows of pews. For a moment the pews swirled dizzily. I scooted sideways into a room where thick, tied-up ropes hung through holes in the ceiling. "This is the bell-ringers' room," Susan said. "Those ropes ring the church bells."

Jamie pretended to pull one of the ropes. Susan frowned. "Absolutely not." Since the start of the war, church bells were only to be rung to signal a German invasion.

Susan, then Jamie, climbed a wooden ladder nailed against the wall. I stared at the ladder. I'd never climbed a ladder before. Couldn't, with a clubfoot. "Hold on to the sides and use the rungs like stairs," Susan said.

I wedged my right foot forward as far as it would go until my toes touched the wall behind the ladder. That brought the weight of the rung under the back of my heel, so climbing didn't hurt so much. It still wasn't easy. When I looked down, the floor again seemed to swirl.

Above the bell-ringers' room, eight bells filled the bottom of the steeple. They were huge—big enough to bathe in. I paused to steady myself. "I didn't expect them to be so large."

"Each bell plays a different note," said Susan. "If they're pulled in a certain order they make music. It's called change-ringing. I was a change-ringer in my father's parish, when I was a girl."

Now my hands were shaking. I went up more

wooden steps between the bells to a small inward-slanting door. Susan opened it. We stepped outside. We were halfway up the steeple, standing on a narrow ledge framed by a waist-high stone wall.

I looked over the edge of the wall. The ground was miles away; I had no idea we'd climbed so high. The churchyard grass seemed to rise and fall. I could feel myself pitching forward. I shrieked.

Susan grabbed my shoulder. "Ada, what's wrong?".

My hands clutched the stone wall. My stomach heaved.

"You're all right," Susan said. "You can't fall. The wall's strong."

I'd spent my life looking out Mam's window, down three stories to the street. You'd think I'd be used to looking down.

Jamie ran from one side of the steeple to the other, squealing in delight. "Jamie!" I said. "Get away from the edge!"

"He's fine," Susan said. "He can't get hurt."

My head rang. Standing in the steeple was as bad as being bombed.

Susan said, "Maybe this isn't a good idea. Let's go back downstairs."

"No!"

"It's all right to be afraid," Susan said.

I gritted my teeth and glared at her. "*Of course* I'm not afraid."

"The fate of the war does not depend on you fire-watching," Susan said.

What if it did? Not the big war, but my own? What if my fear kept me safe? "I am going to fire-watch," I said. I stood, locked my knees, and steadied myself against the steeple with one hand.

If I looked up instead of down, it wasn't so bad. On one side hills rose covered in brown winter grass. On the other, the ocean spread flat and clean. I took a deep breath, and filled my lungs with the scent of the ocean. I felt the wind on my face. The sky seemed safe.

As long as there weren't any bombs.

Going down was harder than going up. Going down, to get onto the ladder, I had to swing one foot out into open air. Either I swung my unreliable right foot, and hoped it could find the ladder, or I had to trust my weight to the right foot while swinging the left.

"You don't need to torture yourself," Susan said, watching me.

"I don't know what you're talking about." I crossed

the bell-ringers' room and started down the stairs. They were difficult for me even going slowly. I could never get down them fast.

If I started letting myself feel afraid I would never be able to stop.

Outside the church, I stood still for a moment, my feet firm on the ground. I let myself settle. I looked out at the stones in the graveyard.

Mam wasn't there. Mam was gone.

A sudden thought struck me. "Where's Becky's body?" I asked Susan. "Where is Becky buried?"

Chapter 15

"Not here," Susan said. "She's buried in the town where she grew up."

"But her funeral was here," I said, with a sudden flash of memory. "Half the village came."

Susan furrowed her brow. "How do you know that?"

"Lady Thorton said so," I said. "Ages ago." *Most of the village came to the funeral.* I hadn't known what a funeral was, but I remembered Lady Thorton saying those words.

"How odd that you remember." Susan took Jamie's hand and shepherded us down the road. She reached for my hand, but I pretended not to see.

"I remember everything people say about Becky," I said.

"Why?" asked Susan.

I shrugged. "She was important. You loved her. She gave you Butter."

Susan took a deep breath. When she blew out, it made a white cloud in the cold air. She walked faster. "After she died her parents made the decisions," she said. "They held her funeral here because she had friends here. Her house had belonged to her grandmother before it belonged to her, so she'd visited the village ever since she was a little girl. But they had her buried in their own churchyard. I suppose they wanted to be able to visit her grave. People often visit their loved ones' graves."

"You said that before," I said. "With Mam." Though Mam wasn't exactly a loved one.

"Yes," Susan said.

"But you don't visit Becky," I said.

"No," said Susan. "I never have."

"Do Becky's parents not like you either?" Susan's parents didn't like her. I didn't understand why.

Susan sighed. "I don't know. I never asked them. Her father certainly never seemed friendly."

I asked, "Is that why you wanted Mam buried here, because you don't get to visit Becky?"

Jamie asked, "If you went to visit Becky's grave, would you feel less sad about her dying?"

Susan's eyes were watering, but it may have been only the wind. "No," she said. I didn't know which question she was answering.

Two weeks passed. Maggie returned to school. Several days later, toward the end of January, I was reading in the front room when someone knocked briskly on the door. I got up and opened it. Lady Thorton blew in on a rush of wind, cold and fierce like the weather. She looked me up and down. "Where's your mother?" she asked.

"Dead."

"I don't—honestly, Ada. I mean, where's Miss Smith?"

"Where's *Susan*?"

"Yes, of course." Lady Thorton sounded right ticked. "Who else could I possibly mean?"

Susan came in from the kitchen, wiping her hands. "Oh," Lady Thorton said. "There you are. I've decided to move in with you."

Chapter 16

"Please don't let her," I said to Susan later when we were alone, chopping vegetables for dinner.

"There's no *let*," Susan said. "This is her house. She's letting *us* stay with *her*. It's not my decision."

The government was kicking Lady Thorton out of Thorton House because they wanted Thorton House for something to do with the war. In wartime the government could take over whatever they liked. Lady Thorton had two weeks to move.

"Can't she afford to stay somewhere else? Somewhere nicer?"

"Of course she can," Susan said. "She doesn't want to."

"I don't see why not."

"It doesn't matter whether you do," Susan said. "But try to imagine how she feels, rattling around that huge empty place. Her husband, children, servants, all gone, most of the rooms shut up. Don't you think she's been terribly lonely?"

It was hard to imagine Lady Thorton having feelings. "She's always busy," I said. "And she has that housekeeper."

"The housekeeper's going to live with her sister in Lyme Regis," Susan replied. "Lady Thorton has friends in the village, everything she's used to is here, and if she stays with us she won't have to be alone. I think living with us will be good for her."

I thought about it. "Does she really have friends?" I asked. "In the village, I mean." None of the women who rode in the paper chase had been from the village.

"Yes," Susan said, with asperity. "She has me."

For a week, Lady Thorton sorted her furniture and belongings, storing things in the attics of Thorton House or having them moved into our cottage. She took one of the two empty bedrooms for herself, but, instead of giving Maggie the other, decided that whenever Maggie wasn't at school she would share my room with me.

Lady Thorton took half my bedroom away, and Susan didn't stop her. Lady Thorton moved my things aside and covered them up and changed them, and Susan let her do it.

Lady Thorton wanted the last bedroom for what she called a guest room, for when Jonathan or someone else came to stay.

The whole cottage looked different with Lady Thorton's stuff in it. We had more pots and pans and dishes than we could ever use. We had a different, bigger kitchen table, extra kitchen chairs, a plush sofa, and a fancy wing chair in the sitting room. A radio again, bigger than Susan's old one. A fender for the fire, rugs everywhere, paintings on the walls. The painting above the mantel, Lady Thorton said, was quite good, but it was of dead game birds and I hated it. A horse painting went into the kitchen. I liked it better.

The first night after Lady Thorton finished moving in we ate dinner together. Susan and I cooked. Lady Thorton sat at the head of the new table, in the place Susan usually took.

I said, "Jonathan doesn't get leave very often. When he does, he can share Jamie's room. Then Maggie could have her own bedroom."

Lady Thorton looked at me coolly. She said, "I imagined you girls would enjoy sharing."

That was true in one way, but in another way it

wasn't. I started to speak again. Across the table Susan shook her head at me, hard. I didn't know why—she never minded my having an opinion—but I closed my mouth.

Lady Thorton didn't even clear her own place at the table. She got up and went out. Jamie started carrying the dishes to the sink. Susan waited until the door clicked shut on Lady Thorton, then said, "Do you dislike sharing your bedroom with Maggie? I never thought you would."

"Of course not," I said. "I'd share anything I had with Maggie."

"Then what's the matter?"

I struggled to find words for my feelings. Susan waited. Finally I said, "I'd never mind sharing my room with Maggie. But Lady Thorton's turned it into Maggie's room, that she's sharing with me." I paused. "I know I'll never be like Maggie. I just never felt this different from her before."

Susan raised her eyebrows. "Show me."

Lady Thorton had put another bed into what had been my room. She'd taken away my dresser, added a glossy wardrobe, and replaced my small bookshelf with a larger one. Two of its shelves were stuffed full of Maggie's books, while my dictionary lay sideways next to my box on the third. Lady Thorton had emptied a drawer in Maggie's wardrobe for my socks and underwear, and pushed Maggie's mass of dresses over to leave room for mine, but as I only had three—two day dresses and a new Sunday one—they hardly took up any room.

Lady Thorton had spread matching coverlets over both beds, and frilly pillows, and strange lacy curtains that hung from under the mattresses to the floor. She'd hung ruffled curtains over the window outside the blackout frame. She'd spread a wool rug from Maggie's old room on the floor between the beds and plastered the whole wall above Maggie's bed with framed photographs.

Susan said, "I see. But you know, before we were bombed you had a rug and curtains. You had more clothing too."

"Not like Maggie's clothes," I said.

Susan reached into the wardrobe and fingered the fabric of one of Maggie's dresses. "Not many girls your age have clothes like Margaret Thorton," she said.

"The Honorable Margaret Thorton," I said. It was Maggie's official title. Not Lord or Lady, but close enough.

"That sounds jealous," Susan said. "Are you?"

"No!" I said. "I don't care about Maggie's things. But this doesn't look like my room anymore, and nobody asked me. Nobody asked if I wanted a different coverlet or lace around the bottom of my bed. Nobody asked what I wanted at all. The whole house doesn't look like ours anymore. It looks like it belongs to Lady Thorton."

Susan pulled me close and kissed the top of my head. I squirmed away. "It does belong to Lady Thorton," she said. "I know you don't want to hear that, but it's true."

"She should have asked," I said.

"I agree," said Susan. "With your room, she should have. I'm glad for the new kitchen things, and a more comfortable sitting room, but I wouldn't have wanted Lady Thorton rearranging my bedroom either."

"I never had my own space before."

Susan nodded. "It was important to you."

"I didn't realize it," I said, "but it was." I leaned into her a little bit.

"Would you rather share my room?" Susan asked. "I'd give you half the space, and you could keep it however you wished."

I considered. "Lady Thorton wouldn't like that."

"Doesn't matter," Susan said. "I'll handle it with her, if it's what you want."

I thought some more. "I don't know," I said. "Let me wait and see how it is when Maggie's here." I loved being around Maggie. It was Lady Thorton I felt anxious about.

"That's fine," Susan said. "Meanwhile, you can do anything to your side of the room that you want. Change it back as much as you like. Just leave Maggie's belongings alone. And keep your door shut—what Lady Thorton doesn't see, she can't grieve over."

It was odd to have Lady Thorton inside our house at night. She took her bath right after supper, then sat downstairs in her dressing gown. *Lady Thorton wearing a dressing gown.* I couldn't help but stare. She sat in the big wing chair, slippered feet on a needlework footstool, silently reading. I watched her turn the pages. "Ada, please," she said, looking up, "I am not on exhibit in a zoo."

I looked at the wall. Jamie said, "What's a zoo?"

Lady Thorton raised her eyebrows. Susan replied calmly, "It's a park where they have all sorts of unusual animals in cages, and people pay money to go look at them. There's a big zoo in London."

"Like a freak show," said Jamie. Who knew where he'd heard that.

"Not especially," Lady Thorton said.

"What sort of animals?" I asked.

"All sorts," Susan said. "Ones you read about in books. Monkeys, zebras. Lions."

"I am not a monkey," said Lady Thorton. "Throw peanuts at me and I will not respond." This didn't make sense to me, but Lady Thorton and Susan smiled.

The very next morning, Lord Thorton came home. He pulled up to our cottage in an automobile, and when he held open its door a girl a few years older than me climbed out. She had dark hair and pale skin and an expression like Jamie's cat: self-contained and wary.

Susan and Lady Thorton came out.

"Hello, ladies," Lord Thorton said, taking a suitcase from the backseat of the car. "Hello, Ada." He put his hand on the girl's shoulder and propelled her forward a step. "Susan, I've brought you the project I promised. Her name is Ruth."

I stared at Ruth. She stared back, indignant—whether at me or at being called a "project," I didn't know.

"She's sixteen," Lord Thorton said. "She's preparing

for her Oxford entrance exams, and you're going to be paid to tutor her in maths. I have a list of topics she needs to thoroughly understand." He cleared his throat and added, "Her father is a statistician from Dresden."

Susan jerked, startled. Lady Thorton froze. I didn't know why. I didn't know what *statistician* meant.

Ruth dropped her gaze to the ground. Her shoulders tightened. Her cheeks turned red.

"Unbelievable." Lady Thorton sounded outraged. "I will not have a German in this house."

Chapter 17

A German? I stared at Ruth, trying to work out which word Lord Thorton said meant German. *Statistician?*

Susan put her hand on my shoulder. "Dresden is a city in Germany," she said.

Lord Thorton sighed. "Her family came to England in June 1939," he said. "Over a year and a half ago. Since the Battle of Britain, her parents have been held in an internment camp. We're doing our best to get her father released. We need his skills on our side."

Lady Thorton said, "No. I won't have it."

"They're Jewish," said Lord Thorton. "They're refugees."

Lady Thorton said, "A German is a German is a German."

Lord Thorton frowned. "You know that isn't true."

Ruth didn't look up. Her cheeks flamed. I stared at her. A German! We saw German soldiers on the newsreels. They reminded me of Hitler with their cold dark eyes. Some of them even had tiny square mustaches. You could tell by looking at them that they were evil.

Ruth had dark brown hair, neatly bobbed. She certainly didn't have a mustache. I couldn't see what color her eyes were, but she looked normal enough to me.

But then, the spy I'd caught last summer looked normal too. He even spoke English without a German accent. He'd still been a spy. Ruth was the enemy. She ought to be in jail, or at least not living with us.

Susan exhaled deeply. She studied Lord Thorton. She said, "It will be fine."

Lady Thorton said, "It will not."

"It will," Lord Thorton said. "This is important."

Lady Thorton's nostrils flared. She said, "We are at war with Germany. Our son is risking his life to defeat the Germans. I will not harbor an enemy in my house."

"I realize we are at war!" Lord Thorton barked. "I understand more than you know." His voice settled as he gathered himself under control. "I would never ask you or Susan to do anything dishonorable. I assure you."

Susan said, "Of course not."

Lady Thorton said, "Education is a luxury in wartime. Jonathan left Oxford to fight. I do not see why this girl's education should be placed ahead of his."

"You must trust me," Lord Thorton said.

Lady Thorton sputtered. "What on earth am I to tell the village?"

"Anything you'd like."

Lady Thorton said, "We don't have anywhere for her to sleep."

Lord Thorton said, "You have a spare bedroom."

Lady Thorton said, "That's for when Jonathan comes home."

Lord Thorton said, "Spare rooms are a luxury in wartime."

Lady Thorton sucked in her breath. I could see we were in for a storm. Susan shot a glance at me. "Ada," she said, "you and Jamie take Ruth upstairs."

Chapter 18

I led the way up the stairs to the brand-new spare room. I guessed it wouldn't be used for Jonathan now. Ruth set her small suitcase unopened onto the foot of the bed. I wondered what Germans carried with them. My spy had had a wireless set.

Jamie had lingered on the stairs. Now he popped his head through the door. "They're arguing about Germans," he said. "Is this the invasion?"

"No," I said. "Remember? That's off."

Jamie said, "Then why've we got a German here?"

It was a good question. I sat down on the desk chair and watched Ruth.

"I hate Hitler as much as you do," Ruth said. She spoke with a heavy accent, but I could understand her. "Probably more. You heard Mr. Thorton say that I'm Jewish?"

I shrugged. I had no idea what that meant. "His

name is *Lord* Thorton. And it's none of my business,"
I said.

"It's not, except that you must know how Hitler
feels about Jews."

I only knew how Germans felt about Brits. They
bombed us. "It's not my business," I repeated. Ruth
would make a lousy spy. Unless she was faking the
accent, to lure us in. "Get out of here, Jamie," I said.
He didn't need to be associating with Germans.

Jamie ignored me. "Say something German," he said.

Ruth did. I shivered.

"What's that mean?" Jamie asked.

"It means," Ruth said, "I used to think I was
German. I don't belong anywhere anymore." She
stared back at me coldly. "May I have some privacy?"

"I'm not sure I'm allowed to leave you alone."

Ruth scowled. "I'm here to learn maths. That's all."
When I didn't respond she said, "Very well. Show me
where the loo is. Do you want to watch me use it?"

I didn't.

As we left the room, I grabbed the framed photo of
Jonathan Thorton off the bedside table.

Ruth said, "Is that your brother?"

"It's Lord Thorton's son. He's a pilot. Fighting the
Germans," I said.

I didn't go into the bathroom with Ruth, but I waited in the hallway outside the door until Susan called me and Jamie down. "Lord and Lady Thorton are taking a walk," Susan said. "Jamie, sweep up all this mud. Ada, set the table. Six places."

"But no one's watching her," I said.

"No one needs to. She isn't a spy."

"How do you know?" I asked. When Susan didn't reply I added, "Is she really going to live with us?"

"Yes," Susan said.

"Is this the project you had in mind?"

Susan sighed. "No," she said. "I hope Lady Thorton understands that."

I didn't think Susan really wanted to work, even if it was something as easy as teaching maths. Taking care of Jamie and me was already more than she ever wanted to do. Now she had to manage Lady Thorton too, and on top of that a German. "I'll help," I said.

"I know," said Susan.

It grew dark. Jamie and I put the blackout up. We tried to go into Ruth's room to put the blackout over the window there, but Ruth had locked the door. I hadn't even realized the bedroom doors could lock.

"It's the blackout," I shouted.

"I don't have a light on," she shouted back. "Go away."

We ran downstairs to tell Susan.

"She's locked herself in," I said. "She must be planning something. She could have a wireless in that suitcase."

Jamie said, "Or a bomb. We don't want bombs."

Susan lifted her eyebrows. "Ruth doesn't have a bomb. She's a child."

"She's older than Stephen," I said. "He's fighting in the war." At least, I assumed he was. I'd written him twice but not heard back.

Susan said, "Ada? Do you trust Lord Thorton?"

"Of course not."

She laughed and covered her face with her hands. "I walked into that," she said. "All right. Let's put it this way. Whom do you trust more, me or Lady Thorton?"

I understood what she was getting at. "All right," I said.

"What's the answer?"

"I'll put up with Ruth."

"You will not 'put up' with her," Susan retorted. "You'll be kind to her. You'll try to be her friend."

I wasn't promising that. I had Maggie. Also, who wanted to be friends with a German?

Susan went upstairs and knocked on the spare room door. "Ruth, would you like to come down for some tea?"

Ruth said, "No, thank you."

"Dinner is in half an hour. Please come down then."

"Thank you. I will."

Susan came back down the stairs, wiping her hands on her skirt. "See? Not difficult."

Jamie and I exchanged glances. Ruth could absolutely still have a wireless set. Or a bomb.

Chapter 19

Lord and Lady Thorton didn't return. Susan said we'd waited long enough and would eat without them. Ruth came down and sat quietly at the place Susan indicated. She put her napkin on her lap. We watched her. She took a sip of water. We watched.

"Stop staring at Ruth," Susan said. "Jamie. Eat your supper." Supper was hot pot, which was sausage, potatoes, turnips, and carrots all baked together in the oven for hours.

Ruth picked up her fork, took a bite, and spat the mouthful out. "Is the sausage made from pork?" she asked.

"Oh, no," said Susan. "I didn't think. Probably. I mean, who knows, these days, but one assumes pork, yes. Next time I'll ask."

Ruth nodded. She picked the sausage pieces out of her serving and lined them up on the edge of her plate.

"It's good sausage," Jamie said.

"Jamie," said Susan. "Hush."

Jamie said, "We're not supposed to waste sausage. There's a war on."

"You want it?" Ruth asked. She transferred her sausage to Jamie's plate. We watched her. "I don't eat pork," she said, looking up at us. "I keep kosher. At least, I try to." She stirred her fork through the rest of her serving. "My father would tell me not to eat anything cooked in the same dish as pork sausage. My mother would say it was more important that I be a good guest, and that I needed to eat to keep up my strength."

I couldn't make sense of any of that.

"I told you," Ruth said. "I'm Jewish."

I said, "So?"

"Judaism is a very old religion," Susan said. "Far older than Christianity. Many Jewish people follow strict dietary rules that include not eating pork. Ruth, you'll have to let me know how to accommodate you. I probably don't have enough kitchenware for full kosher but I'll do my best."

"What's Christianity?" I asked.

Ruth gaped at me. I ignored her. Susan took a deep breath. "Christianity means any of the religions that believe Jesus Christ was the son of God. You're a Christian, Ada."

I said, "How do you know?"

Ruth snorted.

"What?" I said.

Ruth said, "How can you not know?"

I glared at her.

"Our village church is Church of England," Susan said. "That's a Christian church."

"What about the churches in London?" I used to hear their bells from Mam's room.

"Mostly Christian," Susan said. "But there are Jewish people in London. I'm sure there are synagogues there." She took a breath. "Judaism is the religion of the Old Testament, Ada. Of Abraham and Moses. Jewish people don't follow the New Testament. They don't believe that Jesus was the son of God."

"How can they not believe that?" I said. "It's true."

Ruth sniffed. "That's not what our rabbi says."

Jamie said, "What's a rabbi?"

Ruth said, "I do not believe this. I did not think English children could be so ignorant."

"Not all of them," I said. "Just us."

Susan turned to Ruth. "Ada and Jamie were

evacuated from the East End of London at the start of the war," she explained. "Until recently their educations have been sporadic."

"I see." Ruth looked slightly less horrified. "They don't belong to you."

"They do," said Susan. "I adopted them."

"Our first mother is in heaven," Jamie said. "Susan's our second."

I glared at him. "That's not true. You know it!" Mam wasn't in heaven and Susan was not our mother. I turned back to Ruth. "How can you not believe Jesus is God?"

Ruth said, "How can you believe he is?"

"You can't choose what you believe," I said. "You can't just say, 'I don't believe that's a chair,' and have it turn into a hedgehog. Plus, our vicar wouldn't lie."

"Ada," Susan said, "people choose their own beliefs all the time. Mr. Collins isn't lying. He preaches what he sincerely believes. Ruth sincerely believes something else. That's all right."

"It can't be," I said. All these things I'd worked to learn, and now they were optional? If this was a joke, it wasn't a funny one.

Susan didn't look like she was joking. "Religion is a matter of faith. You always have to choose what you believe."

Ruth nodded, a touch defiantly. "I choose to be Jewish," she said.

"Are there other people like her in the village?" I asked Susan. "People who don't believe in Jesus?"

"Yes," said Susan. "I'm not one of them, but there are probably people in our village who don't even believe God exists. Not in any form."

"You're joking."

"No."

"How do they get to heaven?"

Susan said, "They probably don't believe in heaven either."

"Do you have to believe in heaven to go there?"

Susan said, "I have no idea."

I felt enormously irritated. "Why didn't you tell me all this? Why'd you make me believe all that stuff about heaven if it wasn't true?"

"I didn't make you believe anything," Susan said. "I can't even get you to trust that I'll feed you. Why on earth would I tackle God?"

I said, angry, "I didn't know I had a choice."

Susan said, "Get over it, Ada. Whether you realize it or not, you're choosing your own beliefs all the time." She wiped her mouth with her napkin. "Let us not monopolize the conversation. Ruth, what can I get you? More potatoes? Or some bread?"

Ruth uncovered another piece of sausage. Jamie looked at it hopefully. Ruth gave it to him. "What do you do with your bacon ration?" Jamie asked, chewing.

"Jews don't get a bacon ration," Ruth said. "We get extra cheese."

Jamie swallowed. He said, "That's too bad."

Chapter 20

As soon as she finished eating, Ruth went upstairs and locked herself in her bedroom again.

"She doesn't like us," I said.

"I don't blame her," said Susan. "Poor girl."

Jamie said, "She looked pretty rich to me."

Lord and Lady Thorton returned an hour later. They wore composed faces and were carefully polite. They were both still angry. I could feel it. It reminded me of how Mam sometimes smiled just before she started walloping me. My stomach hurt. I edged closer to Susan.

"If you want to, Ada," she said, "you can read in bed for a while. I'm not going to read to you and Jamie tonight."

"Mum!" Jamie protested.

"Not tonight," Susan said. "You may read in bed or you may stay down here for the news broadcast.

Your choice." We always went to sleep after the nine o'clock radio news.

I went upstairs. My bedroom was cold but I had blankets enough. I snuggled with my dictionary.

Christianity: the religion based on the person and teachings of Jesus of Nazareth, or its beliefs and practices.

Jew: a member of the people and cultural community whose traditional religion is Judaism and who trace their origins through the ancient Hebrew people of Israel to Abraham.

Judaism: the monotheistic religion of the Jews.

Monotheistic: relating to or characterized by the belief that there is only one God.

None of this helped. Our vicar said there was only one God. God came in God-the-Father, God-the-Son, who was Jesus, and God-the-Holy-Spirit, but it was all supposed to be only one God. I'd asked him about that once when his sermon hadn't made sense. His answer hadn't make sense either, except that he promised me it was really all one God.

So if I believed in one God, and Ruth believed in one God, which one of us believed in the wrong God?

I didn't quite dare ask Ruth.

Lord Thorton left the next morning. Susan taught Ruth at the kitchen table alongside Jamie and me.

The moment Susan finished, Ruth gathered her books, disappeared into her bedroom, and locked the door. At meals she and Lady Thorton sat silently at opposite ends of the table.

On the third day Ruth noticed my jodhpurs at lunch. "You ride?" she asked.

I said, "I have my own pony. I work at Lady Thorton's stables in exchange for his keep."

Ruth said, "I like horses. I like to ride."

I didn't say anything.

Ruth said, "Could I come to the stables with you?"

"No." Lady Thorton swiped her hands as though brushing dirt off them. "A German at Thorton House! When there's war work being done there!"

"Just the stables," Ruth said. "I wouldn't go near the house."

Lady Thorton sniffed. "Absolutely not."

People in the village distrusted Ruth too. Susan and I got dark looks when we queued for food. Susan explained why Ruth was living with us, but only once. "They'll get used to her or not, without me," she said. "I'll save my breath."

In the first week, at least, Ruth didn't kill us in our sleep. Jamie rummaged through her suitcase and

141

dresser drawers one day while she was taking a walk, and reported that they contained nothing but clothes, her schoolbooks, a hairbrush, and a toothbrush. Susan was mad as fire that Jamie'd snooped, but I was glad he'd done it. I said so. Susan said she was disappointed in us both. Lady Thorton looked pleased.

"Why does Hitler hate Jews?" I asked Susan. "Do Jews believe in the wrong God?"

If Ruth believed in a different God from Hitler, did Hitler and I believe in the same God? The thought made me queasy. Hitler'd killed Mam, and very nearly me.

"No," Susan said. "Jews don't believe in the wrong God. No one knows why Hitler hates anything. Hitler defies explanation."

Jamie got his cast cut off. His arm muscles were skinny from not being used, but his bones really had healed good as new. His entire arm would be good as new in just a little while. Dr. Graham promised. Bones healed, when doctors took care of them. Jamie wouldn't even have a scar.

"If your clubfoot had been treated when you were born," Susan said, "it would be like it had never happened either. You wouldn't even remember being different."

I would always remember it.

Ruth overheard. "Is that why you limp?" she asked. "You had a bad foot? What is a clubfoot?"

I gave her a look I'd learned from Lady Thorton. "I don't limp. I don't have any idea what you mean."

Chapter 21

The new fire-watching rota finally came out. Susan handed me a copy of it when she came back from working at the WVS, and I scanned the paper for my name. "Lady Thorton!" I said. I pushed it back at Susan. "They've got me going up with *Lady Thorton*!"

"So?" said Susan. "You knew fire-watchers worked in pairs."

I didn't want to fire-watch with Lady Thorton. The idea of fire-watching with anyone made me anxious enough, let alone her. "You know," I said.

Susan shook her head at me. "I don't."

She did, she just wouldn't admit it.

We were assigned an early shift, eight o'clock at night until ten. On the proper night we bundled up and set out together into the darkness. Gasoline was rationed now, and even Lady Thorton no longer drove anywhere she could reach on foot.

Heavy clouds blanketed the black sky. Wind

whistled through bare branches and dead leaves in the hedge. A faraway bird made a soft, low noise. "That's an owl," Lady Thorton said.

I looked up at her. "What's an owl?"

She raised her eyebrows, but after a moment answered, "A nocturnal bird. You almost never see them in daytime."

I nodded. Yet another thing I didn't know.

At the doors of the church, Lady Thorton paused. "On a night like tonight, the way up will be very dark," she said. "Follow me closely. We'll go slow."

The inside of the church smelled of smoke and candle wax. It was so quiet I could hear Lady Thorton breathe, but once we began climbing the staircase, I couldn't see anything at all. The stairwell was utterly dark. I clutched the handrail with one hand and the back of Lady Thorton's coat with the other. I tried to feel my way up, but I wasn't used to trusting how things felt beneath my feet. Any moment I could miss a step and fall.

Lady Thorton missed a step, and stumbled. I pitched forward into her. "Careful!" she said.

We sidled into the bell-ringers' room. I made myself breathe deep, as quietly as I could. Now the ladder. Up. Up. At the top, the sideways jump to the other stair. Lady Thorton swung the little door open. I followed too close; the edge of the door hit my fore-head. I gasped, startled, and nearly slipped.

"Sorry." Out on the steeple's ledge, Lady Thorton ran her thumbs over my face. They felt cold and hard; I didn't flinch. "You're not bleeding, that's good." She pulled the door shut behind us. "So we don't go tumbling into the night."

She sounded perfectly calm, as though the idea of falling down that dark hole was nothing to worry about. As though we weren't standing out in the high, open sky waiting for Germans to come and bomb us. Watching for their bombs and fires.

Lady Thorton had something called binoculars to look through. "They make faraway things seem closer," Lady Thorton said. "Would you like to try them?"

I shook my head. I'd need both hands to hold the binoculars, and then I wouldn't be able to steady myself against the stone wall.

"Walk around and watch for light or movement," Lady Thorton said. "We're almost guaranteed not to have any bombers tonight. Too dark." She smiled thinly. "It's very dull up here most of the time. Good of you to want to take a turn."

"I like to be useful," I said.

"Yes, I know," Lady Thorton replied. "Susan's

turning you into a regular little housewife, isn't she? With all the cooking and sewing she's taught you."

She almost sounded scornful of Susan, which I didn't appreciate at all. Since she'd come to live with us, Lady Thorton had not cooked any part of a single meal, though she'd done her full share of the eating. "I like to cook," I said. "I like having good food."

Lady Thorton put down her binoculars. My eyes had adjusted to the dark enough that I could see her face, unruffled as always. "Of course," she said. "I understand. I suppose your mother was a good cook too."

"Not really," I said.

"I'm sorry," Lady Thorton said, "I shouldn't have mentioned her. I know you must miss her terribly."

"No," I said. "Why would you think that?"

She had stopped listening. She walked around the far side of the steeple and aimed the binoculars at the leaden sky. The wind blew hard. I thought I could feel the steeple sway. Surely not. Surely the steeple was safe. It had been atop the church a long time—

A sound like a gunshot below us. I bit my lip hard and stifled a scream.

"Just a tree branch," Lady Thorton called, from the opposite side of the steeple. "Those old trees round the graveyard. Sometimes they lose a limb when the wind gets heavy."

My speeded-up heart rate refused to slow down. Minutes crawled like hours. My toes and fingers went numb. Lady Thorton opened a thing called a thermos flask and gave me a drink of wonderful still-warm tea.

"I've realized that I like to feel useful too," Lady Thorton said. She smiled. "Before the war, I had a lot more fun, but I wasn't anywhere near as useful."

I supposed that was true. All Lady Thorton's WVS work was voluntary—she didn't have to do any of it. She could have gone off somewhere posh and waited out the war.

"I remember you on evacuation day," I said. She'd been so commanding that I nearly mistook her for an army officer. Her WVS uniform looked like something an officer would wear.

"Yes," Lady Thorton said. "I was never taught to cook or sew, and unlike Susan, I can't do maths past arithmetic. But I'm a good organizer. I don't mind standing out here in the cold either. I'll help with the war however I can." After a pause she added, "I'd do anything to bring Jonathan safely home."

Chapter 22

On the day Lady Thorton moved in with us, she had handed Susan her ration book and said, "Don't worry. I intend to do my bit."

She might be willing to do war work, but her house-keeping bit was not large. Jamie mopped and dusted more than she did, and Susan and I did nearly all the shopping and cooking. Lady Thorton never even helped with washing up. She said, "You all under-stand that sort of thing so much better than me." Of course she could only start to understand the shop-ping by sometimes actually doing the shopping, and I suppose she did know it. The day after our fire-watch she took everyone's ration books, including Ruth's, and spent two weeks' worth of meat coupons on one pound of lamb. Five tiny elegant pieces of lamb.

"Lovely chops," Lady Thorton said. "With a bit of rosemary—"

"Ten shillings!" Susan shouted. It was the first time in months I'd seen her so angry.

Meat was rationed by price, not amount. Each person in Britain, no matter whether they were rich or poor, was only allowed to spend one shilling per week on meat. If you wanted lots of meat, you stuck to the cheap stuff. If you wanted higher quality, you got hardly any at all.

"Susan, dear, you're a marvelous cook, but the cuts you've been choosing are dreadful." Lady Thorton held up a chop. "Only look. The butcher said it was the best he'd had in weeks."

"We can't afford the best," Susan said. "These children need to eat meat more than once a fortnight. What am I supposed to feed them tomorrow?"

Lady Thorton set the chop down. "Well, perhaps—eggs."

The new egg ration was one egg per person per week.

"Or something," said Lady Thorton.

Susan sighed. "We can't give them back," she said. "I suppose we might as well enjoy them."

Lady Thorton smiled. "I'll select a bottle of wine." She'd brought crates of wine over from Thorton House.

Susan seared the chops in a hot pan with a sprinkling of pepper and rosemary and made a fancy kind of gravy. The chops smelled fantastic, but were half the size of my fist. That was all the meat we'd get for the next two weeks.

"A good meal lifts the spirits," Lady Thorton said as we sat down to eat. I stared at her. Her face froze. "Ruth," she said—whenever Lady Thorton said Ruth's name her face screwed up like she was smelling something nasty—"Ruth, what is that by your plate?"

It was an envelope. Ruth looked down, saw it, and picked it up. She started to smile.

"It came in today's mail," said Susan.

Lady Thorton held out her hand. "Give it to me."

"No," said Ruth. Her smile disappeared. "It's mine." She started to tuck the envelope into her pocket. Lady Thorton snatched it out of her hand.

"Eleanor!" Susan protested.

"I consider it my duty!" Lady Thorton replied. "Mail delivered to a German in my house!" She ripped open the envelope and shook out the piece of paper inside. Ruth cried out, soft, like an owl. Lady Thorton's face went red. "I can't read a word of it. I should have known. It's all German—"

Ruth pushed back from the table. "How dare you!"

she shouted. Bright red spots bloomed on her cheeks. She grabbed her letter, ran up the stairs to her room, and slammed and locked the door.

Jamie whimpered. I reached under the table and squeezed his hand.

Susan said, "That was completely unnecessary."

Lady Thorton said, "I agree. Her behavior was reprehensible."

Susan looked her in the eye. "I meant your behavior."

It was impossible for me to eat after that. I hated fighting. Susan never hit me, but Lady Thorton might. She looked ready to wallop Ruth for sure.

"Eat your chop," Susan said to me.

I pushed my plate away. "I'm not hungry."

"Eat it," Lady Thorton commanded, through a mouthful of meat. "In wartime we do not waste food."

I looked at her. I couldn't eat that chop, not even to keep her from walloping me. Not when Ruth's chop sat untouched on her plate.

"Ada is my responsibility." Susan's voice had an edge I didn't understand. "I'll be the one who decides what she does." She swept up my plate, and Jamie's, and Ruth's. "Ada, Jamie, you may be excused. We'll save the rest of this for tomorrow."

Jamie and I washed the dishes like always. Susan and Lady Thorton sat at the table, drinking tea and talking in hard, quiet voices. I tried like anything to hear what they were saying, but Jamie splashed too much and they kept their voices down. When Lady Thorton went into the sitting room, Susan went to the larder. She cut three big slices of bread and spread them with some of the gravy she'd made for the lamb. "Take these upstairs," she said to us. I nodded. She meant, *where Lady Thorton couldn't see.*

I knocked on Ruth's door. "Go away," she said.

"It's Ada. I've got something for you."

"Go away."

"I know you're hungry."

"Do your ears work worse than your foot? Go away."

The next morning, at breakfast, I said to Ruth, "There's nothing wrong with my foot."

Ruth shrugged. "You can say that if you want to."

"My foot's fixed!"

"Susan called it a clubfoot," Ruth said. "You limp. You always limp, and some days you limp more."

"I do not." I was lying. I knew I limped even though I tried hard not to.

"Ruth," Susan said, "Ada prefers to keep her foot private."

"Ah," said Ruth. "Like my letters."

Lady Thorton sat down in time to hear that. She didn't flinch. "I have a right to know with whom you correspond."

"So next time, you can ask me instead of opening my mail." Ruth began to eat. She didn't say who her letter was from. Lady Thorton tapped her fingers against the table. Silence stretched out. Jamie looked at me anxiously.

"Who wrote to you, Ruth?" Susan finally asked.

"My mother," she said. "My mother, who is by herself in an internment camp."

"What's an internment camp?" asked Jamie.

"Jail," I said.

"Certainly not," Lady Thorton said. "Internment camps are merely places to keep watch on enemy aliens. Tell me, Ruth. What did your letter say?"

Ruth sniffed. "None of your business. They have censors in the internment camp. If my mother wrote anything controversial, I wouldn't have gotten the letter."

Lady Thorton frowned. "Is that true?"

"Of course it's true!" said Ruth. "Why do you think it took her so long to write to me? Not because she was writing things she shouldn't—because she's only allowed to write one letter, one single piece of paper, each week. And she has to write to my father and my grandmother and our family back in Germany—and now she finally got to write to me, and I will never tell you what she said! I will go back to that camp myself first!" Ruth's voice rose until she was shouting.

"We want you to stay here," Susan said. "Lord Thorton"—Susan glared at Lady Thorton—"wants you to stay here."

I hadn't even realized that Ruth hadn't received any letters. Maggie wrote her mother three times a week, and me nearly as often.

Jamie said, "Why doesn't your mother come live with us? We've got a big enough cave."

Lady Thorton made a noise in her throat, but Ruth answered first. "She can't," she said. "The British government won't let her."

I said, "In case she's a spy."

"Yes," Ruth said wearily. "In case she's a spy."

Chapter 23

That night Susan filled our dinner plates herself and carefully set one down in front of each of us. Lord Woolton pie, the baked mess of oatmeal and vegetables. Only mine—and, I saw, looking around the table—Ruth's and Jamie's, had cut-up pieces of lamb mixed with it. Lamb and the lamb gravy, with wine and rosemary. Susan's and Lady Thorton's did not.

With the addition of meat, the Lord Woolton Pie wasn't half bad.

Lady Thorton picked through her serving. "Is this supposed to be some sort of punishment?" she asked Susan.

"Of course not," Susan replied. "You and I ate our share yesterday. The whole point of rationing is that everyone gets their fair share."

Ruth's eyes flicked to mine. She didn't smile, but I felt like she was thinking a smile. I thought a smile back at her.

That really was all the meat we got, though, for the next two straight weeks. We'd used up our coupons and we couldn't get more, not without buying meat on the black market, which meant illegally outside the ration. Lady Thorton had enough money to do that but she said she also had too much honor.

February continued cold and bleak. The sun rose late and set early, and between that and the blackout, it really did seem like we were living in a cave. Susan fell into a gloom. She was never as sad as she'd been when we first came to live with her—she got out of bed every day, but she rarely smiled, and she slept more than I thought she should.

One morning my schoolwork felt unbearable. Ruth was squirreled away with her maths and Jamie outside trying to dig a garden plot in the frozen ground. Susan sat dully in front of her sewing machine, rearranging some pins but not stitching anything. I shoved aside my grammar book and said, "Why don't we train the dragons?"

Susan looked up. "What?"

"Fred says horses fought in the last big war."

"Yes," she said. "And in every war before that. They're not much use in modern times, though, not against tanks and aircraft and heavy artillery."

"Right," I said. "So why not dragons?" I'd been

thinking it through. "The kind that can fly. If we took them out of the zoos and we trained them, maybe they could attack German planes without even needing pilots on board." It would be much safer for Jonathan.

A grin spread slowly across Susan's face. "Ada," she said, "you do understand that dragons are mythical creatures?"

As if I knew what she meant by *mythical*. I stared at her.

"Imaginary," said Susan. "Made-up. Pretend. The stuff of fairy tales." She coughed, then started to laugh. "My dear—oh, I'm sorry—it's wonderful— *Why don't we train dragons?*" She laughed harder. "That'd serve Hitler. A couple of ranks of dragons, and the ghost of St. George—"

I'd never seen Susan laugh like this.

I picked up the closest thing at hand—the grammar book—and threw it hard across the room. It narrowly missed Lady Thorton coming through the front door. She bent to pick it up and smoothed it in her hands.

"Ada," she said sternly, "we do not throw books."

Susan was still laughing. "I know I should stop— I'm not being kind—"

"Stop what?" asked Lady Thorton.

Susan said, "She wants to train dragons to fight Hitler."

"Nobody told me they aren't real!"

Lady Thorton considered. "A pity they aren't," she said. "It would be an excellent plan. Except I suppose the Germans would also have dragons."

"Bigger dragons," Susan said. "Stronger, taller, blonder dragons—" She looked ready to laugh again.

"How am I supposed to know what's real and what isn't?" I almost shouted. "Nobody tells me! Nobody tells me anything!"

"Ada," Susan said, recovering herself, "I'm sorry I laughed. But be fair. I tell you things all the time."

"Fairy tales," Lady Thorton said. "What you need is a proper dose of fairy tales. Then you can move on to mythology. I'll fetch some books from Thorton House."

I said, "You have more books than what you brought here already?"

"Oh my, yes. We left most of them on the shelves in the library."

Imagine. Their own library. Thorton House had a library.

Lady Thorton brought over volumes of fairy tales. Susan read them to Jamie and me all through the rest of that dreary month. She explained after each story what was real and what wasn't. I could have guessed most of it—I already knew that animals couldn't talk, and that people couldn't really fly or weren't born so small they could sleep in a teacup. But it was hard to see how unicorns, for example, were less real than horses. Dragons still seemed dead useful to me. Winged lizards? Why not? Angels were people with wings. It was hard to see the difference.

Ruth stayed downstairs to listen to the fairy tales. "I've never heard them in English before," she said.

Jamie said, "They have stories in Germany?"

You never thought of Germans telling stories.

Ruth looked offended, but then, she usually did. "Of course we have stories in Germany," she said. "Most of these stories *came* from Germany. They were German *first*."

I didn't want to believe her, but Lady Thorton pursed her lips and said it was true. "The Brothers Grimm were German," she said.

I didn't think anything good came from Germany. When I said so, Lady Thorton disagreed. "I traveled through Germany extensively when I was younger," she said. "Dresden is a beautiful city, very cultured. You can't judge the whole country by Hitler."

I said, "But you judge Ruth by Hitler."

Lady Thorton's head snapped up, angry. Ruth bit her lip, and Susan outright smiled.

Susan finally found a book about dragons at the village library. St. George, the patron saint of England, was supposed to have killed a dragon, and so was a saint named Margaret of Antioch. It amused me to think that Maggie had been named for a dragon-killer. But saints were supposed to have been real people, not imaginary, and dragons were imaginary, not real. How could a real person kill an imaginary animal?

"The stories get a little mixed up," Susan said. "These particular saints lived a very long time ago."

"Back when people were stupid like me?"

"Ada," said Susan, "if you say things like that, I'll make you write lines."

I didn't know what *write lines* meant. I didn't care. I repeated, "Stupid like me."

Susan made me sit at the table until I'd written the sentence "I will not continue to conflate lack of intelligence with lack of knowledge" one hundred times. It took hours. I considered refusing to do it, but the expression on Susan's face made me pick up a pencil instead.

"What's *conflate*?" I asked.

"Combining two ideas that ought to be kept separate," Susan said. "You are going to stop doing it."

"Tell me all the things that are imaginary," I said. "When I'm done with these stupid lines I want to make a list."

"I can't," Susan said. "It would be an infinite list. Anything you can make up inside your head is imaginary."

I thought about this. "So love is imaginary?"

"No, no," Susan said. "Love exists outside your head. Think harder, Ada. Stop being so cross."

Every day Ruth saw me wearing my jodhpurs. Every day she saw me going to the stables. Every day when I came back smelling of horses and hay she sniffed the air longingly. She looked enormously sad.

Butter made me happy every single day.

Lady Thorton hardly ever went to her own stables. She said she was too busy with the WVS to ride often, and she never ever did chores.

"You can't take Ruth with you if Lady Thorton won't allow it," Susan said. "She does have that authority."

I wasn't used to being envied. To my surprise, I didn't like it at all.

Chapter 24

Lord Thorton telegraphed that he was coming home for the weekend. We tried hard to make things nice for him. Instead of ducking her share of the housekeeping, Lady Thorton actually mopped the kitchen floor and polished the brass on the fireplace, and she queued for three hours to get our bacon ration while Susan stood in a separate queue for fish.

Lord Thorton arrived in his car, to our surprise. I wondered how he'd gotten the gasoline. He brought gifts for all of us. A piece of chocolate for Jamie. A potted plant for the kitchen table. A small bottle of perfume for Lady Thorton, and four new bars of smooth, silky scented soap, one each for Lady Thorton, Susan, Ruth, and me.

To my astonishment I was actually happier to get nice soap than I would have been chocolate. Soap was on ration, and all we could usually get was war soap, unscented and harsh. It made me itch. I'd gotten used to daily baths and nice soap, living with Susan. Odd when you thought about it. Mam hadn't been much for keeping us clean.

Ruth stared at her soap as though she were afraid of it. She looked close to tears. I wondered what she was thinking. I didn't understand her at all.

Lord Thorton was still scary, very tall in a looming sort of way, but now he spoke to me as though I was someone he knew well, and also as though he rather liked me.

"You look as though you're getting around quite easily," he said. "Even better than at Christmastime."

I realized he was talking about my foot. I didn't want him talking about my foot.

"Thank you," I said. Across the room, Ruth looked up, interested.

"Does it hurt anymore?" he asked.

"Of course not," I said, though it did, sometimes.

"Good," he said. "Very good."

"What happened to your foot?" Ruth asked that night as we climbed the stairs to bed.

"Nothing," I said.

"Susan called it a clubfoot," Ruth said.

"I know," I said, and closed my bedroom door.

Chapter 25

A week later Maggie came home for half-term. I met her train at the village station. "I can't believe my father brought home a German," she said. "What's she like?"

"Not as odd as I thought she'd be," I said. "Course, she might be pretending. Trying to trick us into feeling safer." Though the longer I knew Ruth, the more ordinary she seemed. "Your mother hates her," I added.

Maggie nodded. "I'm not surprised."

Maggie stood in the middle of our bedroom, her hands on her hips. I stood beside her. The two halves of the room no longer matched.

I'd stripped the frilly coverlet and pillows from my bed and removed the lacy curtain-thing that went around the bottom of it. I'd taken the curtain off my side of the window. I'd thrown my dictionary in with

Maggie's books on the shelves, moved my box to my bedside table, and scooted the rug partially under Maggie's bed so it didn't lay on my half of the floor at all.

"Did my mother do this?" Maggie asked.

"Yes," I said.

She shook her head, lips firmly pressed together. "I can't believe it. It's not fair." She grabbed the edge of the rug and tugged on it. "Help me," she said. "This needs to go in the middle. It's for both of us."

"It's not," I said. "It's yours."

"That's ridiculous. As if I wouldn't share anything I had with you." She centered the rug on the floor. "I thought we had two of those coverlets," she said. "I know for a fact we had two sets of pillows." She flung open the wardrobe door. There, stuffed against the back on the floor, were the extra pillows.

"Your mother did put them on my bed," I said. "I just didn't like them."

Maggie looked at the pillows, and back to me. "Oh," she said. "Well. You don't have to take them. I thought my mother didn't want to let you use them, that's all."

"No," I said. I felt a little uncomfortable. "She wanted to share. She just went ahead and did everything without asking me."

Maggie nodded. "I know. She's always like that." She sat down on the edge of her bed. "What do you want? I think we should both use the coverlets. That way our beds would match. Like we were sisters."

"Sisters?"

Maggie scowled. "Don't sound so horrified. I always wanted a sister."

I never thought about having a sister.

"I don't mind the coverlet," I said, "if we can get rid of those lace things around the beds."

"The dust ruffles? Deal."

Maggie and I rode out together to the top of our lookout hill. It was lovely to have company on my rides again. "I missed you," I said.

Maggie nodded. She scanned the sea from side to side, the way we always did, checking for spies. "I missed you too," she said. "I miss everything. School's wretched in wartime. I'd give anything to be home.

"Three girls have gotten telegrams so far," she continued. "There's this long drive from the road leading up to the school, and you can see the whole of it from every classroom window. Whenever the telegraph boy turns down the drive, all of us are watching him by the time he gets to the door. We all stand at the windows, not breathing, hoping his message isn't for us."

I'd seen a messenger bicycling around the village. I said, "When Mam died I got a letter, not a telegram."

"The military sends telegrams," Maggie said. "Sometimes they say *wounded* or *missing in action.* The three that came to our school all said *dead.* Two brothers and a father." She paused. "We watch the boy bicycling up the drive and then the head calls someone out of class and we all know what's happened. And we're just glad it wasn't us that was called. We don't feel sad as much as relieved. It's horrible."

Jonathan wasn't my brother and I still worried about him. I couldn't imagine having to think about telegrams and Jamie.

"Getting a telegram here would be just as bad as getting one at school," I said.

Maggie turned to me. Her eyes looked dark in her pinched face. "That's not true," she said.

When we got home there was a letter waiting for Maggie. I looked at it anxiously but Maggie's face lit up. "It's from my grandmother!" she said. "From Scotland!"

Ruth spun around. For one brief moment her face glowed with joy. Her expression fell so quickly into her usual solemnity that I wouldn't have believed it if I hadn't seen it. "Oh," she said, "your grandmother.

Not mine." She turned and went up the stairs. I heard her lock her bedroom door.

Maggie was laughing. "My grandmother's got a bunch of evacuees staying with her," she said. "A whole dozen boys. She says it's worse than when my father and his brothers were small."

Maggie's grandmother in Scotland was Lord Thorton's mother. Maggie had explained it to me. Before the war, Maggie used to visit her every summer and every Christmas.

Grandmothers sounded cozy. But so did mothers, and my mother had been dreadful. It was hard to imagine how my grandmother might have been. Anyhow, Susan had made inquiries. No one knew of any other family for Jamie and me.

At dinnertime I asked Ruth, "Are you expecting a letter from your grandmother?"

Ruth shrugged. "My mother says there is still hope."

She hunched over her plate and wouldn't say anything more.

Chapter 26

"Can't I stay here?" Maggie asked her mother, the day before she had to return to school. "Susan could teach me like she teaches Ada and Jamie."

"Of course not," Lady Thorton said. "We must not impose."

"Susan wouldn't mind," Maggie said. "You could pay her."

Lady Thorton's eyes flashed. "I think not."

"It would be fair."

"It's out of the question," Lady Thorton said. "You're far safer at school. I nearly didn't let you come home for your holiday."

Maggie's mouth dropped open. "That would have been dreadful."

Lady Thorton sipped her tea. "It would have been prudent," she said.

I looked it up. *Prudent: acting with or showing care and*

thought for the future. I read the definition to Maggie.

"Oh, please," Maggie said. "She just doesn't want to have to deal with me herself. Her life's easier when I'm gone." She hugged me. "Take care of her for me."

"Me, take care of your mother?"

Maggie nodded. "Someone should."

"I can't," I said. "I wouldn't know how. Besides, she'd never let me." Also, it was all I could do to take care of myself and Jamie and Susan. I didn't have room in my head to worry about Lady Thorton.

"Just keep an eye on her, is what I mean," Maggie said. "Write me if you notice anything odd."

I doubted I would notice anything new that was odd about Lady Thorton. Everything about her seemed odd to me.

"Please," Maggie said.

I nodded. "I'll try."

Without Maggie the house felt empty again. I missed her snoring in the bed across from mine. I missed having someone to ride with.

I told Fred about Ruth. He spat on the ground. "We don't want Germans here," he said.

"She's just a girl," I said. "She's younger than the Land Girls." The Land Girls worked on the Thortons' home farm, in place of workmen who'd joined the army. Fred didn't like them. "She's Jewish," I added. "Does that make a difference?"

Fred looked at me down the side of his nose. After a long pause, he nodded. "Some."

Ruth loved horses. I didn't think someone who loved horses could do us harm.

"That's a logical fallacy," Susan said when I told her. "Hitler himself could love horses for all we know."

Fallacy: a mistaken belief, especially one based on unsound argument.

"So Judaism is a fallacy?" I brought my dictionary down to the sitting room.

Lady Thorton laughed. I didn't know why.

"Of course not," Susan said. "Religious beliefs are complicated. You can't call someone else's religion a mistake."

I didn't see why not. I did see that it was complicated.

"There isn't a right and a wrong," Susan said. "There are just different ways of thinking."

"I think Mam's in heaven," Jamie said. He'd been playing on the floor with Bovril. I hadn't thought he was listening.

"I don't," I said. "I think she went to hell." Fred had told me about hell. It was the opposite of heaven, the place bad people went when they died. In hell Mam's soul would burn for all eternity. Forever.

"Ada," Susan said, "we don't know that. We can never know that. Your mother was clearly incapacitated."

"What's that mean?"

Susan considered. "The root word comes from *capacity,* which means being able to hold. Your mother wasn't able to take proper care of you. She didn't have the ability to do it."

"Maybe she just didn't want to."

Susan said, "I don't think anyone wants to be a horrible person. I also like to think that God shows mercy."

"What's *mercy?*" I sounded angry. I was.

Jamie said, "Being nicer than you should be."

I had no idea how he knew that. Susan nodded. "Yes. *Mercy* means that you have the ability and the right to hurt someone, or punish them, and you choose not to. Maybe it would be right for God to punish your mother, for the way she treated you. But maybe God chooses mercy. I like to hope so."

I picked at the dry skin around my fingernails. Susan hated it when I did that. "Why?" I asked.

She sighed. "Perhaps because I've always wanted

mercy for myself. Or perhaps I just think it would be kinder. Ada, your mother can't hurt you now. She can never hurt you again."

She could, though. Mam had never loved me and never would. That would hurt forever.

Jamie dropped Bovril into my lap. "Everyone loves everyone once they get to heaven," he said.

Bovril jumped down. He stalked away, twitching his tail. It would take getting to heaven for Bovril to love me.

Chapter 27

Lady Thorton hated Ruth and Ruth hated all of us. Not that I blamed her. A few days after Maggie left, in the middle of another silent, awkward meal, Ruth took a swallow of water, then belched. I could tell it was an accident, not an impertinence, but Lady Thorton rolled her eyes and sighed as though belching Germans were far too much for her to bear.

"Oh, stop it!" I said. "Ruth can't help belching, but you can help the rude noises you make!"

Lady Thorton lowered her chin, looked down her nose at me, and glared. "I hardly think—"

A sudden crash shook the table. I jumped. It came from Susan—*Susan*—who'd picked up her plate and slammed it down hard. "Ada's right," she said calmly. "Eleanor. You *can* help the noises you make. Also, I will not continue to be the referee in this house. Nor the sole cook, nor the tweeny. Nor do I wish to live in the middle of a battlefield. Bad enough there's a war outside our home. We don't need a war inside as well."

Lady Thorton's mouth formed a thin grim line. "I'm doing the best I can."

"I don't believe so," Susan said. "When Becky died I thought I was doing the best I could too. Then the children arrived and it turned out I could do better. It wasn't easy, but I could do it." She stood. "Let's take a walk," she said to Lady Thorton. "You and I. Children, when you're finished eating I expect all three of you to do the evening work in a calm and cooperative manner." She grabbed Lady Thorton by the elbow and walked her out the door.

Jamie, Ruth, and I stared. Jamie said, "Cor."

When we finished eating, Ruth cleared her place, then started to walk up the stairs. "No," I said. "You heard Susan. Come back here and help."

Ruth sniffed. "I'm supposed to study, not do housework."

I said, "I do both."

Ruth said, "That's because you live here."

Ruth lived here too, as far as I could tell. "Wash or dry?" I asked. "Jamie's going to bring in coal."

Ruth looked at me. She folded her arms across her

chest. I folded my arms across mine. Finally, Ruth looked away. "Dry," she said, and did.

Susan and Lady Thorton returned while I was taking my bath. I came downstairs in my pajamas and dressing gown. "Ready for our story?" Susan asked. Jamie was curled up beside her. Lady Thorton sat as usual in her wing-backed chair, knitting a stocking. Her face was flat and calm.

I wasn't sure what to think. Susan sounded normal now, but at dinner she had not been normal. I felt anxious. "Are you finished being angry?" I asked.

"Yes," she said, "and you survived it. You're okay."

Maybe.

"Tomorrow," Lady Thorton said, "you and I are doing the shopping, Ada. Together."

Next morning Susan taught us, the way she always did.

Lady Thorton came down late. "Good morning, Susan. Good morning, children. Ada. Jamie. Ruth." She said Ruth's name stiffly, but at least she didn't sneer.

Ruth glanced up from her textbook. "Good morning," she said.

"Ready, Ada?" Lady Thorton pulled on her gloves.

In the village the women in the queue outside the butcher's shop were all politeness toward Lady Thorton. If they were surprised to see her doing the shopping with me, they didn't let on. We stood for an hour; when we finally reached the front of the queue the only choices left were beef shin bones or a ragged piece of liver.

"Sorry," the butcher said, wiping his hands on his grimy apron. "All I've got."

Lady Thorton peered into the glass case, then down at me. "Do you know how to cook liver?" she asked.

I shook my head. "Susan would." I didn't like liver; I thought it tasted muddy.

Lady Thorton grimaced. "I told her you and I would make dinner tonight."

"I can do shin bones," I said.

She raised her eyebrows. "Really?" She shuddered. "I never thought of shin bones as something people actually ate."

I said to the butcher, "A shilling's worth of the beef shins, please."

"You want them sliced like your mother gets them?"

"Susan's not my mother."

"Right," said the butcher. "You want 'em sliced like she gets 'em?"

Lady Thorton looked amused. I gave the butcher a dignified nod. "Please."

At home Lady Thorton watched while I browned the shins in leftover dripping. She chopped carrots while I chopped celery and a slice of onion. Then I put the shins in a pan with water, added the chopped veg plus salt and pepper and some herbs and things, covered the whole mess, and stuck it into a slow oven.

"That's it?" Lady Thorton asked.

"It takes a couple of hours to cook," I said, "so we should put some potatoes in too, and maybe some apples." In wartime you were never supposed to use your oven to cook only one dish. It wasted fuel.

We found other things that could be baked and put them in the oven. "What next?" Lady Thorton asked.

"I've got to go help Fred." I couldn't imagine Lady Thorton on the business end of a pitchfork. On either end, actually.

Apparently, neither could she. "I want to finish some paperwork for the WVS," she said. "We can just leave all this to cook?"

I nodded.

"That's not so hard," she said, with a wide smile.

I knew she didn't really feel cheerful. I knew she was pretending. I liked her better for being willing to pretend.

As I pulled on my coat, Ruth came in from outside.

"Where are you going?" she asked.

"Stables. To do chores."

"Can I come?"

I looked at Lady Thorton. She pursed her lips. I shook my head. "No."

Beef shins are just about the least expensive kind of beef you can buy, but if you cook them right, they taste lovely. By the time I got home from the chores, the whole house smelled savory and good. I took the leftover oatmeal from breakfast, formed it into lumps, and dropped them into the stew's gravy. Just as I hoped, they swelled and turned into something like dumplings. As I was finishing, Lady Thorton walked in.

"Why didn't you let me know you'd come back?" she asked. "I would have done that with you."

I hadn't even thought about it. I wasn't used to Lady Thorton helping in the kitchen. She said, almost apologetically, "It wasn't ever part of my training to learn to cook, you know. When I was growing up, before the first war, girls of my class were expected to assume we would hire a cook."

I didn't reply. Was I supposed to feel sorry for her? She wouldn't have hired me to be her kitchen maid before the war. Not me nor any girl like me, who grew up poor in the London slums. I started to take the potatoes out of the oven, one by one, using a towel to protect my hands.

Lady Thorton said, "I suppose where you grew up you often ate beef shin."

I said, "We could never afford beef shin. We were lucky to get bacon once a week."

Lady Thorton said sharply, "I wasn't joking, Ada."

I straightened and looked her in the eye. "Neither was I."

She looked as uncomfortable as I'd ever seen her. After a long pause she said, "Was that true for your neighbors too?"

I shrugged. "Maybe. Probably. Most of them had fathers that worked, but most had more mouths to feed. Jamie wasn't any skinnier than the rest of the kids his age." Dirtier, maybe, but not skinnier.

I sliced the potatoes open and arranged them on

plates. Lady Thorton spooned beef shin stew over the steaming potatoes. "What about you?" she asked. "Were you worse off than Jamie?"

Even now, thinking about it made me want to send my mind far away. "I stayed in the one room," I said. "I never left it."

Lady Thorton paused, her spoon dripping stew. "Susan told me that once," she said. "I didn't believe her."

Susan always believed me about Mam.

"I never thought a mother could be like that," Lady Thorton said. "Cold, yes. I've known unaffectionate mothers. My own was quite remote. But not evil. What you describe is evil."

I said, "Susan said she was incapacitated."

Lady Thorton nodded. "Very much so."

That night, while we ate beef shin, Lady Thorton asked Ruth quite civilly how her studies were progressing. Ruth swallowed and returned a civil answer. Later as we were washing up I overheard Susan thank Lady Thorton for the meal.

"Don't thank me," Lady Thorton said. "I'm beginning to learn how much I never realized I didn't know."

Chapter 28

Lady Thorton tried harder but she didn't thaw all the way. She quit opening Ruth's mail, but she always asked Ruth who her letters were from. If Lady Thorton had known how to read German, she would have insisted on reading them. "They're all from my mother or my father," Ruth said. "My mother's have already been cleared by a censor. I told you. You don't need to be afraid."

"I'm being cautious," Lady Thorton said. "Of course I'm not afraid."

Ruth cut her eyes at me. I grinned. Of course Lady Thorton was afraid.

It made sense to be wary of Germans. On the other hand, if Ruth really planned to kill us in our sleep, I thought she would have done it by now.

A week later Ruth and I were studying at the table when someone knocked at the door. Ruth got up.

"Hello!" said a voice I recognized.

I jumped out of my chair. *"Jonathan!"*

"Ada!" It was Jonathan, tall and thin, in his RAF uniform and leather flying jacket. He grinned. "Is my mother home?"

Lady Thorton came halfway down the stairs. She saw Jonathan, screamed, and ran the rest of the way. A *happy* scream: I'd never heard one before.

Jonathan swung Lady Thorton around in a hug. He said, "Sorry I couldn't warn you. I only got leave at the last minute."

"Oh!" Lady Thorton stood back from him, beaming. "It's so good to see you! I'm so glad!"

"This is Ruth," I said.

Jonathan held out his hand. "I've heard about you," he said. Ruth grimaced and darted a glance at Lady Thorton, but Jonathan continued, "My father says you're brilliant at maths."

Ruth smiled. She almost never smiled. Brilliant? I hadn't thought she was brilliant.

"You must be starving," Lady Thorton said to Jonathan. "Let's get you something to eat." She led him into the kitchen and put the kettle on. She started rummaging through the cupboard. "Where is Susan hiding those eggs?"

Jamie had finally gotten two hens named Penelope

and Persnickety. They each laid an egg every single day. It was glorious, having that many eggs again.

Lady Thorton poked her head out the back door. "Jamie! Come here!" Susan was in the village doing WVS work. She wouldn't be home until time for tea.

Jamie ran in covered in mud. He saw Jonathan, drew himself up, and saluted.

Jonathan saluted back. "At ease," he said.

"Yes, sir!"

Lady Thorton said, "We need a treat, Jamie."

"I told you already," Jamie said, "we are not eating my hens."

"Of course not," said Lady Thorton. "I was thinking omelet. What happened to the extra eggs?"

Jamie shrugged.

"Susan's saving them," I said. She'd tucked them out of Lady Thorton's sight. She was going to preserve them in isinglass, she'd told me, so we had a reserve, in case a fox got the hens or Lady Thorton bought lamb chops again.

Lady Thorton laughed. "She won't mind if we splurge for Jonathan."

I wasn't sure, but I fetched the eggs from their hiding place. There were eight of them. Lady Thorton threw the entire week's butter ration into a frying pan and cooked a vast omelet using all eight eggs.

Every. Single. One.

Susan was going to be livid.

On the other hand, the omelet smelled delicious. "Sit down," Lady Thorton said. "Everyone, sit down."

"I'll take my work to my room," said Ruth.

"Sit and eat," said Jonathan. "Don't you like omelet?"

She hesitated. "I don't want to eat your food."

He grinned. "I'm pretty sure I'm eating yours."

Ruth let Lady Thorton serve her a tiny portion of the omelet. Jamie and I had small portions too. Lady Thorton didn't take any, which left nearly half the omelet for Jonathan. He ate it all in six quick bites. We watched him. He was thinner than he had been at Christmas, his face sharp angles and lines.

Lady Thorton said, "Perhaps we can manage a cake for tea."

Ruth and I exchanged glances. There went the sugar ration. We'd be eating our oatmeal salted for a month.

Jonathan wiped his lips on his napkin. "I brought us a treat." He reached into his jacket pocket, pulled something out, and placed it on the table. It was thin and long and smooth, yellow speckled with small brown spots.

"Jonathan!" his mother said.

"Where did you get that?" Ruth asked, sounding thrilled.

"What is it?" asked Jamie. He picked it up, carefully, and handed it to me. I didn't know what it was, either. It felt leathery and a little bit squishy. I put it back on the table.

"I don't want to know where you got it," Lady Thorton said. "Black market, I'm sure. I don't need to hear about that."

"No," Jonathan said. "There's no ration on fruit."

I said, "That's a fruit?"

It was called a banana. Lady Thorton had had no problem using up every egg in the house, but she wasn't greedy about the banana. "We'll have it for tea, when we're all here," she said. "I won't cut it before Susan comes home."

We all went into the sitting room. I poked up the fire. Lady Thorton fussed over Jonathan, smoothing his hair and wondering if he needed more tea. "Stop," he said, "I'm fine."

He didn't look fine. He looked tired down to his bones. Whenever he was still, his face fell into tense and anxious lines. Even when he smiled at Jamie the smile didn't reach his eyes.

Jonathan tugged off the green-and-brown scarf wrapped around his neck. "Take a look at that," he said, tossing it to Jamie. "It's made out of a piece of a camouflage parachute."

"Cor!" Jamie grabbed the scarf by its corners and pulled it, fluttering, around the room. He got one of his tin airplanes and tied it to the edges of the scarf.

"He'll wreck it," I said.

Jonathan shook his head. "He won't." He turned to Ruth. "Tell me what it was like in Germany," he said.

Ruth shrugged. "We left almost two years ago."

"Right," he said. "What made you leave?"

He leaned forward. He looked like he was really interested, not just trying to be polite.

"We're Jewish," she said.

"Yes. My father told me."

"My father was a university professor in Dresden. In statistics. He lost his job because Hitler decided that Jews could not teach at universities anymore."

Jonathan nodded, as though this was the answer he expected. "How bad had it gotten?"

Ruth's voice stayed flat and emotionless. "Jews could not vote. We no longer counted as German citizens. We weren't allowed to go to parks, or restaurants, or public swimming pools. We weren't allowed to ride bicycles, go to the movies, attend concerts, visit the beach. A mob burned down our synagogue. I was expelled from school."

"You did something wrong?" I asked.

Ruth said, "I'm Jewish. Jewish children were no longer allowed to go to school."

"Just because you don't believe Jesus is God?"

"It didn't have anything to do with my religion," Ruth said. "It didn't have anything to do with what I personally believe, with whether or not I practice Judaism. According to Hitler, if my grandparents were born Jewish, I'm a Jew. If my grandparents converted to Christianity on the days of their births, and my parents and I had always been raised to believe Jesus was God, I would still be Jewish according to Hitler. It's not about religion. It's about race. Hitler sees the Jews as a separate race."

Lady Thorton was staring at her hands. Had she known any of this? I said, "So it really isn't anything about your God."

"It's the same God," Ruth said. "Christians read the Old Testament too."

Jonathan said, "Christ himself was raised a Jew."

"Jonathan!" Lady Thorton said.

"What? It's a fact." After a pause he said, "One of my best flying mates is Jewish. Grew up in Liverpool. He's got family in Poland he's worried about." He said to Ruth, "I'm glad your family escaped."

"We searched for months to find a country that

would take us," Ruth said. "America wouldn't. France wouldn't. Finally, England did. Then we weren't allowed to sell our home. We had to leave all our money and everything we owned behind." She swallowed. Her voice trembled. "We had to leave my grandmother behind."

Chapter 29

"I'm sure she's fine," Lady Thorton said. "Even the Nazis wouldn't harm an elderly woman."

"We haven't heard from her," Ruth said. "Not one letter in almost two years. My mother is sick from worry."

Lady Thorton said, "I'm sure she's all right."

Ruth's eyes glittered. "You don't really understand anything, do you? That, or you choose not to." She stood. "Excuse me. I will take my work upstairs."

I watched her go. Across the room, Jamie made airplane noises. Jonathan raised his eyebrows at his mother.

"How can she say that?" Lady Thorton demanded. "When you—my son, my only son—are risking your life every single day? When the government's taken my home, when our village has been bombed, when we deal with queues and shortages every day?"

Jonathan pressed his fingertips together so hard the

pads of his fingers turned white. "Because we haven't faced anything like what she has," he said. "You've lent our house, you haven't lost it. None of us know how she feels."

Jamie looked up. "Can you rescue Ruth's grandmother?" he asked Jonathan. "Can you go get her with your plane?"

"Not with a Spitfire," Jonathan said. "I'm afraid we'll need infantry for that."

"Will you do it?" Jamie asked.

Jonathan said, "We'll certainly try."

Susan was not cross about the eggs. She wasn't even cross about the butter. "Of course you had to celebrate!" she said. She threw her arms around Jonathan, as though she were thrilled to see him, as though he were someone really important to her.

Maybe he was.

"I thought perhaps a cake?" Lady Thorton suggested.

"Mmm, yes, we could manage a small one," Susan said. "Jamie, quit pestering Jonathan. Run over to Fred's or the Ellistons' and see if you can't borrow one more egg. Tell them I'll pay it back. And invite them all to tea. Tell them we have a banana."

The thick skin of the banana peeled away. Inside was a long, slim, cream-colored fruit. It was soft like pudding and didn't have seeds or stones—you could cut it the way you would a block of warm butter. Susan divided Jonathan's banana into slices and handed them around on a plate. Jamie's eyes widened when he tasted his. "I like banana!" he said.

I wasn't sure. Susan laughed when she saw my face. "Ada's thinking, 'This is very different,'" she said, and she was right, I was.

"What's flying like?" Jamie asked Jonathan. He scooted his chair over until he was nearly touching Jonathan's side. He was wearing Jonathan's scarf; Jonathan had shown him how to knot it the way a pilot would.

"Extraordinary," Jonathan said. "Free. You can go up, down, sideways—any direction at all. Everything's beautiful from above. The ocean is like an endless sparkling blanket of blue."

I turned toward him. "That's how it looks from the church steeple."

Jonathan nodded. I said, "When you're flying, are you afraid?"

Maybe it wasn't a question I should ask. Jonathan's face went very still. "I'm not afraid because I'm flying," he said at last. "Let's leave it at that."

Jamie leaned into him. "Everyone's shooting at you," he said.

"Yes," Jonathan said. "We're all shooting at each other."

After our baths we came downstairs to listen to the radio news. Jonathan was slumped half-asleep in his mother's wing chair. He started when he saw me. "Ahh!" he said. "Ada, I promised to take you riding!"

"Me and Maggie both," I said, "and she's not here."

"Still," he said, "I did promise, and I don't like to waste the chance. Maybe really early tomorrow morning? Only I've got to catch the train before nine."

With wartime daylight savings, it didn't even start to get light until seven. I said, "We'll do it next time. Maybe Maggie will be home then."

He looked relieved. "You aren't disappointed?"

I was disappointed not to have the ride, but happy he remembered his promise. Plus, he looked so tired. I said, "I'm fine."

Next morning it rained. Penelope and Persnickety laid two more eggs, and Susan fried them in the still-buttery omelet pan for Jonathan's breakfast. All the rest of us ate toast with tiny scrapings of jam.

Jonathan seemed even more tired than he had the day before. I thought of what it meant to be a pilot, to go out and try to kill Germans.

To kill people like Ruth.

Except that Ruth had been kicked out of Germany. Hitler had kicked her out.

If our pilots hadn't won the Battle of Britain, Hitler and the German Army would have invaded England for sure. That's what everyone said, even Winston Churchill. I was pretty sure Winston Churchill wouldn't lie.

War was as complicated as religion, when you started to think about it.

Jonathan shook my hand good-bye. "Next time," he said, "we'll have our ride. I won't forget."

I nodded. "Be careful," I said.

He grinned ruefully. "I can't afford that. Remember? There's a war on."

Chapter 30

The fire-watching rota had us each going up once every two or three weeks—too often to forget how frightening it was, but not often enough to get used to it.

The next time I was scheduled after Jonathan's visit, I got the midnight shift—midnight to two a.m.—and the WVS woman paired with me was Susan. I preferred Susan to Lady Thorton or to someone I didn't know, of course, but at the same time I dreaded going with her.

Susan woke me after a few hours' sleep. We bundled up and walked to the village through deep darkness in air so cold it was like breathing knives. "Nothing's going to happen tonight," said one of the men we replaced. "It's a new moon. Too dark to fly."

Nothing except standing exposed in the middle of the sky. The climb to the steeple was the worst yet. Inside the staircase, I couldn't see anything, not even Susan right in front of me. The cold air made my insides shiver, and that felt like fear. It was hard to breathe. It was hard to make myself stay present inside my head. By the time we'd reached the outdoors again, I felt numb inside and out.

I clutched the stone wall and stared down at my feet, my heartbeat pounding in my ears.

Beside me, Susan tilted her face to the sky. *"Oh!"* she said.

I looked up. I gasped too. Thousands of stars pricked the sky—more than that, tens of thousands, hundreds of thousands. Thousands of thousands. More stars than I'd ever seen, so many that they made a broad streak of light across the middle of the sky. I stared and stared. I'd seen stars lots of times since living with Susan. They'd never before looked like this.

"It's such a clear night," Susan said. "No clouds, no moon, and of course the blackout."

My face felt warmer under the starlight even as my breath blew out in a frozen cloud. "I wish I had paper," I said. "I'd draw a map of the stars."

"People have done that," Susan replied. "They've named patterns in the sky. Constellations. Look for the brightest stars. See that one—and there—and there—and those—how they make a square and then a crooked line? That's the Plow."

I looked, but I couldn't see what she meant. There were too many stars to concentrate on only a few. "What's a plow?"

Susan looked down at me. She smiled. "A tool for tilling the earth."

She tried to show me other shapes: an archer, twin brothers. "And Draco, the dragon," she said.

A dragon on the edge of the map of the sky.

"A real dragon or a story-dragon?" I asked.

Susan put her arm around me. She said, "All the dragons are story-dragons."

I forgot to be afraid until I stumbled on a rough piece of slate and fell against the parapet wall. Then fear came rushing back so quickly I nearly vomited.

Susan pulled me back from the wall. "You're shaking," she said.

I was. I couldn't stop.

"What about this frightens you so much?" she asked.

"I don't know." I looked up again. Susan wasn't afraid. "The stars are fantastic." I never saw stars looking out the window of Mam's flat. You couldn't look up out of Mam's window, not really, or at least I never did.

"You don't have to do this," Susan said quietly. "We can find you other useful war work."

This is why I had dreaded going with her.

I shook my head. It felt like a bargain I'd made: my fear in exchange for Jamie's safety. For mine and Jamie's and Susan's safety.

"Are you sure?" Susan asked.

"Don't stop me."

"I won't," she said, "because I don't believe you're in danger up here, not any more than anywhere else. Think about it. You don't have to feel safe to actually be safe."

I supposed. I'd never felt safe, so how would I know?

A few days later, midafternoon, I banged on Ruth's door.

"I'm busy!" she yelled.

She'd become even more of a hermit since telling us about her grandmother.

Then she stuck her head out her door. "Did I get a letter?" she asked.

"No," I said.

She went to shut the door again, but I stuck my foot in the way. "Tell me about your grandmother," I said.

Her eyes narrowed. "Why?"

"I want to know about grandmothers," I said. "They sound nice. I don't have one."

"You did."

"Not to know them."

Ruth sighed. She opened the door a tiny bit farther. I pushed myself forward. "It's cold in your room," I said.

"This entire country is cold." She sat down at her desk and picked up a pencil. "I'm working."

"Do you have any pictures of your grandmother? Of any of your family?"

"None of your business," Ruth said.

I said, "I'm not your enemy."

She looked up at me silently.

I said, "I'm not."

She said, "But I'm German. I'm *your* enemy. Remember?"

I said, "You hate Hitler more than I do."

Ruth nodded. "Very true. But I still won't tell you about my grandmother."

I waited. After a pause she spoke again, looking down at her desk. "If I start letting things out of my heart," she said, "if I talk to you, if I bring out the photographs, I will fall to pieces. I won't be able to endure living here. I won't be able to learn what I need to learn to help my family. If I crack at all, I will come undone."

She kept her voice absolutely quiet and even.

I said, "I know how that feels."

"I thought you did," she said. "Now go away."

Chapter 31

That was the last cold snap. Spring arrived with bits of green, and an enormous white pig came to live in the pen in our back garden. Susan and Lady Thorton named her Mrs. Rochester. In a few months she was going to farrow, which meant have babies, and the babies were going to be pig club pigs.

Pig clubs were a war thing. Groups of people combined their food scraps and fed them to a baby pig. When the pig was grown and slaughtered, the whole group shared its meat. Pig clubs turned leftovers no one could eat into pork chops and bacon. You could almost never find pork chops in the shops anymore.

Every day, Mrs. Elliston, the wife of the man who farmed the Thortons' estate, collected her potato peels and gristle and other leftovers in a bucket. Fred added his, and I carried the bucket home from the stables.

Susan added our scraps and boiled the stinking mess into slop for Mrs. Rochester. It was a lot of work.

Jamie loved Mrs. Rochester. He fed her, gave her water, scraped up her manure, spread fresh straw for bedding, scratched her back with a stick, and sang to her, for all I knew. I avoided her as much as possible. Ruth, on the other hand, liked her. "She's a very friendly pig," Ruth said.

Ruth moved a small table and one of the old kitchen chairs out to the back garden. She studied there, in a patch of sunshine beside the pigpen, with Bovril on her lap and the chickens pecking the grass near her feet.

"Did you have pigs in Germany?" I asked her.

"Of course not. Jews don't eat pork."

"I meant for a pet," I said. "Not to eat them."

She looked up. "No one keeps pigs for a pet. We had horses and a dog. That's all."

"How many horses?"

"Three. One each for my father, my mother, and me." She scratched behind Bovril's ears. The cat kneaded his claws into her leg. She didn't mind. "When I was very small I had a gray pony named *Schneeflocke*. Snowflake. When I outgrew him we gave him to my younger cousins."

"What are cousins?" I reached for Penelope. She scuttled away.

"My mother's brother's children," Ruth said. "If you have a child one day, and Jamie has a child, they will be cousins."

It was irritating that Ruth knew English words I didn't. I said so. "I started learning English in school," she replied. "The rest I learned fast at the internment camp. I worked hard. I knew I needed to be fluent to go to university."

"Why do you care about university?"

"I want to be like my father," Ruth said.

My father had worked on the docks. All the fathers I grew up with did.

"Where are your cousins now?"

"You're asking a lot of questions," Ruth said. I didn't respond. She sighed. "They're still in Germany," she said. "My mother's father and brother were both cavalrymen in the German Army. My uncle fought for Germany in the First World War. So he feels safe in Germany, even though he's Jewish. He thinks other Germans will respect his service to the country."

"He's fighting against us?"

"He's not fighting anyone," Ruth said. "He's too old to fight now."

"But he fought against us before?"

"Yes," Ruth said. "He's a good German. You can't blame him for that."

Of course I could. Germans were the enemy. Every time I was about to forget that, Ruth reminded me.

Ruth shook her head. "I know it's very difficult to get mail from Germany right now."

"Still nothing from your grandmother?"

"Nothing from any of them."

Maggie came home for the two weeks surrounding Easter. Her first night back we stayed awake late in our bedroom. "I'm worried about Jonathan and I'm worried about Mum and I'm lonely and I want to be home. You're here. It isn't fair." She whispered to me across the space between our beds. We'd left the blackout down and moonlight streamed through the window. "I really hate school. I didn't used to, but I do now."

I told Maggie about Ruth's grandmother. I said, "Jamie and I must have had a grandmother too."

"Well, of course," said Maggie. "Two of them."

I shivered. Perhaps my grandmothers had been as nasty as my mother. Perhaps it was lucky I couldn't remember them.

"It's too bad you don't have anything from your

home in London," Maggie said. "Your mother must have left some things behind."

Maggie loved me, but she could never understand what my life in London had been like. Only Stephen White and Jamie had known. I didn't hear from Stephen and I hoped Jamie had forgotten. "My family didn't have anything extra," I said. "Photographs or books or anything like that." I stuck my right foot out of the bedcovers. "I have this scar. That's how I remember my mother."

"Susan gave you that scar. Not your mother. It's a good scar."

"I suppose."

"You've got other scars, though too, don't you?" Maggie rolled onto her back. I could see her hands clasp the edge of her bedsheets. "Everyone does. Invisible ones."

I took a deep breath. In, out. I thought of being up in the steeple, where it hurt to breathe. I could not really imagine Maggie having scars.

She kept talking. "So you understand what it's like at school, everyone afraid, and all the news of people dying. That wretched telegraph boy bicycling up the drive."

Ruth was even quieter around Maggie than she was around me. "Does she ever talk?" Maggie asked.

I shrugged. "Sometimes. Not really."

Jamie said, "She talks to me. When you two go ride."

Susan said the Friday before Easter was called Good Friday. It was a special day to remember Jesus dying on the cross. "But this year," she said, that morning, "it also happens to be a special day for Ruth. It's the first day of a Jewish holiday called Passover." Before dinner Susan poured salt water into several small bowls. She had Maggie set one next to each of our plates. She handed me several sprigs of parsley. "Put one beside each bowl," she said.

"Where'd you get the parsley?" We'd started planting our garden, but the only things sprouting so far were radishes and lettuce.

"Mrs. Elliston had some wintering over in her cold frame," Susan said. She opened a bottle of Lady Thorton's wine, something she rarely did, and poured a small amount into a glass set by every place. "It's not much but at least Ruth will know we are thinking of her."

When Ruth saw the table with the wine and the parsley, her hands flew to her mouth. Her eyes filled with tears. "Oh, thank you," she said.

"I don't know how to do a real seder," said Susan.

Ruth said, "But you knew it was Passover." As we sat down, Ruth said that on the first night of Passover, her whole family would get together for a special meal called a seder. Wine, parsley, and salt water were part of the seder meal.

"I went to a seder once at university," said Susan. "Would you like to ask the four questions?"

Ruth looked at Jamie. "Usually the youngest person asks them."

"What are the four questions?" Jamie said.

Ruth took a deep breath. She said, "The first is, 'Why is this night different from all others?'"

Jamie put down his fork. He settled his hands in his lap. He repeated, "Why is this night different from all others?"

Ruth sat very still. After a pause she said, "We dip parsley in salt water because we replace our tears with gratitude." She picked up her parsley, dipped it into the bowl, and ate it. So did Susan and Jamie, Maggie, and, after a pause, Lady Thorton, and me.

Salty bitterness filled my mouth. It tasted like tears.

Chapter 32

I couldn't take Ruth up the church steeple—the village would never let a German fire-watch—but on a clear night a few weeks later, I stayed up until dark and took her outside. There were trees all around the cottage, but we went down the lane until we had an open view of the night sky.

"Susan showed me pictures in the sky," I said. "A plow and a dragon."

Ruth shrugged. "Sure. I know about them. You think the English invented astronomy? Kepler was a German."

"Who's Kepler?" Sounded like Hitler.

Ruth laughed. "Oh, Ada. Why did you drag me outside?"

"I wanted you to see this." The stars made me feel better. Perhaps they would help Ruth too. I said, "Maybe your grandmother is looking at these stars. The same ones. Maybe right now."

Ruth pressed her lips together. "What do you want me to say?" she asked, after a pause.

"Nothing," I said. "I thought you needed to see them, that's all."

She walked back toward the house. "Don't worry about what I need."

On May 13, 1941, I celebrated my real birthday for the first time. I was twelve years old.

I hadn't known my birthday until I'd found my birth certificate last September. Susan had made up dates to put on our identity cards. She had celebrated our pretend birthdays too.

Mam never celebrated birthdays. Mam never celebrated anything.

Maggie was back at school, but Ruth and Jamie picked flowers from the hedgerows and covered the breakfast table with them. Susan gave me a piece of bacon and a whole fried egg for breakfast. She and Lady Thorton stacked presents by my plate—new books, three of them.

It was too much. Church-steeple panic crawled across my skin. I handed the bacon to Jamie. I pushed the books out of sight. I made myself choke down the egg. Susan would be angry if I wasted it.

I should have been used to birthdays. Mam should have celebrated my birthdays.

"It's okay," Susan said, watching my face. "Whatever you feel, it's okay." She put her arms around me.

"Why didn't she love me?" I whispered.

"Because she was broken," she said. "Remember that. She was broken, not you."

I had the bad foot, but the foot worked better now. The foot wasn't the reason. Something else must be wrong with me. Most mothers loved their children.

I went out to the garden. Ruth followed. "Why are you afraid?" she asked.

"I'm not afraid," I said. "I'm never afraid."

"Huh," she said. "You also say there's nothing wrong with your foot."

"That foot," I said, "is a very long way from my brain."

She arched her eyebrows. "Of course," she said. "Who thought it wasn't?"

"I'm going to the stables," I said. "I'm going for a ride." I took two steps down the path, then turned back to Ruth. "Want to come?"

Chapter 33

"It's my birthday," I told Fred. "Ruth's riding with me to celebrate."

Fred's mouth worked back and forth. "Does Lady Thorton know?" he asked.

"No," I said. I'd found a pair of Maggie's old jodhpurs in our wardrobe. They were a little short for Ruth, but she pulled her stockings over them. We'd run to the stables without saying anything to anyone. "Ruth can ride Butter," I said. "He's my pony and I can decide who rides him. I'll ride Ivy." Maggie wouldn't mind. Any of the other horses Lady Thorton could get snippy about. "Lady Thorton went to the WVS office," I said. "She won't find out. We'll never tell her."

Fred looked at me grimly. "It's not right," he said.

"It is," I said. "What's right and what's permitted are sometimes different things."

Fred scratched his head and sighed. "You two be sure to stay away from town."

On Butter, Ruth could not quit smiling. I'd never seen her smile so much. I said so. "I know," she replied, laughing as we trotted down the edge of a field. "My cheeks hurt." She patted Butter's neck. "What a lovely pony." She rode with competent ease; Butter looked like he was smiling too.

I took Ruth to the top of the lookout hill. The sun shone hot and bright. The air smelled like salt and new grass. The sea stretched out wide and blue, with white waves close to shore and nary a fishing boat in sight. Ivy tossed her head. Her long mane brushed my knees.

"I caught a German spy last summer," I said. "I was up here, and I saw him in a boat rowing into shore."

Ruth raised her eyebrows. "An actual spy?"

I nodded. "He had a wireless set."

"Well, you can rest assured that I am not a spy. I do not have a wireless set."

"I know," I said. "Jamie searched your things when you first came."

Ruth looked angry for a second, then burst out laughing. "That's terrible!" she said. "You are horrible children!"

It seemed funny, out in the sunshine. We turned

the ponies. Ivy began to bounce. "Want to gallop?" I said. "We usually gallop down."

"Please!" Ruth shot Butter forward. I followed on her heels.

I showed Ruth the beach where my spy had landed. We skirted the village, then took a long route through land Maggie's family owned. Most of the pastures were planted in crops now. Lady Thorton said Mr. Elliston had doubled how many acres he'd put under plow. The government told Mr. Elliston exactly what to grow. "Potatoes, swedes, and flax," I told Ruth.

Ruth frowned. "I don't know *flax*. What's that taste like?"

I shrugged. "Dunno." I supposed we'd be eating it soon. I'd eaten all sorts of odd things since living with Susan.

We circled a copse of trees and came upon a tractor stopped at the edge of the field. One of the Land Girls was fiddling with something under its bonnet. The bonnet wouldn't stay up; it kept slamming onto her elbow.

"Oi, help me, can't you?" the Land Girl said.

I jumped down and gave Ivy's reins to Ruth.

"Hold the edge of the blasted bonnet," said the girl. "It's not hard to fix, I just need a minute."

The Land Girl was barely older than Ruth. She

wore a green shirt and rubber boots and pants that had been cut off, short and ragged, above the knee. She banged the engine with a spanner.

"There, that should do it." She nodded to me, and I dropped the bonnet. It clanged. "Now to get the blasted thing restarted." She held her hand out to me. "Thanks for your help. You must be Miss Margaret. I'm Rose."

"I'm Ada," I said, shaking Rose's hand. "Ada Smith."

"Oh. Well, thanks anyhow. Cheers."

"Will she tell?" Ruth asked when I climbed back into the saddle.

"Tell who?" I said. "The Land Girls barely speak to Fred, let alone Lady Thorton." We picked up a trot. "Fred doesn't like the Land Girls. He says they're lightfoots."

"What does that mean?"

"No idea," I said, "but I think it sounds fun."

We trotted past the potato field now covering the big front lawn of Thorton House. Ruth studied the house. "It's very grand."

"Yes," I said. "Like a train station."

Ruth laughed again. "Very much like a train station," she said. "You are terrible, Ada. I like you."

When we finished riding and had put the ponies away, Ruth changed back into her skirt in the tack room. "I will help with the chores," she said.

"Better not," I said.

"Yes, I will."

"You'll smell like a horse."

Ruth sniffed appreciatively. "Yes. The best smell in the world." She grinned at me. "Don't worry. I will visit Mrs. Rochester before I come inside. I will smell like the pig by the time Lady Thorton can sniff me."

"You look happy," Susan said to me at dinner. She had made me a birthday cake, a tiny one, with a single candle on top because twelve wouldn't fit and candles were hard to come by. "Did you go for a ride? Did you have an adventure?"

I was careful not to look at Ruth. "Butter was marvelous," I said.

Lady Thorton smiled. "How nice."

After that I let Ruth ride Butter once or twice a week, on days Lady Thorton spent in town. Fred muttered until I told him how Ruth's grandfather and uncle had been in the cavalry. "German cavalrymen were some of the finest horsemen who ever lived," Fred said. "I was batman to a British cavalryman in the Great War myself, so I know. And just look at her— lovely seat, wonderful hands."

Ruth rode with strength, patience, and liquid grace. Butter went better for her than he did for me. When I said so, Ruth nodded. "Swing your hips," she said. "Loosen your muscles. When you try to sit still, the horse bounces you."

I tried. "My muscles don't loosen," I said.

"I see that. You're very stiff."

I felt indignant. "Most people tell me I'm a good rider."

"Oh, yes," she said, "by English standards."

Which was an insult no matter how you thought about it.

"I haven't been riding very long," I said. "Just since I came here. And you know I had a clubfoot."

Ruth looked at me appraisingly. "The clubfoot that doesn't ever make you limp? The one there's nothing wrong with?"

"I'm better now," I said. "I had surgery last year. Before that my whole ankle curled sideways. Without crutches, I could barely walk."

Ruth studied me. "Drop your feet out of your

stirrups," she said. "Swing your legs. Like this." She demonstrated. I tried. "No," she said, "swing from the top of your legs. The very top."

It hurt, in a good sort of way. "Better," said Ruth. "Now loosen your knees."

"Fred tells me to keep my knees in," I said.

"In, but not pinching. When you post, lift from your stomach instead of your legs. From your muscles. Like this." She demonstrated.

I tried. "That hurts."

"Yes. Practice will make you stronger."

It hurt, but it was better. Even I could tell that. We rode down the length of a field.

"Why do you hate to talk about your foot?" Ruth asked, her eyes on Butter's mane.

I took a deep breath. Loose legs, strong stomach. Ivy relaxed. I said, "Why do you hate to talk about your grandmother?"

"I'm worried about her," Ruth said. "Talking makes me worry more."

"Oh." We rode on in silence. At last I said, "I'm tired of feeling ashamed. About my foot."

Ruth frowned. "A clubfoot is nothing to be ashamed of."

"My mother was ashamed. Mam, I mean."

Ruth said, "She was wrong."

I shrugged. "I can say that," I said. "It's harder to believe it."

Ruth kept riding, though not every day, and not always with me. We knew that if we were always gone from the cottage at the same time, and only when Lady Thorton was away, Susan would start to suspect. Some days I rode Butter alone, and other days Ruth did. I drew her a map of the Thortons' estate and the roads around the village, just as Susan had once done for me. *Dragons*, I wrote, with an arrow pointing to the WVS office, Lady Thorton's lair.

Ruth chuckled. "I will be like St. Margaret. I am not afraid."

Chapter 34

In July Maggie came home for two whole months. "At *least* two months," she said. "If I get my way, I'm never going back."

The two of us walked to the stables on her first morning back. "I've been exercising Ivy for you," I said.

"Oh, thank you," she said. "That's super."

"I've been letting Ruth ride Butter."

Maggie froze. She turned toward me with her hand in the air. "Stop talking," she said. "I didn't hear what you just said. I do not want you to tell me again. When my mother finds out—and she will find out—I want to be able to say I didn't know anything about it."

"I think you'd like—"

"My mother would be far angrier with me than she will be with you," Maggie said. She started walking again. "I'm not joking. I don't want to know."

"I thought maybe you could ride Oban, and that way the three of us—"

Maggie shook her head. "Not on your life."

"Coward."

"Realist."

"Ruth's not afraid."

"Ruth has nothing to lose."

"Sure she does," I said.

"Less than me. Why should I get in trouble for her?"

"I thought you were named after a dragon-slayer," I said. "St. Margaret the Brave."

"No," said Maggie. "I was named after her great-grandmother. Plain Margaret the Sensible. Not a saint, but also not a martyr."

"Ruth's like us," I said. "Horses help."

Maggie shook her head. "It's not my job to help her, is it?"

"Your father might think so. Your brother might."

"*Might,*" Maggie repeated. "But they aren't here. While my mother is, and we all know how she feels."

Weeks passed full of sunshine. The days were so long and the nights so short I rarely had to go fire-watching. I made sure Ruth still got to ride Butter sometimes, but only by curtailing how much I rode myself. Maggie wouldn't let Ruth take out any of the Thortons' horses and she wouldn't let me do it either. "We'd have more fun with the three of us," I said.

"I need to stay on my mother's good side," Maggie said. "If I annoy her I go back to school in September for sure."

Maggie and I picked berries on the wild hillsides, and Susan taught us how to make them into jam. You could get extra sugar rations to preserve fruit. Susan had bought three whole kilos.

Jamie flew in, banging the back door behind him. "Mum, Mum!" he said. "Mrs. Rochester had her babies! Mum, come see!"

I flinched. All these months of Jamie calling Susan *Mum,* and I still couldn't get used to it. "Mum!" Jamie said, pulling on Susan's hand. "Come see, come see!" He dragged Susan outside.

"Why do you mind what he calls her?" Maggie asked, watching me.

I shrugged. Some things were too complicated to explain.

Mrs. Rochester gave birth to eight piglets. She lay on her side, grunting, suckling them all in a long row and looking pleased. "What should we name them?" Jamie asked.

"We aren't naming them," Susan said. "They're pig club pigs. We don't name animals we plan to eat."

"I don't mind," Jamie said.

Susan said, "I do."

"Mum loves us," said Jamie. He sat curled on the sofa at night, reading *Swiss Family Robinson* again. Maggie was upstairs in the bath. Ruth had said she was going for a walk but was actually riding Butter, and Susan and Lady Thorton had taken chairs outside to sit on the lawn. It was a beautiful evening. "And Becky," Jamie said. "Becky loves us too."

"Oh, Jamie." I sighed. "That's a stupid thing to say. Becky never met us." She'd died before she could.

"She loves us from heaven," Jamie said.

"What about Mam?" I said bitterly. "Does Mam love us from heaven too?"

"Probably," Jamie said. "I think she's capacitated now."

Jamie repeated to Susan that Becky loved us. Susan put her arm around Jamie and said, "Of course she does."

When I complained about it later, Susan looked at me and said, "Do you really want me to tell him that he isn't loved?"

What was I supposed to say to that?

I wouldn't have told Susan I loved her even if I thought it was true. Words could be dangerous, as destructive as bombs.

"Do you think Mam's capacitated, now that she's dead?" I asked instead.

Susan tilted her head. "That's a nice thought," she said. "Maybe we all become better versions of ourselves after we die. Maybe we all reach heaven eventually."

Chapter 35

In mid-August Lady Thorton and I were supposed to fire-watch, but I convinced Maggie to go up with me instead. The moon was half-full and the air clear and warm. The wind blew in from the sea.

The sky was still so light that even the brightest stars were faint. I held on to the parapet and steadied myself. "Have you ever had a bomb, or an actual fire?" Maggie asked. She walked around the steeple, completely at ease.

"No." Since the end of the Battle of Britain, most of the fighting had moved to other parts of England. The Germans had only dropped three bombs anywhere near our village in the past year. None had hit buildings and the only thing that died was a sheep.

Maggie looked at me. "Then why are you afraid?"

"I'm not—"

"Be honest. I see you're afraid."

"I'm not afraid of the bombs," I said. "I'm afraid of being trapped."

My own words startled me. I didn't know where they came from, but I knew they were the truth.

I was afraid of being trapped.

"Trapped by what?" asked Maggie.

"I don't know, I—" I spread my hands out. "Everything. I have dreams about walls falling down on top of me. Pinning my leg again. Or bombers come, and I can't move—or I'm back in our flat, stuffed under the sink—I can't ever get away." I took a deep breath. "I grew up like that. In our flat. I couldn't get out."

Maggie said, "But you did."

My laugh came out shaky and close to tears. "I suppose," I said. "Only I still have to keep watch. I have to be careful, to keep bad things from happening again."

Her eyes were dark with sympathy. "You couldn't keep bad things from happening before," she said. "You still can't. It isn't really up to you."

I walked to the corner of the parapet. I looked out at the coal-black sea. "I'm fire-watching to keep Jamie safe," I said. "Jamie and me and everyone."

"You aren't," Maggie said. "You're taking a turn watching for fires. That's all. If you weren't doing it, someone else would be. You could be home sleeping and you'd be just as safe."

"Please stop talking," I said.

Maggie didn't. "It isn't all only up to you."

I looked at her. "It feels that way."

"So?" She handed me the binoculars. We kept watch. No bombers came.

Chapter 36

Very early one morning near the end of August, a rattling against the bedroom window startled me awake. I jumped out of bed. Maggie did too. I thought the noise sounded like gunfire, but Maggie was grinning. "Pebbles," she whispered as she took the blackout down.

It was almost dawn. Indigo shadows stretched across the back garden. A quarter moon still hung low in the sky. Jonathan Thorton stood beneath our window, looking up.

"Shh," Maggie hissed, before I could shout. She opened the window and put her head out.

"Get your jods on," Jonathan said, low. "It's a secret. Not a word."

Jods meant jodhpurs. We slipped into them. "What are we doing?" I whispered to Maggie.

She whispered back, "No idea."

At the top of the stairs I heard a door creak behind

us. I turned to see Ruth standing in her nightgown, wide-awake. She looked us up and down.

Maggie and I froze. Then I grinned. "Get your jods on," I whispered.

Ruth looked from me to Maggie. Maggie shook her head. I said, "You expect her to keep quiet if we leave her behind?"

Maggie sighed. She nodded at Ruth. "Jods," she whispered.

Ruth slid back into her bedroom. Maggie said, low, "You'll be the death of me."

Ruth reappeared, grinning, dressed to ride. We crept down the stairs and out the back door.

If Jonathan minded that Ruth was with us, he didn't say. He lifted his finger to his lips, then led us down the path toward the stables. A little ways from the cottage, we met a second pilot standing beside two parked motorcycles. "Hop on," Jonathan said to Maggie. He straddled one of the motorcycles. "You get behind me. Ada, you sit in front. Ruth, you get on behind Stan."

"What're—"

"Just do."

I balanced myself on the front edge of the seat of Jonathan's motorcycle. Jonathan gripped the handlebars. I held on to his arms. We roared down the road until we were almost to the stables. Jonathan lifted a hand, and he and the other pilot coasted to a stop. "Wait just here," Jonathan said to him. "Back in a bit." To Maggie and Ruth and me he said, "Quiet, now."

"What are we doing?" Maggie asked him, but he didn't answer. We almost had to run to keep up with his long stride.

He looked, I thought, terrible. Run to earth. Even thinner than before, and every muscle of his face clenched tight. The sparkle in his eyes held an edge that was almost frightening, but when he saw me staring at him he smiled, and his eyes smiled too.

In the stable yard, the dogs greeted us quietly. Jonathan opened the tack room. He directed Maggie to tack up Ivy, me to tack up Butter, and Ruth to tack up one of Lady Thorton's horses.

"Ruth should take Butter," I said. "She's used to him."

"Sure," Jonathan said. "Whatever suits."

Jonathan tacked up his own horse, Oban. Next we walked the horses very slowly over the cobblestones— if we were trying to be secret, which it seemed we were, this was the trickiest part, since the clank of shod hooves against stone might wake Fred. In a moment, though, we were on dirt again. Jonathan shortened the stirrup leathers on his saddle. "Here you go," he said, handing me Oban's reins. "I'll give you a leg up."

I froze. "Me?"

He chuckled. "What do you think I've cycled through the night for? I promised you we'd go riding."

"I didn't think you'd let me take Oban," I said.

"Scared?" he asked.

I laughed. I loved Oban. "No. Well, maybe. Some. Not so scared that I don't want to."

Jonathan laughed too. He legged me up, then quickly mounted the horse I'd saddled. "Away quiet like, then we'll have a run."

"How long are you here?" Maggie asked. "Mum'll—"

"No," Jonathan said. "I have to be back at the airfield by ten. It's going to be tight enough as it is. This'll be our secret. You're not to tell her. Promise me, all right?"

"All right," Maggie said. Flicking a glance at me, she added, "Ada's been letting Ruth ride. All summer."

"Good," said Jonathan. "Why shouldn't she?"

"Mum said no," said Maggie.

"That's silly," Jonathan said. "When our horses are just standing around. They could use the exercise. I'll write Mum about it."

Mist rose with the sun over the green-gold fields. The broad leaves of potato plants stretched far and wide, and in the hedgerows birds sang loudly. Oban walked beneath me with a marvelous loose swinging stride. I gathered the reins until I could just feel the edges of his mouth, and he softened his neck and relaxed into my hands. I let my hips swing and made myself breathe quietly.

"See?" Jonathan said to his sister. "How could we miss this?" He nodded at me. I smiled. It was so glorious, so unexpected, so perfectly right, the walk, the fields, the horse—

—the hedge exploded.

It was a grouse, not a bomb. A grouse with a nest in the hedge, who took exception to the horses coming so near, and flew out squawking and flapping straight for Oban's head.

Oban spooked, and ran.

I nearly came off him with the first leap, but I saved myself with a double handful of mane. The hedge flew past. Maggie screamed. Oban stretched out. He ran faster and faster, swallowing the ground. I pulled myself up like a jockey, legs straight in the stirrups, fighting panic. I hauled on the reins. I wasn't strong enough to stop him, not when he'd lost his head so completely. "Sit up!" Jonathan roared, far behind me. "Hold on!"

The wind made my eyes tear. The hedge blurred. My breath caught in my throat and the pounding of the horse's gallop echoed in my bones.

We were flying.

Flying, really flying. Butter never in his life could have gone so fast. Oban was a Thoroughbred, bred to run. He stretched his neck out farther, lengthened his stride even more.

Suddenly my fear fell away. Oban was flying, and I was flying with him. *Flying.* I was flying! It was the best, most joyful feeling in the world.

I dropped my hands to Oban's mane. I let the reins run out, let my hands surge with the movement of his mouth. Instead of pulling him in, I kicked him forward. He bunched his hindquarters and ran harder.

Oban loved to run. I loved Oban running.

I kicked again. I whooped. His speed increased until his stride began to feel as smooth as rushing wind, as effortless as flowing water. I moved with him, effortlessly.

On the day I was evacuated, I'd looked out the window of our train and seen a girl galloping a pony, racing the train. Now I was that girl, galloping, laughing, my head thrown back, the wind tugging my hair.

I'd become the person I'd longed to be.

At the far, far end of the field, Oban's breath started to come in gasps, like mine. I sat up. He dropped to a trot, and then a walk, his sides steaming, dripping with sweat. I turned him toward Maggie and Ruth and Jonathan, who were cantering toward us half a mile away.

"You all right?" Jonathan called. I waved to him, then ran my hand down Oban's sweating neck.

"Good boy," I whispered, patting him. *Good girl.* "Good boy."

"Sorry," Jonathan said, coming closer. "Are you really all right? The grouse spooked him, but I don't know what made him keep running like that."

"I did," I said. "I told him to go faster."

"You did?"

I nodded. "It was wonderful!"

Ruth laughed, and so did Maggie. "Told you," Maggie said to Jonathan.

He grinned at her. "Yes, but I didn't believe you."

We turned and walked back toward the stables through clouds of the horses' own steam. "Are you always so brave?" Jonathan asked.

"That wasn't brave," I said. "I just—I didn't fall

off, and then we were flying. We both wanted to run, so we did."

He lifted his gaze briefly to meet mine. "I'm glad I came today," he said. "I'll tell the boys at the airfield about you. You'll give them courage, you will."

I doubted that, but it didn't matter.

We got the horses back without anyone waking or hearing. Jonathan and his friend drove away. Maggie and Ruth and I rinsed the horses down, and wiped the tack and dried it. By the time Fred woke, we had a story ready about the horses getting loose and coming down to our cottage, and the time we'd had rounding them up and getting them back in. If he didn't believe us, Fred never let on. Susan and Lady Thorton believed us.

Jonathan wanted our ride kept secret, and I understood why. He meant for it to be a gift, a tiny piece of his time that belonged only to me, Maggie, and Ruth. It didn't belong to Lady Thorton or anyone else.

It was a gift. It was the best single hour of my life.

Chapter 37

September came. Despite Maggie's careful behavior all summer, Lady Thorton insisted she return to school. "You're safer there," she said.

"I'm just as safe here," Maggie said. "We haven't had a bombing for ages."

"Bombs aren't the only danger," her mother said. Later I overheard her say to Susan, "At school she's surrounded by good girls. It's the kind of environment I want for her."

"What am I?" I asked Susan. "The wrong environment?"

"I don't actually think she meant it that way," Susan said. "Lady Thorton never went to boarding school. She seems to imagine it as a sort of jolly holiday."

Susan had gone to boarding school. "Was it?"

"No," Susan said. "Mind you, I didn't hate it. But sometimes being in a group of girls is just as lonely as being alone."

Three days later, Ruth and I rode out together. We were trotting along the road that led to the lookout hill when I saw something red coming toward us. It was Lady Thorton's automobile.

I couldn't believe it. Lady Thorton almost never drove anywhere. Plus, I thought she'd walked into town.

Ruth's eyes narrowed. She glanced sideways at me. "Is that her?"

"That's her." There were hardly any cars on the roads these days. It was easy to recognize Lady Thorton's.

The car slowed to a stop. Lady Thorton stared at us through the windscreen.

My first impulse was to gallop away, but I knew it was no use. I drew rein and halted on the edge of the road. So did Ruth. "Maybe she won't be angry," I said.

Ruth looked perfectly composed. "She'll be furious."

Lady Thorton *was* furious. She got out and stood with her arms crossed, her upper lip twitching. She glared at Ruth and me for a very long, silent minute.

"I promised Maggie I'd exercise Ivy," I said.

"How long have you two been doing this, without my permission?"

I stared at the ground. Ivy mouthed the reins against my stiffened hands.

"Ada?" prompted Lady Thorton.

"I've been riding all summer," Ruth said.

"Only Butter," I said. "He's my pony. I can let anyone I want ride my pony."

"You've allowed a young German woman to come onto my property, against my explicitly stated orders, despite the fact that the house is being used by a government agency during a war against Germany?" Lady Thorton's voice had an edge that could have sliced steel.

"Jonathan said—"

"I never stepped foot into your house," Ruth said quietly. "I never spoke to anyone there. I'm not a spy. I hate Hitler."

Lady Thorton said, "That is entirely beside the point. I'm quite sure I made myself perfectly clear. I am disappointed in you both." She shook her head bitterly. "I hope my daughter wasn't involved."

"No, ma'am," I said, thankful it was mostly true.

"Go along home," Lady Thorton said. "Put those ponies up and come straight back to the cottage. Susan and I will deal with you there."

We walked back silently, our ponies' hooves clopping against the road. Swallows dove and swirled around us. I felt awash with indignation. "Butter is too my own pony," I said at last.

"We knew it wasn't allowed," Ruth said. "We took a chance and we got caught."

"But it's silly! You're not a spy!"

"I'm not," Ruth said. "It doesn't matter."

"Lord Thorton trusts you. So does Jonathan."

"Lady Thorton doesn't. She never has."

I looked at her helplessly. "I'm sorry. I didn't mean to get you in trouble."

Her face looked serious, even worried, but suddenly she laughed. "I'm not sorry," she said. "I got to ride for a few months, at least. Lady Thorton's angry, but she isn't Hitler. She won't kill us or throw us into jail."

"Susan'll be angry." My stomach twisted. I'd never done anything to make Susan really angry before. *Horses are good*, I thought. *Ruth needed horses.*

We put the ponies up, avoiding Fred. We walked slowly back to the cottage. We'd just rounded the last turn when Ruth sucked in her breath. "Oh, no," she said. I looked.

The telegraph boy was cycling up the drive.

Chapter 38

Ruth and I stopped walking. Her fingers reached out and grabbed mine. "Maybe it's not about Jonathan," I said.

The messenger got off his bicycle. He knocked on the door.

Ruth said, "He could be captured. He could be injured. He could be missing in action."

Lady Thorton came to the door. She saw the messenger. Color drained from her face.

I said, "Maybe he had to bail out over enemy lines."

Lady Thorton plucked the telegraph from the boy's hand. She opened it with trembling fingers. Her eyes closed, and she sank to the ground.

"He was just here," I whispered. "He was just fine."

Ruth squeezed my fingers. Tears trickled down her face.

Susan took Lady Thorton upstairs to Lady Thorton's bedroom. Ruth and I sat downstairs. I didn't know where Jamie was. I dreaded having to tell him.

"A telegraph boy will come for Maggie too," I said. He would cycle up the drive to her school's front door while Maggie looked out the classroom window, her heart filled with dread.

"We can't fix it," Ruth said.

From upstairs we heard a long, drawn-out wail. I buried my head in the sofa cushions and choked back tears.

"I hardly knew him," Ruth said, "but I think I would have liked him."

"I liked him," I said. "I liked him very much."

Jamie came in with a basket of vegetables he'd picked from the garden. "Where's the slop?" he asked. "It's time to feed Mrs. Rochester."

The slop was still on the stove, boiling. It was burned on the bottom, but Mrs. Rochester wouldn't care. I poured it into Jamie's bucket. "Let it cool before you give it to her," I said.

Jamie studied my face. "What happened?"

I couldn't say the words. Ruth said them for me. "Jonathan Thorton died."

"No," Jamie said. "No! No, no, no!"

"Yes," I said, grabbing him, holding him tight while he shook and sobbed.

Ruth and I cooked supper, but only Jamie ate it. We made a pot of tea. When Susan came back downstairs, I handed her a mug.

She took a sip, and tears came to her eyes. "You sugared it," she said. "You always do." She rubbed her face with her hands. "What a terrible, terrible day."

"What will they do with his body?" I asked. It was dreadful to think of Jonathan Thorton in a box.

"His plane blew up over the English Channel," Susan said. "They won't recover his body."

Jamie wailed. Susan pulled him onto her lap. "It's fitting," she said, wrapping her arms around him. "It has always been a custom for warriors to be buried at sea."

We went to bed. I put the blackout up and lay in the empty darkness of my room. I thought of Maggie. When would the telegram reach her? What would she do?

Jamie opened the bedroom door. He stood in the doorway in his pajamas, hair tousled, clutching his cat. He said, "Bovril's too sad to sleep."

"Oh, Jamie." I held my arms out to him, and he cuddled against me, breathing hard. Bovril lay between us, utterly limp. I supposed he knew Jamie needed him.

Ruth came in a few minutes later. "I can hear her through my bedroom wall," she said. "Lady Thorton. Susan said she was sleeping, but she keeps making noise." Ruth climbed into Maggie's empty bed.

A few minutes after that, Susan put her head into the room. "All right, you're being sensible," she said. "Stick together. I'm going to sit with Lady Thorton."

In the morning we woke and it was all still true.

Maggie had gotten her telegram. She was on her way home.

Chapter 39

It was a terrible, unending week. It was unendurable, but we endured it. We didn't have a choice.

Lord Thorton got a telegram too. He picked Maggie up at her school and they came home. They sat on our sofa. Lord Thorton wept.

I'd never seen a man cry before. It was horrible.

WVS women and Mrs. Elliston and the vicar's wife and other people who knew the Thortons brought food to our house and sat with us. Ruth locked herself in her bedroom whenever we had company. Otherwise she took long walks through the countryside. Neither of us rode. I did the chores every day as usual. I brushed Oban's sleek back and remembered every heartbeat of our gallop across the fields.

Instead of a funeral, the Thortons held a memorial service in the church. All the village came. Lord and

Lady Thorton and Maggie sat in the very first pew, looking like they might shatter at the slightest touch. We sat toward the back, Susan wearing all black on my one side, Ruth silent and downcast on the other. Jamie held tight to Susan's hand. I felt as fragile as Maggie looked. I wondered if I had any right to feel that way.

Mr. Collins, the vicar, stood by the church door shaking hands as people filed out. I looked past him to the graveyard. I asked, "Can't we at least put Jonathan's name on a stone?" Jonathan had been part of the village; he had gone to the church. He should be remembered there.

Mr. Collins said, "I'm sure we will in time." He took my hand and led me down the steps, along the path to the center of the graveyard, to a tall stone column engraved with a long list of names. "These are the village boys who perished in the First World War," he said. "None of their bodies were sent home. The soldiers from the first war were all buried where they died."

Twenty-three names. I counted. And two toward the top: Corydon Collins Jr. and Charles Collins. I touched the names, then looked at Mr. Collins.

"Yes," the vicar said. "Those were my sons. Lovely boys, both of them." His voice dropped to a whisper. "Lovely, lovely boys."

I hated war.

Lord Thorton returned to his work, wherever that was. Maggie went back to school, though she begged and pleaded to stay home. Lady Thorton became like a wild animal trapped inside our cottage.

She never slept. Far into the night, we could hear her moving about inside her bedroom. She paced from side to side. She opened her window. She closed it again. Sometimes she went down the stairs, the fifth and sixth steps creaking violently, and then she might stay awake on the sofa, staring into the darkness, or she might pace back and forth in the sitting room. In the daytime she sat at the table, cradling cups of tea in her hands until they grew cold. I never saw her eat, only sip at the tea. She was running through our tea ration, but Susan brewed fresh pots and said she didn't care.

"What does she think when she looks at me?" Ruth asked Susan.

I didn't think Lady Thorton thought about Ruth at all. I didn't think she thought of anyone but Jonathan.

Ruth and I confessed to Susan about our riding. "Lady Thorton was angry," I said. "I know you'll be angry too."

Susan blew out her breath. "Not really," she said. "I don't think you should have done it when you knew you didn't have Lady Thorton's permission. Butter may be your pony, but he lives on the Thortons' property. However, it all seems terribly irrelevant now."

I said, "You mean no one cares very much about who rides which pony now that Jonathan's dead."

"That's right," Susan said.

I would rather have gotten in trouble.

Whenever I felt overwhelmed I could go away inside my head. The problem was that sadness kept taking me by surprise. I'd be doing the breakfast dishes, not thinking about anything, and suddenly my stomach would clench and I'd want to sob, and it would be all I could do to get my mind to shut down. I wasn't sure I had any right to feel so sad. Compared to the Thortons, I hadn't lost anything.

"This isn't a contest," Susan said when I said so. "You're allowed to grieve too."

Ruth left for two weeks at the internment camp to celebrate Jewish holidays I'd never heard of with her mother. I wished I could go with her. I wanted to escape.

"Bear it," Susan said. "That's all we can do."

"You mean just *feel* it?"

Susan pulled Jamie onto her lap. "Jonathan's in heaven," she said, holding Jamie tight.

I said, "Is believing that supposed to make this better?"

Susan looked up. "Yes," she said. "Most people are in fact comforted by the idea of eternal life."

"Now Jonathan's like Mam," Jamie said.

I said crossly, "He's not anything like Mam."

"They're both dead," Jamie said. "They're in heaven. With Billy White."

I hoped heaven was a big place. I hoped Jonathan would be smart enough to stay far away from Mam.

"One of the Land Girls said people who go to heaven turn into angels," I said. "She said everyone in heaven wears a white dress and plays the harp." Susan had shown me a picture of a harp in the Bible. It looked ridiculous. If I was supposed to be happy in heaven, I wanted horses there.

"No one knows what heaven's like," Susan said. "No one's ever come back to say. But I don't think people turn into angels. I think angels are different."

"Why?" asked Jamie.

Susan said, "I just do."

It was a crummy answer. All the questions were

impossible and all the answers insufficient. "I don't even know why we're fighting this war," I said. "Why couldn't Hitler just stay where he belonged?"

Jamie said, "We're fighting so Ruth can have her grandmother back."

"That's right," Susan said. "We're fighting for Ruth's grandmother, and for all the people like her. For all the people Hitler wants to hurt."

If I could see heaven on a map I would feel better. On the very edge of a map, maybe, far away from Germany or even England. Out beyond where the dragons were. Maybe Jonathan could fly there. Or get there on a very fast horse. Galloping into heaven. I liked the sound of that.

Chapter 40

Susan still read to us in the evenings. We were partway through *The Jungle Book*. The second week after Jonathan died, Lady Thorton sniffed when Susan began. "Must we do this every evening?" she said, from the depths of her wing chair. "Can we not have one solitary night of peace?"

We stared at her. We never read all night. We quit and turned on the radio for the nine o'clock news. "Just one chapter," I said.

Susan had already closed the book and gotten to her feet. "I'll take Ada and Jamie upstairs."

It wasn't as nice upstairs, away from the fire, though it was warm enough we didn't need the heat. Jamie kicked the banister on his way up. Susan gripped his shoulder hard. He said nothing, but made a face.

"We'll be fine up here," Susan said.

"We were fine down there," I said.

Jamie said, "She's being horrible."

"She's grieving," Susan said. "It's very early days, and you're to let it go."

Lady Thorton's grief had begun to look like rage. I knew how that felt. "She's angry at everything now," I said. Angry at nothing, or everything. Sometimes I had felt so out of control. I didn't get like that anymore, not even when I thought about Mam. I could clamp a lid on my feelings and keep them under control.

Susan squeezed my hand. "Yes," she said.

Jamie walked up the rest of the steps in silence. When we'd settled ourselves on the bed in Jamie's room, he said quietly, "Mam was angry at everything too."

My head snapped up. "Because of me," I said. "Because of my foot." She'd said so, over and over.

Jamie shook his head. "No. She was angry at *everything*."

I stared at him. His words soaked into my brain.

A knot I hadn't known I was carrying untied itself inside my belly.

Mam had always been angry.

About everything. All the time.

Mam had never been anything but angry. Even when she smiled, she always stayed angry inside. No sadness, no joy. Just anger.

It had *never* been about me.

I couldn't breathe. I went to the window and looked out, seeing nothing, gripping the windowsill hard.

It hadn't been my fault.

Jamie drummed his bare feet against the counterpane. He asked Susan, "Were you angry when Becky died?"

"Yes," said Susan. "I felt all sorts of things. Anger was certainly one of them."

"Would you be angry if I died?"

"Yes," said Susan. "Very angry indeed."

I could hear Susan say that, but I didn't have to believe her. Grieving for me the way she grieved for Becky? I didn't want to matter so much. "I'm not that important," I said.

"Fortunately, you are not in charge of how I feel," Susan said. "Come back here, and we'll have our story." She patted the bed beside her. "We all loved Jonathan."

"I didn't," I said. "Of course I didn't." That was preposterous. I barely knew him.

Susan shook her head at me. She said, "Love isn't as rare as you think it is, Ada. You can love all sorts of people, in all sorts of ways. Nor is love in any way dangerous."

Sure it was. Jonathan Thorton was dead.

Dear Ada, Maggie wrote from school, *How is my mother? I'm counting on you to tell me the truth.*

What could I possibly say?

Dear Maggie, I miss you. Your mother never sleeps. She never seems awake either. It's like she's stuck halfway.

I wrote Maggie every week. I wrote all the truth I could, but I could never tell her everything.

Dear Maggie, We try to make your mother eat, but she never does. Hard to blame her when the food's so bad. On Wednesday Susan made her do the shopping because she thought the walk would do her good. She came back with a piece of whale meat. Really, actual whale meat. She said it was all the fishmonger had by the time she got to the front of the queue. Susan was angry, but when she went shopping herself the next day she found out it was true.

The whale meat was dire. In the end, we fed most of it to Mrs. Rochester. It gave her gas. The whole village laughed about how awful it was.

Dear Maggie, I miss you. Last night your mother actually fell asleep. She had a nightmare and started screaming. It woke us all. Jamie was so scared he ended up sleeping the rest of the night in Susan's bed. Susan

*says if your mother could let herself cry in the daytime
it might be easier.*

Of course I could never write that.

Dear Maggie, What about you? How are you?

*Dear Ada, I don't mean to sound horrible. I am sad,
very sad. It turns out I liked Jonathan quite a lot and
of course I loved him too. But I'm used to him not being
around, especially when I'm at school. I mostly didn't
live with him. So I don't actually miss him even though
I'm sorry that he's dead. Sometimes I realize that for a
few hours I've forgotten all about him. I think I miss the*
idea *of him more than miss his real self. Does that make
me a bad person? I'm afraid it does.*

*You're the only person I can say this to. I don't trust
the girls here, not the way I trust you. I figure you
already know how bad people can be, so I'm not as likely
to shock you.*

*Dear Maggie, Of course you don't shock me. Nothing
about you could shock me. I hate this awful war.*

Chapter 41

Ruth returned looking more solemn than ever. She told us that her mother had finally gotten a letter from Germany. Ruth's grandmother had been taken to a German internment camp called Ravensbruck.

"That sounds all right," I said. "Your mother's in an internment camp, and she's fine."

Ruth's eyes blazed. "Hitler's camps are very different from the ones in England," she said. She pushed past Susan and me. "Excuse me."

I followed her up the stairs and sat down on her bed. "Take Butter up the hill," I said. "You'll feel better."

"She won't let me."

"She only said you can't go onto her farm. I'll tack up Butter and Ivy and meet you on the road."

Ruth looked at me warily. "Why would you do that?"

"Horses help," I said.

"I know. Why do you care?"

"Why wouldn't I care?" Ruth lived here.

"I'm German. I'm Jewish. I'm everyone's enemy."

"I grew up in one room. You're not my enemy." I took a breath. "I never had a sister."

Ruth stared at me for a long moment. She said, "Me either. I always wanted one."

We rode to the top of the hill and stood in the wind, looking out to the sea. "I can never go back to a country that imprisons old women," Ruth said. "I no longer have a home."

"You have a home," I said.

"In Lady Thorton's house? Not likely."

Lady Thorton continued to grieve. As the days grew shorter Susan fell into one of her bleak periods too. She made herself get up every morning to teach us, but she was sad and disinterested.

"Honestly, Ruth," she said one morning. "Linear interpolation is not that difficult of a concept."

I looked up. It sounded difficult to me.

"Sorry," Ruth mumbled.

"Don't apologize," Susan snapped. "*Concentrate.*"

When Susan got up to get some tea, Ruth looked

at me. "Did I do something wrong?" she said. "Other than the maths, I mean."

"I don't think so," I said. "She gets like this."

Ruth nodded. "I'm glad it's not about me."

At breakfast one morning, Lady Thorton said, "Margaret's coming home tonight for the potatoes."

"What potatoes?" I said.

Lady Thorton frowned. "What do you mean, 'what potatoes'? Blasted things are everywhere. They've even planted up my lawn."

"But why—"

"She has to pick them," Lady Thorton said. "I suppose you and Jamie will too."

We'd missed the previous potato harvest because of my surgery. It turned out that England's potato crop was so important to the war effort that all the schools still running—even posh ones like Maggie's—let out for two weeks so that children all over England could help with the harvest.

"And me," said Ruth. "I will work."

Lady Thorton looked up. "I think not. Just because I never punished you for your exploits doesn't mean I've forgotten them. I've made it clear that you do not have permission to be on my farm."

Ruth set her mouth in a stubborn line. "I won't go to your stables. I *will* pick your potatoes." When Lady Thorton didn't reply, Ruth persisted. "It's something I can do. I want to be useful too. Hitler took my grandmother, and I couldn't stop it."

Lady Thorton finished her piece of toast. "Very well," she said, at last. "I suppose I will allow it."

Maggie came home that evening. She looked taller and thinner, the skin of her face pulled tight the way Jonathan's had been when we last saw him. Her uniform skirt hung loose around her hips. I wanted to hug her but I was afraid she might break. Lady Thorton, who had walked with me to meet Maggie's train, gave her a stiff kiss.

"How are your studies?" she asked Maggie.

Maggie hadn't brought her trunk, just a satchel. I offered to carry it, then staggered under its weight. "Books," Maggie explained. "All I brought home are books, socks, and underpants." To her mother she said, "I can't study. I haven't learned a thing."

"How are your friends?"

"I don't know. I haven't asked them."

"How are your marks?"

"Hideous."

Even I knew that *marks* meant grades, and that hideous grades were a bad thing. But Lady Thorton was trying hard. I shook my head at Maggie. Maggie rolled her eyes and stayed silent in return.

In the living room Susan had stoked the fire high. Dancing flames brightened the gloomy blacked-out walls. Lady Thorton sank onto the sofa as though exhausted. Susan handed her a cup of tea. Maggie took her bag from me and went up the stairs. I followed. Ruth's bedroom door was shut tight.

Maggie stood in the middle of our room. She said, "Mum's not as bad as I thought she'd be."

"We're watching her," I said. "Susan and me."

"I thought about running away from school," she said. "Running away to come home. But I don't know if it would do any good. Heaps of girls have had someone die now—so many different places have been bombed. It's not like I'm somebody special."

In the middle of the night, I heard Maggie crying. I didn't say anything. After a bit she sniffed and said, "I know you're awake. I can hear you breathing."

"I'm trying to be quiet," I said.

"I'm not," she said. "It's such a relief not to be in

that dorm. Did you tell Mum or Susan about our ride with Jonathan?"

"Of course not," I said.

"Good," said Maggie. I heard her roll over. "Potato picking's awful," she said. "I did it last year. You're going to hate it."

Chapter 42

Potato picking was tedious, dirty, exhausting, and cold. I rather liked it.

Mr. Elliston pulled a plow down the rows of potato plants, halfway digging them up and loosening the soil around them. The rest of us followed on foot, scrabbling through the heavy, wet dirt to unearth the potatoes. We filled buckets with potatoes, then emptied the buckets into a wagon on the edge of the field. We worked from dawn to dusk, with only short breaks, and we were filthy and half-frozen by the end of each day.

We were useful. Potato picking was real work, important war work, and I had become a strong girl who could work hard for hours. I had become a tough girl who could ignore the aches in my shoulders and the blisters that sprang up on my palms.

Besides the three Land Girls, it was only Jamie, Ruth, Maggie, and me for all of the Thortons' vast fields. The first morning, Maggie lagged behind. When I finished my row I went to the top of hers to help. "Go away," she said. "I'll catch up. I don't need you."

"Give over, Maggie—"

She glared at me. "I'm doing my best. My fingers are frozen. I hate this."

Which had nothing to do with anything, did it? No one asked us did we want to pick potatoes. It was war work, and we were expected to get on with it. I said, "My fingers are frozen too."

Maggie looked as though she was about to cry. She said, "I wish my father were here. I wish this was still my front lawn. I wish Jonathan—"

I looked up at Thorton House, majestic on the edge of the potato field, with strangers' cars parked in front of it and unknown men in uniform walking in and out. Maggie'd lived there all her life. Now she shared a bedroom with a slum-born orphan in her family's former gamekeeper's cottage. Maggie'd started out in life with more good things than anyone I ever knew. She'd lost and lost in the war.

I'd been a crippled, ignorant prisoner looking out the window of a dingy London flat. Now I walked on two feet and rode and read and shared a bedroom and bookshelves with the daughter of a baron. Except for losing Mam, I'd done nothing but gain. Did Mam dying count as loss or gain?

Maggie bent over her row. My fingers found another potato. "Incoming!" I shouted, and lobbed it at Maggie's head. She jumped, startled, and whirled to glare at me. "Please laugh," I said. "That was funny."

She did laugh. "You're an idiot," she said.

"So are you." We grinned at each other. Then we both threw potatoes at Ruth.

Ruth fired back. Jamie and one of the Land Girls joined in. We smacked each other with filthy, squishy, mud-covered potatoes. One of Ruth's hit me square in the mouth.

"Stop that!" shouted Rose. She was the oldest Land Girl, and the most in charge. She flew at us, waving her empty bucket. "Stop it! Stop! You pick those up right now! *Stop throwing potatoes!* We are not wasting food. We're in the middle of a war!"

Jamie chucked a potato at Rose. She snatched it out of the air.

"Don't try me," she warned. "I've five brothers, and better aim than you."

Maggie picked faster after that. It was easier to pick once you'd been laughing.

At lunch we sat together on the long table in the Ellistons' kitchen. Mrs. Elliston's food was hot and good. Ruth had hardly spoken all morning, and I didn't blame her. "You're the German girl?" Mrs. Elliston asked her.

Ruth nodded. I said, "Her father lost his job and her family lost everything and now her gran's imprisoned in a place called Ravensbruck. Also she's Jewish."

The Land Girls exchanged glances. Mrs. Elliston said, "My two boys are fighting in the army." She looked at Ruth appraisingly. "I can't say I'm glad you're here," she said. "I'm being honest. I can see you're only a bit of a girl, and I'm sorry for your family's trouble, but it's hard to trust you, no mistake."

"I know," Ruth said. "I don't blame you."

"My mother didn't want to let her pick potatoes," Maggie said.

"I'd not go that far," Mrs. Elliston said. "We haven't got nearly enough help as it is."

"When my mam locked me up," I said to Ruth as we walked back to the field, "she told all our neighbors it was because I was simple. So they wouldn't try to help me."

Ruth looked at me. "It's not really the same. I *am* German, and we *are* at war. I understand why they're afraid."

"I'm sure your gran will be fine," I said.

Ruth said, "I'm sure she will not."

Ruth picked more potatoes than any of us, including the Land Girls, who were used to hard work. At the end of the day, Rose made a point of shaking Ruth's hand. "I'll see you tomorrow," she said.

"You will," Ruth said, with a hint of a smile.

I dumped my last bucket of potatoes into the wagon. Rose gave me a perplexed look. "Why'd you do that?" she asked. "You know you're allowed to take potatoes home."

I didn't know it. "Really? How many?"

Rose grinned. "As many as you can carry. Did you think you were working this hard for free?"

"Sure," I said. "It's war work. I thought we had to."

Rose shook her head. "You'll be paid too."

"*Really?* Actual *money?*"

Maggie had come up behind me. "Two shillings a day. That's what it was last year."

Two shillings a day! And she'd been unhappy about it? I'd do just about anything for two shillings a day. Finally, a chance to earn. "Ruth!" I said. "We're getting two shillings a day!"

Ruth grinned. Jamie came running up. "Me too?"

"You too," Rose said. "You worked hard."

Jamie smiled. He was mud from head to toe. Only his teeth were still clean.

I filled our picking buckets to the brims. Maggie stared. She said, "I am not carrying that many potatoes all the way home."

"Maggie," I said, "they're food. For winter. We earned them."

"We *earned* them," echoed Jamie.

"I have blisters," Maggie said.

I spread my oozing palms faceup in front of her. Ruth came over and held out her own hands. One of them was actually bleeding.

Maggie sighed and reached for her buckets. "Sometimes, Ada," she said, "I get very tired of you setting the example for us all."

"If I'd known you all wanted pocket money," Susan said at dinner, "I would have found a way to give you some."

"That wouldn't be right," Ruth said. "I can't take money from you. You're being paid to teach me."

"I don't want money from you either," I said. "I want to earn."

"Ada," said Susan, "I've told you and told you. You don't have to worry about money."

Of course I did. If something bad happened, we were all better off with money put by.

She glared at me. "Can't you learn to trust?"

I took a bite of bread. Shrugged my shoulders. Looked away.

"Mum," Jamie said, with profound satisfaction. My fingers itched to smack him.

That night I heard a sound on the other side of my bedroom wall, the wall I shared with Ruth's room. "Maggie," I said, sitting up. "Ruth's crying."

Maggie sat up too. "She won't want us bothering her," she said, after a moment.

"She never cries," I said. I got up and went out to the hall. Knocked on Ruth's door. "Come be with Maggie and me," I said.

Ruth didn't unlock the door. "Please go away," she said. The crying stopped. At least, I couldn't hear it anymore.

The second morning of potato picking, I woke up stiff and aching everywhere. It was worse than the days when I first taught myself to walk. The second day of potato picking, my hands hurt so badly by lunchtime that I could barely hold a fork. We all hurt. It was hard work. At night we took baths and went to bed early. Lady Thorton sniffed over the blisters on Maggie's hands. "You ought to wear gloves," she said.

"My hands are no worse than everyone else's," Maggie said. "Have you looked at Ruth's?"

Of course she hadn't. Since Jonathan's death, Lady Thorton barely acknowledged Ruth. But at dinner she divided the meat on her plate and shared it out between us—Maggie, Jamie, Ruth, and me. Lady Thorton helped herself to more potatoes. We had plenty of those.

We picked potatoes for twelve days. We each carried home ten pounds of potatoes every day, which meant by the end, we had earned nearly five hundred pounds of potatoes. They filled the little back room. We could eat them all winter. We wouldn't have to queue for them or carry them home from the village.

A back room full of potatoes! In Mam's flat we never had anything extra stored away.

Each of us also earned twenty-four shillings.

Twenty-four shillings. More than a pound. I never in my life expected to have so much money all at one time. For certain Mam never did. I counted the shillings out on the table. Four piles of six. Eight piles of three. Six piles of four. Shillings, shillings, shillings.

Money could be a kind of ward.

"Ada." Susan sat down beside me, sighing.

"You could die," I said.

"I won't."

"You could," I said. "Jonathan—"

"Was a pilot—"

"Stephen's mother—"

"That was the Blitz," she said. "It's over."

"Becky," I said.

Becky's name lay between us. Becky, who Susan loved. Becky, who I'd never met. Never would. Becky, who was dead like Mam.

Susan reached for my hand. I let her take it. "You know so many hard things," she said. "I forget sometimes how much you've endured. Save your money, if it helps you feel better."

"Please let me stay home," Maggie begged. "I'm not learning anything. I can go back after Christmas."

"Don't be ridiculous," Lady Thorton said. "You're safer at school."

"The village hasn't been bombed in ages! You're just trying to be rid of me. Susan doesn't make Ada leave."

"Susan knows my position," Lady Thorton said. "As do you. The matter is not open for debate."

"Don't speak to me like I'm one of your WVS women," Maggie said. "I'm your daughter. Pretend you have some compassion."

That was low, but I didn't blame Maggie.

"I'll watch her," I said to Maggie when she left. "I'll let you know how she does."

"Thanks," Maggie said, hugging me.

"Who's watching Maggie?" I asked Susan.

"She has friends at school," Susan said. "She has teachers."

I shook my head. "She needs her mother."

Chapter 43

A week or so later, all of us except Lady Thorton, who had gone early to bed, were sitting by the fire at night, listening to the nine o'clock radio news. Suddenly someone hammered on the door. Susan leaped up. I leaped up too. A telegram, at this hour?

It was Fred. He gagged, groaned, and vomited in a wide arc across the floor.

"Oh!" Susan jumped sideways, but still got spattered by sick. "Oh, Fred, do you need a doctor?" Which didn't make sense, since Fred could have phoned for a doctor from the stables. Our cottage didn't have a telephone.

"Sorry," Fred said. He clutched the doorjamb. "We're all sick—bad fish—and the horse is down. I can't walk him. I need help. Ada."

I stood with Ruth and Jamie, staring at Fred and the puddle of vomit. "Butter?" My voice rose high and quick. "Something's wrong with Butter?"

"No. It's Oban."

I ran for my coat and shoes. Fred grabbed his gut and vomited again.

"*Kolik?*" asked Ruth. It was a word I'd never heard. "Is it *kolik*?"

"Yes," said Fred. "Colic. Yes." He wavered and sank to the ground.

Ruth shoved her feet into her shoes. She said, "I know what to do."

Susan was leaning over Fred with a towel. "Are you sure, Ruth?"

Ruth nodded. "Ada will help me."

We ran along the path through the moonlit woods to the stable yard. Oban lay on his side in the stall, his dark coat slick with sweat. From the looks of his bedding, he'd been thrashing.

Ruth threw open the door. She kicked Oban, hard. "Up! Up!" she shouted. "Get up!"

I flew at her. "Stop that! Don't hurt him!"

Ruth knelt to buckle Oban's halter around his head. "You must do what I say." She clipped a lead rope to the halter and pulled hard. Her dark eyes glinted in the dim light. "Kick him," she said. "Get him up. We must make him walk, or he dies."

It made my stomach hurt, but I hauled back and

kicked Oban, hard. He gasped and moaned, then lurched to his feet. "Good," said Ruth. "Find another lead rope. Help me walk him." She pulled him out of the stall, into the stable yard. Oban staggered and nearly went down. "No!" Ruth said, kicking him again. He pulled away from her, nearly yanking the lead from her hands. I came at him from the other side, smacking my lead rope against his hip.

"Good," Ruth said. "Keep him walking."

We made Oban stagger the length of the yard between us. His sides dripped sweat. "He's bad," Ruth said. "Very bad."

"Should we cover him?" It was a cold night for the horse to be so sweaty. Horses chilled easily, and Oban's thick coat was soaked through.

"A blanket, yes."

I found a horse blanket in the tack room. I threw it over Oban while Ruth kept him walking. "Good," she said. She walked him to the end of the yard, turned him, and walked him back. When he staggered, she yelled at him and smacked him with the end of the lead. It looked awful, but she seemed to know exactly what she was doing.

"Water?" I asked her.

"No. No water, no food. Only walking." Ruth

turned Oban, started him forward again. "Colic, this means he has a stomachache. In a horse it's very serious. Horses die from colic."

Oban tried to pull away from Ruth. His knees began to buckle. I went to his far side and shoved. "Oban!" I shouted, and smacked him.

"Good," Ruth said. "We keep him moving, he has a chance. If he lies down in his stall and rolls, he can twist—twist his insides, his stomach. Then he dies for sure.

"Oban?" she said. "The horse is named Oban?"

I nodded. "He was Jonathan's horse."

Ruth said, "The one you galloped. I remember."

Ten minutes later, Ruth said, "If he gets much worse we'll need a gun. Do you know where we can get one?"

"A gun! You mean to—" I couldn't make myself say it.

Ruth nodded. "We will not let him suffer if there is no hope."

It was horrible how the hardest things could be the truth. "Is there hope?" I said.

She shrugged. "A little."

"Fred has a gun," I said. "I don't know where it is. I don't know how to use it."

Ruth said, "I do."

A half an hour later, Susan came to check on us. She said that all the Land Girls and the Ellistons were puking too. They'd all eaten dinner together— an enormous piece of what must have been rotten fish.

Oban was sweating a tiny bit less. "We're managing," I told Susan. "Ruth knows what to do."

When Susan left, Ruth said to me, "Maybe the horse also ate the fish."

I realized she was making a joke, and I smiled. Then I asked, "Could you really shoot him?"

She nodded. "I think so. I know how. My father shot one of his horses, once, when it broke a leg. It was mercy, not cruelty. You understand?"

"*Mercy* means not punishing someone when you should," I said.

"It also means putting an end to suffering," said Ruth.

We took another lap of the yard, one on each side of Oban. "I understand," I said, "but I couldn't do it."

Ruth regarded me for a long minute. "You could," she said. "You are strong and honest, and you love them."

After the next lap she said, "You make an X between their eyes and the bottom of their ears." She crisscrossed her finger over Oban's face. "Then shoot the center of the X. That way they die instantly, no pain. Don't shoot between the eyes. It hurts them but they don't die right away."

I stored this information in my head in the bulging file titled "Things I Wished I Didn't Know." It included what it felt like to walk on a clubfoot for ten years, and what it sounded like to have your mother say she never wanted to see you again.

"Horses don't fear death," Ruth said softly. "No animal does."

Horses were lucky that way.

We walked miles that night, back and forth across the stable yard. "Do you believe in heaven?" I asked Ruth.

"Yes," she said. "Do you?"

"I think so," I said.

Clop, clop. Oban's feet struck the cobblestones. I wasn't having to smack him as often. "My mam died," I said. "She was not a good person. But Susan says maybe God has mercy."

"I think that too," said Ruth. "Perhaps your mother's soul will suffer for a while. Perhaps she will repent. Then she can be with God forever."

Perhaps. I liked that word. Perhaps.

After a few hours, Oban began to walk more easily. His sweaty coat dried. Ruth pressed her fingers under his jaw, then showed me how to feel a small pulsing sensation there. "That's his heartbeat," Ruth said. "Count the beats out loud when I say so."

I counted. Ruth checked them against her wristwatch. She nodded. "Fast, but not terrible. When horses are in pain, their hearts speed up." She let Oban drink a tiny sip of water. Then I walked him alone to give her a chance to rest. Back and forth, back and forth. When I grew tired she took over again. We wrapped horse blankets around ourselves and kept walking, back and forth across the dark, cold yard.

We talked through the night. I'd never heard Ruth talk so much before. She told me about her own horse back in Germany. "He looks like this one," she said, stroking Oban's face. "What is the English word for this coloring?"

"Bay," I said. "He's a Thoroughbred."

"Yes," Ruth said. "Mine is built heavier."

"Where is he now?"

Her face clouded. "We didn't tell anyone we were leaving. We had to be able to get away. The horses were at a livery stable, with their board paid for the month. Someone will have taken them. They were good horses."

I told Ruth about the day I jumped Oban out of Butter's field. That made her laugh. "Sounds like something I would have done," she said. "We are like each other, you and I."

Oban stopped walking. I tugged on the lead. He tugged back, lifted his tail, and deposited a steaming pile of manure onto the cobblestones. "*Wunderbar!*" Ruth shouted, leaping up. She threw her arms around me, then rubbed her hand hard on Oban's forehead. "Beautiful! Good! Good boy!" She said to me, "That's a good sign. He's better. Maybe he won't die!"

"He won't?"

"Not tonight," Ruth said, hugging me. "Not tonight. We saved him."

Chapter 44

In the morning, when she heard about Oban, Lady Thorton's face went red with anger. "Why on earth didn't you wake me?" she said. "I know how to deal with horses and colic. Of course I do. Honestly—why on *earth*?"

It had never once occurred to me. When I'd started riding, Lady Thorton had steered me toward Fred for help, not offered to help me herself.

I said, "Ruth knew what to do."

Lady Thorton drew herself taller. "Why didn't you wake me?" she said, more loudly. "Susan!"

Susan opened her mouth, then shut it again.

"You didn't think I would be useful?" Lady Thorton demanded. "You didn't think I should be told?"

Susan looked uncomfortable. "I didn't think at all," she said. "I'm sorry."

"What if he'd had to be put down?"

Susan's mouth fell open. "I didn't think—"

"We would have done it," I said. "Ruth said so. She knows how."

Lady Thorton shouted, "You would have left these children to make that decision on their own? You would have let them bear such a terrible thing?"

"I didn't know," Susan said. "They said they knew what to do. I didn't know it could be that bad."

"I did!" Lady Thorton said. "I am not incompetent! I do not need to be treated with kid gloves! Extend to me the honesty and forthrightness you extend to everyone else, and for God's sake, the next time something goes wrong, *get me out of bed!*" She looked back at me and Ruth.

"It was Ruth, really," I said. "I didn't know anything about colic. Ruth saved him."

"Thank you," Lady Thorton said to her. "Thank you very much." She held out her hand. Ruth shook it. "That horse means a great deal to me. I'm angry that I wasn't called, but it wasn't your responsibility to do so and I'm not in any way angry with you. I'm very grateful. Please know that."

"I'm glad I could help," Ruth said. "He reminds me of the horse I left behind."

I went with Lady Thorton to do the shopping. She and Susan took it in shifts now, and I often went along. "You were wrong about Ruth," I said.

"Thank you, Ada," she said. She marched down the road, her heels clomping the pavement. "I will draw my own conclusions."

"Oban would have died without her," I said. I had to run a bit to catch up. "I never heard of colic. I wouldn't have known what to do."

"I would have," Lady Thorton said. "In future you will remember that."

"But Ruth did it," I said. "She did everything right."

"And I am grateful," she said. She looked at me sideways. "I know you're still letting her ride your pony. I asked Fred Grimes."

"She doesn't come to the stables," I said. "I meet her on the road."

"Except of course for last night," Lady Thorton said drily. She said, "None of you think me competent. That's clear."

"Ruth needs horses the way I needed horses," I said. "The way Maggie needs them. You aren't using them. It'd be like letting the cottage sit empty and not letting Susan and us live there."

Lady Thorton made a face. "It's not the same. She's Ger—"

I interrupted. "It's not her fault where she was born."

A week later, Ruth received a letter from her mother. She opened it at the dinner table, and we all watched as her face fell. Tears filled her eyes and overflowed down her cheeks. "She's dead," Ruth whispered.

I grabbed her hand. "Not your mother?"

Ruth shook her head. "My grandmother. She died in that camp." She threw the letter onto the table. "'Died peacefully,' the Nazis said."

Lady Thorton cleared her throat. "For the elderly, a peaceful death can be a blessing," she said.

Ruth glared at her. "If you think my oma died peacefully," she said, "you still don't understand Hitler at all." Ruth stood and marched up the stairs. She locked herself in her bedroom until morning. At breakfast she stared at her oatmeal, hollow-eyed. "It's the start of bad news," she said. "If they can kill my grandmother, none of my family in Germany will survive this war."

Lady Thorton wiped her lips on her napkin and

excused herself from the table. She went upstairs, and when she came back down, she dropped a pair of her own jodhpurs into Ruth's lap. "Oban seems fully recovered," she said. "I hope you would be willing to exercise him for me. He does best when ridden every day."

Ruth opened her mouth. She closed it. Opened it again. "Yes," she said at last. "Thank you."

Ruth and I rode out together on Oban and Butter in the brisk October wind. "Only walking, for now, until we really know he is well," Ruth said. Walking was cold, but I agreed. We went up the hill and stared at the white-capped sea. I wished Maggie were with us.

"Let's ride through the village," I said. "You can now."

Ruth smiled. She rubbed Oban's neck. "Let's not push our luck that far."

I studied her. Calm as always. "I'm so sorry about your gran," I said.

Ruth nodded. "You would have liked her."

Chapter 45

It was nearly time for Ruth's examinations. Nights, now, she worked maths problems in front of the fire. She and Susan discussed maths using words I'd never heard of. *Algorithm. Interpolation. Optimization.* When I asked Susan to explain them, she couldn't do it in a way I could understand. I said, "There is just no end to the things I don't know."

"The whole world's like that." Lady Thorton spoke from the depths of her wing chair. "Full of things we don't understand."

I hadn't expected her to be listening. I said, "Ladies like you understand everything."

Lady Thorton said, "You of all people should know better—when it's you who's been teaching me how to cook. And here's Susan with her Oxford degree, and me half taught by an undereducated governess. My own ignorance shames me."

I had been showing Jamie how to knit a washcloth.

I set down the needles to stare at Lady Thorton. I said, "Susan says ignorance is nothing to be ashamed of."

"At your age, perhaps," Lady Thorton said. "Not so much at mine."

I never thought of Lady Thorton as being ashamed of anything. I never thought of anyone besides myself feeling ashamed. "Susan can't ride like you can," I said. "And you're better at the WVS."

"Thank you," said Susan.

"We all have our strengths," Lady Thorton said. "Most of us also have our weaknesses."

"You've traveled," I continued. "Susan hasn't. You said you'd been to Dresden." Across the room, Ruth raised her head.

"Yes," Lady Thorton said. "It's a beautiful city."

"It was," Ruth said. "I don't think it's beautiful anymore."

"I knew about the part of the world I grew up in," Lady Thorton said, looking directly at me. "You knew about the part you grew up in. Now we both know more."

When the weather became cold enough, Mr. Elliston slaughtered our pig club pig. He cut it up into pieces and salted down the bacon and ham. I expected

Jamie to be sad, but he wasn't; he helped with the butchering, saying he needed to learn how to do it. Mr. Elliston loved teaching Jamie.

On Pig Day, Susan roasted pork chops and invited everyone from the farm to the feast. We roasted potatoes too, and parsnips and carrots; we made rich gravy from the pork fat in the pan. Ruth, of course, didn't eat pork, but Mrs. Elliston brought her a piece of lamb, and Susan roasted it for her in a separate pan.

In between the pig feast and Christmas was Jamie's eighth birthday. I went to the shops with my shillings but didn't find anything I wanted to buy him, so I saved my sugar and butter rations and made him some toffee. Fred gave him a spade and Lady Thorton a book. Susan pulled off the best gift. She'd found a pair of actual rubber boots—secondhand, but still sound. New rubber boots weren't being made because of the war. No more cold, wet feet for Jamie.

"Farmers' boots!" he said when he saw them. "Proper farmers' boots!" They were a little too big, but that was good; Susan stuffed the toes with rags and said if we were lucky he'd wear them for a few years. I doubted we would be. Jamie grew faster than the piglets.

One night in early December, we switched on the radio as usual for the nine o'clock news. The announcer was always vague about anything to do with the war, because of course Nazi spies listened to the broadcast. He'd say things like, "Bombs fell in parts of London today," or "A mid-sized city was hit by bombs."

This time he said specifically that Japan had attacked the United States at a place called Pearl Harbor. They had also attacked a British colony called Singapore. The United States and Britain had declared war on Japan.

I handed Susan the book of maps Lady Thorton had brought over from Thorton House. "Show me," I said.

Pearl Harbor was in Hawaii, a group of islands far out in the ocean. Singapore was an island near Japan. It was hard to imagine that such small islands were worth fighting for. "England is a small island," Susan said.

Germany and Japan were allies, so Germany declared war on the United States. The United States declared war right back. Unimpressed, Susan shook her head. "Might be useful," she said, "having the Yanks on our side."

Lady Thorton sniffed. "One hardly supposes they were going to side with Hitler. Did you think we'd win this war without the Americans? I didn't."

Jamie's eyes lit up. "So now we win?"

Susan said, "Not yet."

Chapter 46

Christmas was coming. I dreaded it. I asked Susan, "Can't we go somewhere?"

We were chopping veg for stew. She looked up at me in amazement. "Where?" she said. "How?"

No one was supposed to travel for fun, because of the war. Big posters at the train stations read: "Is Your Trip Really Necessary?"

"Anywhere," I said. "Away from here." The cottage was full of gloom and darkness and memories of Jonathan. "Maybe we could visit your family," I suggested. "Your brothers and your dad." It would be a little like having cousins. Cousins and a grandfather.

Susan shuddered. "Not on your life. I wish that was a good idea, but it's actually a very bad one." She set down her knife. "I know you don't understand," she said, "but I think someday you will. My family truly hates me for things that I can't change. I wish they didn't, but they do."

"I don't understand," I said. "You're not a cripple. There's nothing wrong with you."

Susan said, "My family has the problem. Not me. Them."

I said, "But they're wrong."

Now Susan looked me directly in the eye. "Yes," she said. "My mother's dead, you know that. My father is wrong. He should love me. He doesn't. I can't fix it. That's hard, but it's the truth."

Like Mam.

I'd never thought of Susan's family as being like Mam.

I could still hear Mam in my head. *Who'd want you? Nobody, that's who.* I sat down at the table and buried my head in my arms.

Jamie barged through the back door. "I'm gonna kill Persnickety for Christmas dinner," he announced, "since she's too old to lay eggs. Ada, why're you crying?"

I lifted my head half an inch. I said, "Because Susan's father doesn't love her. And our mother didn't love us."

Jamie snorted. "Course she does," he said. He slung his arm around Susan's neck. "You do love us," he said. "Don't you?"

Susan kissed him. "I do," Susan said. "I love you both very much."

That was the second time she'd said she loved us. It made me cry harder, though I'd no idea why.

The next morning, instead of doing my schoolwork, I drew myself a different kind of map. I started on the left side, with a dark box and a girl trapped inside. Then a train. Butter. Susan's old house. The cottage where we lived now. Maggie and Ruth and Lady Thorton. Jamie hanging from a tree with two good arms. Above us, dragons circling in the sky. In the center, Susan, brave like St. Margaret, a gleaming sword in her hand.

"What comes next?" Susan said when she saw the drawing. "That's your map of the past. What's in the map of your future?"

I stared at her. "What do you want?" she persisted.

I had no idea. When I'd first been evacuated I'd wanted to be like the girl riding the pony, racing the train. Now I was. Parts of me were still jumbled—but maybe that girl had been jumbled too. I'd only seen her from the outside.

"I want to go places," I said. "I want to travel. I want to see Dresden."

Susan put her arm around me. "When the war is over, you will."

"What do you want in the future?" I asked Jamie.

He looked thoughtful. "More hens."

Chapter 47

Maggie came home for Christmas. She looked wretched.

"Last year we ate Christmas dinner together inside Thorton House," I told Ruth. "Jonathan was nice to me and Jamie. He was nice to everyone."

Ruth nodded. "When I went to see my mother for High Holy Days, all we could think about were past celebrations, with all our family in our home in Dresden."

"What did you do to feel better?" I asked.

"Nothing," said Ruth. "We were miserable." She took a deep breath. "Better to be miserable together than miserable apart. I suppose."

I supposed too. We tried to be cheerful. Maggie and Jamie and I cut down a lovely Christmas tree— much bigger than the ragged one I'd cut the year before. We trimmed its bottom branches and used the clippings to decorate the fireplace mantel. I'd saved up colored paper over the year and we made strings of colored paper rings, and shiny paper stars. Maggie and I rummaged in the attic of Thorton House and found electric lights and glass ornaments like Susan once had. The tree looked beautiful. None of us really cared.

"It still feels like a cave in this house," Maggie said.

"It *is* a cave," said Jamie.

I said, "It's less gloomy than it used to be."

Maggie shook her head. "If only the blackout didn't have to be black."

"It doesn't," I said, in sudden realization. "Not on the inside."

Maggie actually smiled. "You're right!"

Our blackout screens were heavy black cloth stretched over wooden frames, exactly sized to cover the windows. Maggie dug up some paints in the attic of Thorton House, and over the next two days we painted the insides of the screens with what we saw when the blackout wasn't up. The trees, with sun shining through their branches. Jamie's bicycle. Mrs. Rochester's shed and pen. The garden asleep in the winter, mounds of straw heaped over the earth. The Anderson shelter beside the house. The new chickens and the rooster.

Ruth took the blackout screen from her bedroom, painted its inside allover white, then took a pencil and sketched and erased until she was satisfied. Then she painted what she'd drawn: a stone path, flowering trees, and a bed of tulips bursting with color. "My home in the spring," she said. "The home I used to have." She smiled at me. "Silly to do so much work for only a short time." Ruth had passed her entrance exams; she was leaving for Oxford at the new year. "But it pleases me to see this view again."

"We'll keep it," I said to her. "You'll visit."

We tried hard to be cheerful, but it didn't take. I felt sad and anxious. Maggie was twitchy, and Lady Thorton and Susan sank into gloom. Lady Thorton's head cold didn't help.

We skipped church Christmas Eve. Lady Thorton said she didn't feel up to it. Susan, who never liked church anyhow, decided to stay home with her, and Maggie wanted to meet Lord Thorton's train, which was supposed to arrive the same time the service started. He'd have to walk to the house; the village didn't have a taxi anymore.

"You can go to church, Ada, Jamie," Susan said.

"I'm staying with Mum," Jamie said.

She was not our mum.

I decided to walk with Maggie to the station. Ruth

came too. "This house feels horrible," she said, pulling her scarf around her face. "I'm glad I'm Jewish, if this is Christmas."

"This isn't Christmas," Maggie said.

Ruth slid her arm around Maggie. She said, "I know."

Trains usually ran late in the war, but this one arrived early. We got to the station just in time to see Lord Thorton, tall and wide in his thick overcoat, step out of the carriage. Another man, equally muffled, came after him, and then a woman in a heavy black coat and headscarf.

Ruth screeched. She threw herself at the man and woman. She clung to them and actually sobbed.

The woman pressed Ruth to her bosom, murmuring words I didn't understand. The man put his arms around them both.

German words. They were her mother and father.

I watched the three of them hug and kiss each other. No one I knew hugged or kissed with such enthusiasm. Lord Thorton embraced Maggie and me, but he seemed incredibly sad. Even when he smiled at Ruth he looked tired. Not that Ruth noticed. She chattered away in German. She pulled her mother over to me, put her hand on my arm and said something that made her mother beam at me and kiss me square on the lips before I could duck.

"My mother says thank you," Ruth said.

Thank you for what? I didn't know how to respond. A total stranger kissing me! I looked at Ruth. "What's German for 'you're welcome'?" I asked.

"*Bitte*," Ruth said, smiling.

"*Bitte*," I repeated. Ruth's mother smiled and kissed me again.

"Why is she thanking me?" I asked.

Ruth said, "I told her all about you."

That could mean anything. Still, given the kissing, it didn't seem like it could be bad.

We went home. Ruth held both her parents' hands. Lord Thorton and Maggie and I walked a few steps behind.

"So they let Ruth's mother out of prison," I said.

"British internment camps aren't prison," Lord Thorton said, "but yes. Her father's been working with me for some time and we've finally managed to get her mother released. She'll be able to live with Herr Schmidt and Ruth."

"Ruth's going to Oxford," I said.

"Right."

"Do you work near Oxford, then?" We'd always

wanted to know what war work Lord Thorton did. He couldn't say, but that didn't mean we couldn't try to ferret it out of him.

He gave me a look down the side of his nose and didn't answer.

Nuts.

Ruth's father spoke a bit of English, her mother less. She said long sentences in German to Lady Thorton and to Susan, bowing and smiling, and Lady Thorton and Susan bowed and smiled back as though they understood.

"What did she say?" I asked Susan.

Susan looked at me. "You understood her as well as I did."

The funny thing was, I did understand her. Frau Schmidt was telling us how happy she was we'd taken care of Ruth, and how glad she was to meet the women who'd given Ruth a home. I couldn't translate the words, but I knew their meaning.

Lady Thorton had been a grudging host to Ruth, but she was gracious now. Despite her head cold and her grief, she smiled at the Schmidts. She said kind things to them. She hung up their coats and directed Jamie to carry their luggage upstairs. She went into the scullery and came back with a bottle of wine, and all the grown-ups drank a glass, toasting each other. It was remarkably civilized. Ruth beamed from ear to ear.

That moment ended up being the best part of Christmas.

We hung our stockings on the fireplace, even Ruth at Jamie's insistence, although she sniffed about it. In the morning, each held a piece of candy and a shilling. We ate a month's worth of bacon and a dozen eggs for breakfast while listening to carols on the radio. We kept the fire bright, dancing off the ornaments on the Christmas tree. The sun shone, and it would have been a glorious day, except for the ghost of Jonathan.

Last year Jonathan had been with us. He'd made jokes at the table and been so funny and kind.

Memories of Jonathan felt like dragons, like real, imaginary fierce creatures with wings. Memories of Mam felt like rocks, or coals. I tried to recall a single happy memory of my mother. If Mam had come to live with us, at Susan's house, could she have learned to be happy? Could anything have made her better? I would never know.

"Breathe," Susan said, her arm around me. "Just take one breath at a time. We'll get through it."

Susan, Ruth's mother, and Lady Thorton started dinner. Lord Thorton and Ruth's father played backgammon. Maggie, Ruth, Jamie, and I went to help Fred with the stable chores and bring Fred back for dinner.

We ate dinner and we opened presents. That's when I got the surprise.

Chapter 48

Susan gave me a book and a sweater she'd knit herself. She gave Jamie a sweater and a new toy airplane. I gave everyone—even Lord Thorton and Ruth, but not Ruth's parents, as I hadn't expected them—hand-knitted hats.

I started to feel a sort of energy coming from Lord and Lady Thorton. It made me nervous. It was a bit like the energy Mam gave off before she started walloping people—friendlier, but still like that. I shifted closer to Susan, who looked as puzzled as I did when Lord Thorton set a wrapped box onto my lap.

"Wait," he said as I picked it up. "I want to read something first." He drew an envelope out of his waistcoat pocket and took from the envelope a letter. It was worn and creased, as though it had been folded and unfolded over and over again.

Lord Thorton cleared his throat. Then he paused,

swallowed, and cleared his throat again. When he first spoke his voice trembled.

"*Dear Lord Thorton,*" he read.

"*I should have written earlier, I know, but it's been a bit—well, I won't make excuses. I should have written earlier. I'm sorry. Your son Jon was a close friend of mine. He was a good pilot and a brave man.*

"*I'm sure you've heard the story of our last little adventure but I thought I'd tell you how it looked from my side.*

"*Being a pilot gets pretty hard after a while, going up night after night, and always some planes not making it back. You start to think you're next, every night, and that wears at you, starts to eat away at your insides. It's not fear exactly, it's more like you can't bear the waiting.*

"*Anyhow, one night Jonnie came to find me pretty late. We were both off that night, and we should have been sleeping, but sometimes you can't sleep no matter how tired you are. Jonnie said was I ready for an adventure, and I said sure. He'd borrowed a couple of motorbikes. He said he wanted to keep a promise he'd made, and he thought he'd better do it while he had the chance. So we set off through the night, pitch dark, colder than it should have been—anyway, in a couple of hours we pulled up near this cottage on a big estate. I didn't realize at first that the estate was your home. Jon didn't talk about stuff like that.*

"He snuck around back and threw pebbles at one of the windows. Next thing I know, out come these school-girls rubbing sleep from their eyes. Jon's sister looked like him, of course. Then there were two dark-haired girls who might have been sisters, one younger, one older.

"We all piled onto the bikes and went along to the back of the big house, where the stables were. Jon asked did I ride. I said, never in my life, mate. I grew up in Liverpool city, not many horses there. So he told me to follow along on the bike, but keep quiet, he didn't want to wake the old groom.

"The girls came out with some horses, and Jon got out one, and next thing he was tossing the smaller dark-haired girl into the saddle of the biggest horse. Her eyes shone—I wouldn't have wanted to sit on that thing, it looked snorty and fierce to me, but this kid was so excited, I knew this was the promise Jon had made.

"They went off down the fields, me following. Then something startled the big horse, and away it ran, fast and furious, like it'd been shot out of a cannon. The little girl bounced around for a moment—honest, I thought she was going to be hurt—and next thing she's up in her stirrups like a jockey running in the Grand National.

She's flying across the fields with the others chasing but not catching her, and me following thinking an ambulance was going to be required.

"Eventually the horse quit running. The girl on his back looked over her shoulder. Her hair had all come loose around her head, and her cheeks were bright pink, and she was laughing. *She wasn't afraid, not one tiny bit. She said, 'That was wonderful, Jonathan! Oh, thank you!'*

"We had to hurry to get back in time. We left the girls with the horses and whatever explanations they'd have to make.

"I assumed the girl on Jon's horse was another of the local gentry, but when we got back to the airfield Jon said no. He claimed she was from the East End of London, the bad part, evacuated at the start of the war. He said when she first came she hadn't been able to walk. He said, 'Did you see her face? Did you see how brave she was?'

"I said I saw.

"Later that day he said, 'That's what we're fighting for. That kind of courage. We can't get beat, not when we're fighting for the spirit of England.'

"I knew what he meant. It made a fellow feel better, somehow, to know that there were still green fields and bold children laughing in them, even in the middle of this

war. Jon said he was going to name his plane Invincible Ada. *He was going to have that painted on her tail.*

"He never got the chance, but he would have done it, and I wanted you to know. And if you could tell the girl named Ada about it, I think Jon would have wanted her to know too."

Lord Thorton folded the letter, replaced it in its envelope, and returned the envelope to his waistcoat pocket. He nodded at me. "Open your gift, my dear."

Inside the box was a leather halter, cleaned and oiled soft and supple. The brass nameplate on the cheek piece read "Oban." It was Oban's halter.

I said, "I don't understand."

Lady Thorton looked fierce, almost angry. She said, "We're giving him to you. We're giving you the horse."

I said, "You can't do that. He's Jonathan's."

I don't think I really understood death until that moment. I mean, I knew what dead meant. I knew that Jonathan, like my father and mother, like Stephen White's family, like Becky, like every other dead person ever, was not coming back. But I didn't get it until then. If that's hard to understand, well, so are a lot of things.

No one said anything. Everyone in the room looked at me. I lifted the halter, rubbed the nameplate, remembered that beautiful, beautiful summer dawn. I said, "I love him very much."

Lord Thorton said, "Good. That's all we ask."

I said, "Do you mean it? Is he really mine?"

"Of course we mean it," Lord Thorton said.

"I can do anything I want with him?"

"Yes," Lady Thorton said, a touch sardonically. "I see where you're going with this. Oban is yours. You can let anyone ride him that you want."

"Thank you," I said. I got up and pushed the halter into Ruth's hands. I said, "If he's mine, then I'm giving him to Ruth. He's her horse now."

Chapter 49

Ruth stared at me. She said, "I'm Jewish. I don't get Christmas presents."

"It's not a Christmas present," I said. "It's a friendship present. It's—it's a sister present. You heard what Jonathan's friend wrote—he thought we were sisters. I have Butter. I don't need Oban. You do."

"I'm leaving next week," Ruth said. She clutched the halter. "I can't take a horse."

"You'll come home sometimes," I said. "I'll take care of him for you until you do."

Ruth bent over the halter. Her shoulders shook. Her mother put her arm around her and said something softly in German. Ruth answered, in German, without raising her head.

"For heaven's sake," Lady Thorton said, annoyed.

"Yes," said Susan. "I'd say so."

I could tell Lady Thorton didn't like what I'd done, but she couldn't undo it. I couldn't tell what Lord Thorton thought, but I didn't care.

Maggie was grinning. Jamie was too. Susan said, "Come help me make tea, Ada," and led the way into the kitchen.

"Are you angry?" I asked her, once it was just us two.

"Of course not," she said. "Why should I be? Only Oban's a far fancier horse than Butter. Even I know that."

"Ruth's a fancier rider than me. Plus, I love Butter. Plus, why would I ever need more than one horse?"

Susan laughed. "You'd be surprised," she said, "how much some people think they need."

I shrugged. "There's a war on."

"Yes," she said, "and you're winning it. Only, fair warning. I don't think Lady Thorton's going to be happy about all this, once she's had time to think."

Susan was right. All Christmas evening, I could feel Lady Thorton's anger building. I could see it coming like a storm across the sea from up on my lookout hill. She was angry that I'd given Oban away, and to a Jewish German. She was angry that Jonathan had come to see me and Maggie instead of her.

She was very, very angry that we hadn't given her the chance to see him one last time.

She was also angry that Jonathan wanted to name his airplane after me. She didn't say so, but I knew.

"You should have told me," Lady Thorton said to Maggie the next morning. It was Boxing Day, the anniversary of the paper chase. I remembered Jonathan stopping Oban when I fell off at the ditch, remembered him saying, "I'm trying to act like a gentleman." I remembered his smile, and felt his loss all over again.

If it was this bad for me, it had to be so much worse for the Thortons.

"I promised Jonathan I wouldn't tell," Maggie said.

"You should have told me before you promised. You shouldn't have promised. You should have told me first thing."

"I couldn't!" said Maggie. She ran back upstairs, choking on half-suppressed tears.

Lady Thorton turned to me. "You should have too."

"I should have ratted Maggie out, or broken my

promise to Jonathan? Which? I'm glad I didn't," I said.

I knew I shouldn't be rude. I should be grateful. But the nastier Lady Thorton acted, the less gratitude I felt.

Ruth and Lord Thorton took Ruth's parents to the stables to meet Oban. The Schmidts were so knowledgeable about horses that Lord Thorton arranged we should all go riding together that afternoon: me, Maggie, Ruth, Lord Thorton, and Ruth's parents. "You too," he said to Lady Thorton.

"I think not," she sniffed.

"It would be good for us," Lord Thorton said.

"No," she said.

The rest of us went anyhow. We galloped and jumped things and for two hours felt happy. Oban went beautifully; Ruth couldn't quit smiling. Afterward her mother petted me and made a fuss. I didn't know what she said, but I rather liked it.

Ruth was sleeping in Maggie's bed while her parents slept in her room, and Maggie was sharing my bed with me. After our ride together I couldn't sleep. I kept talking, about Butter and Oban and how we'd saved him from colic, and about our ride that day.

"Ada," Maggie said, "be quiet."

"It's like having sisters," I said. "I never had family except Jamie."

"You had your mother," Ruth said.

"I didn't," I said. "Someday I'll tell you."

Ruth extended her hand across the space between the beds. We'd taken the blackout down, and I could see dimly in the shadowed light. I held my hand out to Ruth. "Maggie too," Ruth said. Maggie sat up on her elbow so that her hand would reach ours. "All three together," Ruth said. "Sisters."

"Say it in German," I said.

"*Schwestern*," Ruth said.

"Schwestern?" Maggie giggled. "That's hilarious."

"Schwestern," Ruth repeated firmly. "You two are my schwestern now. So I will tell you a secret. I'm not going to Oxford."

I dropped her hand and sat up in bed. "You said you passed your exams!"

"I did," Ruth said. "I learned all the maths. I'm ready. But Lord Thorton said that if I wanted to, I could work where he and my father are working instead. I will go to Oxford after the war."

"Real war work?" Maggie said.

Ruth laughed. "Yes. Very real."

"Where?" I asked. "What are you doing?"

"I can't tell," Ruth said. "But I will write to you, and you will both write to me, and, Maggie, you need to exercise my horse for me whenever you are home from school. You're starting to outgrow your pony."

"You'll come home when you can," I said.

Ruth lay back on her bed. I could hear her smiling. She said, "Your government has decided we aren't spies. My family will live together, and my father and I will work together. And yes, I will come home when I can."

The next morning, Lady Thorton started in on Maggie first thing. Susan, Ruth, and I escaped to the kitchen to make breakfast. Lady Thorton came to the table in a cloud of fury, stiff and upright. Maggie sank into the chair beside her, her eyes red and swollen from crying.

Suddenly I blew up a cloud of fury of my own. None of this was Maggie's fault, or mine. "I don't see why you're being so horrible," I said to Lady Thorton. "You've known about that letter for weeks." She had. Lord Thorton had sent her a copy. He'd said so.

"Hearing it read aloud again was difficult," Lady Thorton said, "and when I think how my own daughter acted deceitfully—"

"You didn't have to read it out again," I said. "You could have kept it secret, or handed it to us to read."

She sniffed. "That was Lord Thorton's choice."

I gathered myself up taller. "Then be angry with him," I said, looking Lady Thorton in the eye. "Not Maggie. You're making her miserable about something she can't ever fix. It isn't fair."

Bright spots of color appeared on Lady Thorton's cheeks. "I hardly think," she said, "that I deserve to be reprimanded by someone like you."

"Oh—" Susan said.

I held Lady Thorton's gaze, even though my heart was hammering. "You don't deserve a daughter like Maggie," I said. "You are a terrible mother."

Everyone in earshot froze. Lady Thorton went white. Then Ruth said, into the cold, dead silence, "Ada, apologize this instant. You know that isn't true."

Chapter 50

I glared at Ruth. She glared back. "She's not doing anything right," I said. "Maggie needs her and she keeps being angry. She's angry Jonathan's dead and Maggie can't fix it and it's not Maggie's fault."

Ruth said, "She's doing the best she can."

"How would you know?" I felt frustration building up inside me like a rising wave. "She's horrid to you! She's horrid to everyone!"

"Ada!" Susan said.

"All the mothers are horrible!" I got up from the table and ran up the stairs to my room.

A few minutes later someone knocked on my door. I didn't answer.

"Ada?"

It wasn't Susan or Maggie. It was Ruth.

She came in and sat on the foot of the bed. I'd

wrapped myself in my coverlet so that only my eyes showed. I wasn't crying.

"Susan said Christmastime is hard for you," Ruth said.

"I did all right this year," I said.

"The whole season is hard," Ruth repeated.

"So?"

"So maybe you can see not everything is Lady Thorton's fault."

"I don't know why you're on her side," I said. "She's never liked you."

Ruth sighed. "I'm not on anyone's side. It was awful, what you said. That she didn't deserve to have Maggie. When Maggie's all she has left."

"She shouldn't be so mean to Maggie. She should listen to Maggie. She should love Maggie, even if Maggie isn't perfect—"

"She does," Ruth said. "Lady Thorton isn't perfect either. She does love Maggie."

"How would you know?" I knew I sounded rude. I didn't care.

Ruth grabbed the edge of my blanket and tucked it over her feet. Our bedrooms were always cold in winter. "My mother is a genius," she said. "That's what my father says. That we're smart, him and me, but that she's smarter than both of us. Only her parents never allowed her to go to university, because she was a girl. So she never got to do anything with all her brains, and sometimes it frustrates her and she gets angry, but it doesn't have anything to do with us."

"So?" Ruth's mother was kind. She kissed me and petted me. She was nothing like Lady Thorton.

"My mother got us out of Germany," Ruth continued. "She persisted. She kept trying and trying until she found somewhere that would take us. She wasn't afraid to leave our home behind. She was sorry she couldn't convince the rest of our family to leave, but she was brave and strong for my father and me."

"My mother was a monster," I said. "I can't remember one good thing about her."

"So your mother was a monster. It doesn't mean mine is. It doesn't mean Lady Thorton is." Ruth prodded me with her foot. "People are complicated. You, yourself, are not the easiest person to love. But you are still my sister."

I glared at her. "You aren't the easiest person to love either," I said.

"I'm sure I'm not," Ruth said, "and yet you love me. I am your sister too.

"When my mother is difficult," Ruth continued, "and she is difficult, quite often—I think about the

look on her face when our boat landed in England—
how grateful she was not just that she was out of
Germany, but that she'd gotten me out of Germany.
That I was safe." Ruth looked at me. "Lady Thorton
is trying to keep Maggie safe."

"She's doing it wrong," I said.

"Maybe," Ruth said. "That doesn't mean she isn't
trying to do right."

I blew out my breath. "So?"

Ruth said, "So you need to apologize."

I didn't want to. I dreaded what might happen. But
after Ruth left, Maggie came in. "You shouldn't have
said that," she said.

"I was trying to stick up for you," I said.

"I know," she said. "You still shouldn't have said
it. Ruth and I are going to the stables with our fathers
and Frau Schmidt. My mother's staying here."

"All right." I understood what she was telling me.
My stomach hurt. My hands felt damp. I sat in my
freezing bedroom and reminded myself to breathe.

After a long time, I unwrapped myself from the
coverlet. I walked carefully down the stairs. Lady
Thorton and Susan were sitting by the fire in the big
room, drinking tea. I didn't see Jamie.

"I—" I didn't know what I was supposed to say. I walked toward them. My knees shook.

Lady Thorton and Susan looked up. They waited.

"I'm sorry I said you were a bad mother," I said.

Lady Thorton nodded. "Thank you." She took another sip of tea.

I waited for what happened next.

"Have some breakfast, Ada," Susan said. "You haven't eaten. There's oatmeal on the back of the stove."

"I can eat breakfast?" My voice came out small and frightened.

Lady Thorton frowned. "We are not in the habit of starving children who misbehave. I've accepted your apology. Go eat."

I walked toward the kitchen in a sort of daze. Was that really the end of it? Mam used to put me in the cabinet—I swallowed hard. I couldn't eat any oatmeal, but I had a cup of tea.

Later in the day, when I'd had a chance to calm down a bit, Lady Thorton sat beside me on the sofa. "What was the worst thing about your life?" Lady Thorton asked. "Before you came here."

I thought for a while. Coals fell in the grate. "My

mother could have fixed my foot," I said at last. "She chose not to. And then she blamed me for it."

Another silence stretched out long and thin. "That's why you're so angry," Lady Thorton said. "You think I'm blaming Maggie for things to do with Jonathan. I'm not. I blame myself."

Chapter 51

In our room that night I still felt fragile. "I thought something worse would happen," I said to Maggie. "I was still willing to defend you, though. I was trying to help."

"I know," Maggie said. "St. Ada slaying the dragon."

"Why do you think my mother was so horrible?"

Across the room Ruth made noise between her teeth. "Why is Hitler horrible?" she asked. "No one knows. Some people are horrible. You were unlucky with your first mother. You were lucky with your second."

"Susan's not my mother," I said.

Ruth shrugged. "You can say that if you want to."

Ruth and her parents and Lord Thorton left. The rest of us walked them to the train station. The government had finally completely forbidden any private use of gasoline. Lady Thorton's car was up on blocks in the corner of the stable yard.

Ruth hugged me good-bye. "Don't look so tragic," she said. "I'll write to you. You'll write back."

Her mailing address was an office in London. It wasn't where she was really going to be. "They'll forward your letters to me," Ruth said. "Don't be sad. I'm not gone forever."

Stephen White seemed to be gone forever. After he left, I'd never heard from him. Not once.

Ruth gave me another hug. "My little *schwester,*" she said. She kissed Jamie. "Little *bruder,*" she said. "Take care of that pig for me."

Maggie and I rode across snow-covered fields in bitter wind. I was riding Oban, for Ruth, for Jonathan. Oban tossed his head, wanting to gallop, but I couldn't let him on the icy, uncertain ground.

"You'll have to trot for hours to work him down," Maggie said. Her pony Ivy puffed white clouds of breath, struggling to keep up. We rode along the field where the grouse exploded. I would never see that field without remembering Jonathan.

"Invincible Ada," Maggie said, so I knew she was thinking of him too.

"That wasn't really about me," I said. "Jonathan wanted something to fight for. He was seeing what he wanted me to be."

When the time came for Maggie to go back to school, she put up a battle that if it had been against Hitler might have won us the war. Unfortunately, it was against Lady Thorton.

Maggie railed and shouted and wept. Lady Thorton never flinched. Finally, Maggie stood up at the dinner table. "If you make me go back," she said, low and hard, "I will never forgive you. I will hate you for as long as I live."

Cor. That was worse than calling her a terrible mother. I wondered what Ruth would say.

Lady Thorton picked up a forkful of food, chewed it slowly, and swallowed before she replied. "To ensure your safety and happiness," she said, "that's a chance I'm willing to take."

"I will not apologize," Maggie said at night in our bedroom. "I am not sorry."

Chapter 52

The house felt sad and empty with Ruth and Maggie gone. Susan swore the days were getting longer again already, but it was hard to believe her when we had to put the blackout up midafternoon. Susan fell again into one of her bleak periods, listless and dull. Then one morning she didn't get out of bed. She coughed repeatedly. Her cheeks were flushed and she could barely speak.

"I'm afraid she's caught my cold," Lady Thorton said. "I've got WVS business all day. Ada, will you be all right? Should I ask Mrs. Elliston to check in on you and Jamie?"

I would take care of Susan. I would be her ward. "We'll be fine," I said.

I took Susan tea and toast. Jamie tended his chickens and Mrs. Rochester. He built up the living room fire and we snuggled close to it, Jamie playing with his tin airplanes and me reading one of Maggie's books.

Susan didn't want lunch. After Jamie and I ate, I took her another cup of tea. She had fallen asleep. Her bedroom was frightfully cold, and frost etched lines across the windowpanes, but when I touched Susan's cheek it was blazing hot. Her breath whistled. I pulled her covers down a bit to cool her off, and left the tea by her bedside. At least she'd stopped coughing.

We'd done the chores and I was teaching Jamie to peel potatoes when Lady Thorton came home. "How's Susan?" she asked.

"I checked on her"—I glanced at the clock—"half an hour ago. She was sleeping. She's been asleep all afternoon."

"Good," Lady Thorton said. "Sleep is the best thing for her."

I sent Jamie up just before dinner. Susan was still asleep. "I hate to wake her," Lady Thorton said. "How did she seem?"

Jamie shrugged. "Asleep."

After dinner we washed up and started the pig slop and swept the floor. Lady Thorton went up to check on Susan herself.

"Ada!" she called a moment later. The sharp urgency in her voice startled me. "Was she like this earlier?"

I went to the stairs. Lady Thorton looked down at

me, her forehead creased with concern. "With such a high fever, and breathing this hard?"

I ran up the steps. Susan's eyes were half-open, glazed and unfocused. Her mouth was open, and I could hear her breath whistling, much louder than before. "She was warm, but I took some of her covers off," I said.

"She has a fever," Lady Thorton said.

Susan groaned. Lady Thorton leaned close. "What is it?" Lady Thorton asked.

Susan whispered, "Hurts."

"How badly does it hurt?" Lady Thorton's voice sounded angry and gentle at the same time.

"Yes." Susan's eyes slid closed.

I stood rooted to the floor. "Did I do something wrong?"

"We'll call Dr. Graham," Lady Thorton said. "Oh. No—where's the nearest—Jamie!" She hurried down the stairs. "Jamie, I need you to run a message over to the stables. Have Grimes telephone Dr. Graham. I'll find a pencil."

"I'll go," I said.

"Jamie's faster." At the kitchen table Lady Thorton scribbled a note while Jamie got into his coat and boots. "Take your bicycle," Lady Thorton said, pressing the note into his hand. "Hurry."

"What did I do?" I asked. "Did I do something wrong?"

"No." Lady Thorton paused to touch my arm. "Either she's gotten worse quickly or you didn't realize how bad her symptoms were. We'll get Dr. Graham here. She'll be fine."

Lady Thorton went into the kitchen, filled the teakettle, and set it to boiling. She rummaged in the scullery until she found a bottle of something. "Here." She gave me the bottle, a big empty bowl, and a clean towel. "Take these and go sit with her."

Susan was sweating all over, the way Oban had when he'd colicked. The room was freezing cold. Susan looked mostly asleep, and when I said her name, softly, she didn't respond. Cautiously I stuck my fingers against her throat. She jumped and pulled away. Her eyes fluttered open. "What are you doing?" The words low but clear.

"Checking for your heartbeat," I said.

"It's . . . still beating," she said, with the ghost of a grin.

"Do you feel very bad?"

She nodded. "Can't . . . breathe."

I didn't know what to do. I had no idea at all what to do. I'd never felt so helpless in my life.

Lady Thorton came in with the steaming teapot

in her hands. She set it down on the floor. "Get me another pillow," she said. When I did she set it behind Susan's head, then reached under Susan's armpits and hauled her half upright. "Now give me the bowl."

She put the bowl against Susan's chest. She dumped something sharp-smelling and astringent from the bottle into the bowl, then added hot water from the kettle. She draped the towel over Susan's head and the bowl.

"What's that?" I asked.

"The steam and menthol will help her breathe," Lady Thorton said.

"I didn't know," I said.

"I know you didn't," she said. "It's all right. I didn't expect you to."

"I thought she was hot because of too many blankets," I said. "Like me at the hospital."

"She has a fever," Lady Thorton said. "That's her body raising its own temperature. Internal heat. It's a sign she's fighting some kind of infection."

"Oh." I should have known. Somehow, I should have known.

"Don't worry," Lady Thorton said.

Dr. Graham listened to Susan's chest with his stethoscope. He felt her heartbeat and measured her temperature and thumped her chest with his fingers. All the while he looked more and more concerned. "Where's the nearest telephone?" he asked, looking up at Lady Thorton.

"Stables," she answered.

I cut in quick. "I can take a message. Fred will make the call."

Dr. Graham shook his head. "We'll stop by on our way, to let them know we're coming," he said. "I'm taking her to a hospital. There's a good one in London for chest and lungs."

"London?"

He looked at me. "It's not far by car." Doctors could still drive cars. "Closest place for what we need. Lady Thorton, you'll come with me?"

"Of course," she said. "Ada, while I'm changing, get Susan's identity and ration cards. Fetch her whole pocketbook. And put together a bag for her—nightgown, toothbrush, that sort of thing."

Dr. Graham carried Susan down the stairs, wrapped in blankets. She couldn't walk. I'd never seen her so helpless and small. She groaned once, and gave a labored cough, but otherwise hardly seemed to care what was happening. My heart beat fast, as though I'd run a mile.

I tucked her bag into the backseat of Dr. Graham's

car. Icy cold pricked through the pebbled drive into my stocking feet. Wind whipped my hair. I leaned against the passenger window. Susan's breath fogged the glass.

Lady Thorton came out, shrugging herself into her coat.

"Let me come," I said, the words raw in my throat.

She shook her head. "I'm sorry. A hospital's no place for children. I'll be back in a day or two. I'll send Grimes down to stay with you." She got into the backseat. Dr. Graham passed me going around the front of the car.

"What's wrong with her?" I asked.

He looked up briefly before shutting the door. "Pneumonia," he said.

Chapter 53

Pneumonia.

Pneumonia.

I'd heard that word before.

Over two years ago, when I'd first come to Susan's house, when I'd learned about Becky, her best friend. "What killed her?" I'd asked, and Susan had said, "Pneumonia. That's a sickness in the lungs."

I was falling, falling. I had no one to catch me. Susan was dying. I had no safe place to be.

The car drove away in a swirl of dead leaves. The wind howled in the trees. I took a step toward the house, and another. Two good feet. I opened the door.

Jamie stood at the base of the stairs, Bovril in his arms. I had to take care of Jamie.

Who was going to take care of me?

I couldn't go to bed. The upstairs was so cold. I couldn't bear to be alone in my room, without Maggie, without Ruth, without Susan in the room between Jamie and me, without even Lady Thorton. I hauled blankets down the stairs and told Jamie to bring in more coal for the fire.

He did it one-armed, clutching Bovril in the other. I didn't blame him.

"If you wrap yourself up tight," Jamie said, pulling the blanket around me, "you won't feel as scared."

It was good advice. We both wrapped up tight. We turned off all the lamps. I moved a low table out of the way and pulled the sofa so that it faced the fireplace head-on. When Fred came in, a bit later, he looked at Jamie and me and the cat huddled right up by the fire. "That's thinking," he said. He pulled off his boots and went to sleep in Lady Thorton's wing chair.

In the morning, as soon as we woke, we tromped over to the stables and used the telephone to phone the number Dr. Graham had left. Fred made the call since I wasn't used to telephones. "Admitted and stable," he said when he'd hung up.

"What's that mean?" I asked.

"Not dead," Jamie whispered.

"No." Fred patted Jamie's back. "She's in hospital and they're taking care of her. She isn't going to die."

"Becky died," Jamie said, so I knew that he remembered too.

I was Susan's ward. I was supposed to guard her. She was supposed to guard me. All that day and the next I felt like I had a band of steel wrapped tight around my middle. I didn't have pneumonia, but I could barely breathe. I could barely function. I did my work—I did all the work I could find to do, every last small thing—but whenever I tried to eat, my throat closed and I couldn't swallow. At night I couldn't sleep. I wrapped up tight on the sofa and cuddled Jamie and his cat and listened to Fred snore from the wing chair.

When Lady Thorton walked in, midday on the second day, I burst into sobs. I didn't want to, but I couldn't stop. I started to ask how Susan was and the words turned into nonsense syllables and those turned into horrible jagged crying sounds and tears.

Lady Thorton stared at me. I stood in the kitchen, sobbing. I didn't want her to touch me. I didn't know how to calm down.

Jamie ran in with one of our blankets. "Here," he said. I draped the blanket around myself. Jamie pulled it tight and hugged me.

"Susan's all right," Lady Thorton said.

We looked at her.

"Not entirely," she amended. "She's very sick. But they have a new type of medicine they're giving her and they hope it will start to show results soon. I'm just back to collect more clothes and things. I'm going to stay in London near the hospital. She needs someone with her."

"I can do it," I said. "I ought to do it. Please let me go." I needed Susan. Oh, how I needed Susan.

"They only allow visitors in to see her once a day," Lady Thorton said. "That's not much. And you have to be at least twelve years old. They won't let Jamie in."

"They did at my hospital," I said.

"Children's orthopedics might bend the rules," Lady Thorton said. "Women's pulmonary never will." She studied me. "Ada, you look awful. You need to take care of yourself."

I had needed all the care I could give myself just to keep from falling completely apart. I said, "Becky died of pneumonia."

Lady Thorton's face clouded. "That's right. I'd forgotten." She thought for a moment. "Jamie, I'll ask Mrs. Elliston if she can keep you. Ada, you can come with me. Pack your things."

"I want to go too," Jamie said. Lady Thorton didn't reply.

I'd always taken care of Jamie before anything else.

He would manage with the Ellistons. I wouldn't.

Chapter 54

Dr. Graham said London was a short trip by car. It was a long one by train. I'd traveled the route three times before in my life—two good, one bad. Now this, the worst of all.

I had to force myself to breathe.

Lady Thorton patted my knee. She said, "No matter what happens, you'll be all right."

I stared at her.

She said, "You and Jamie won't be left alone in the world. If it comes to the worst, I would be willing to take custody of you."

I couldn't speak.

"Lord Thorton and I," she said.

Still couldn't speak.

"It doesn't matter," Lady Thorton said. She opened her purse and rummaged inside it. "It won't come to that. She'll be fine."

It could come to that. Otherwise Lady Thorton wouldn't have said so.

I knew I should be grateful. I was certain I should feel grateful, that Lady Thorton was willing to guard Jamie and me.

Someday I would be grateful. Right now I had no room.

By the time we reached London, it was black dark. I was surprised to see taxis outside the station. Lady Thorton hailed one. "Claridge's," she said to the driver. To me she said, "We've missed visiting hours. I'll call the hospital from the hotel."

I fidgeted with the belt on my coat. "I need to see her."

"Yes," Lady Thorton said. "We'll go tomorrow, first thing, and see if we can speak to a doctor. Visiting hours are in the afternoon."

"I need to see her today."

"I understand," Lady Thorton said. "You can't, however. I can't fix that."

At least Lady Thorton heard me.

I don't know how the taxi driver navigated the blacked-out streets. We rushed through complete darkness and when we stopped, there was still no light to see where we were. On the sidewalk, a uniformed man held a small, dim flashlight. "Welcome, madam," he said, opening a blacked-out door.

Immediately beyond the first door was a pitch-dark space and a second blacked-out door. Immediately beyond the second door was an enormous, astonishingly bright room, with a smooth, shiny, black-and-white floor and a huge electric light hung with hundreds of pieces of sparkling glass.

Lady Thorton twitched my hand. "Don't ogle," she said.

I dropped my eyes and moved to stand beside her. She spoke to a man behind a counter, and then another man picked up Lady Thorton's suitcase—it held my things too—and led us into a small room like a closet. Lady Thorton and the man turned around, so they were facing the door we'd come in. The little room shook for a moment. Then the door opened, on its own, onto a different place. As though the entire building had shifted while we stood in the closet.

"It's a lift," Lady Thorton said, pushing me forward. "Haven't you been in a lift before?"

The closet had moved, not the building. The closet had moved *up*.

The man opened one of a long series of doors with

a key. He showed us into a room with flowered carpet and colored walls, and two beds made up fancy. It reminded me of Thorton House.

The man left. "Put on your church dress and wash your face," Lady Thorton said. "We'll go down and eat."

I said, "I thought we'd stay in rooms over a pub."

"I've always preferred Claridge's," Lady Thorton replied.

Dinner was served in an impossibly grand room, but the food itself was quite normal, probably because of the war. "Can't you eat more than that?" Lady Thorton asked.

I shook my head.

"No, I suppose not," she said. "Never mind." She glanced at the newspaper she'd asked the waiter to bring her. "What else shall we do tomorrow?"

"Susan," I whispered.

"Yes, my dear, but besides that?"

The hospital was a red brick building, tall and thin. Inside, it smelled exactly like the hospital where I'd had my surgery. We checked in at a desk by the front door, and a nurse came downstairs to tell us that Susan had had a difficult night. Her fever was still high. They were continuing to treat her with sulfa drugs. They hoped to see improvement soon.

Visiting began at three p.m.

I studied the walls and the stairs. If I could escape Lady Thorton, just for a moment, I could run up those stairs and find Susan.

"It's difficult," Lady Thorton said. She took hold of my hand and led me back outside. She wouldn't let go, not even when I tried to pull away.

The London near the hotel and the hospital was not a London I had ever seen before. Even in war, even with sandbags lining the sidewalks and storefronts, and glass missing from windows and whole chunks of buildings bombed, even in drab winter, this London was prettier and greener than I ever imagined. Stores still had goods in the windows. There were evergreen bushes, and sometimes trees. There was grass.

"The first thing we should do," Lady Thorton said, "is buy you a new coat."

"I don't need a new coat."

"Nonsense," she said. When I glared at her she added, "What do you think Susan would say? Would she want you to have a new coat?"

It wasn't fair play. I was still wearing the coat Susan had bought me over a year ago when I was in hospital.

It had been small for me then, and even though Susan had altered it repeatedly it was hopelessly tight on me now. We'd not been able to find a coat my size for sale in the village, used or new, and we'd not been able to go elsewhere.

Susan would love me to have a new coat.

We went to a place called a department store. It was huge, a city of shops under one roof. In the children's section, a woman measured me and brought out four different coats for me to choose from, all well-made of good new wool. One by one I tried them on.

"Very suitable," Lady Thorton said, nodding. "Which do you prefer?"

Red, navy, gray, and a sort of brownish green. "I don't know," I said.

Lady Thorton said, "I'm not choosing for you. It's your coat, I want you to like it."

Susan said I looked washed-out in red. I reached toward the gray coat. "Good," Lady Thorton said. "We'll take it."

Lady Thorton told the store clerk I would wear the new coat now. She gave her my old one, and asked that it be delivered to Claridge's. The woman said, "Very good, ma'am," with a sort of mushed-up voice.

I looked away when Lady Thorton paid for the coat. I didn't want to know how much it cost.

Less than my surgery, but still.

Next we took a bus to a huge building Lady Thorton called a museum. She did not explain what a museum was. "They've taken the paintings away, for safekeeping," she said, "but now they have concerts here every weekday at lunch." We joined a long, slow-moving queue. Inside, we found seats among rows of little chairs. Lady Thorton bought us each a sandwich from a table at one side.

Eventually a woman came out to play the piano at the front of the room. Lady Thorton told me it was called a piano. I'd not seen one before, though it looked similar to the organ at church. Its music wasn't quavery like church music. It wasn't like any music I knew. It was all sounds, running together without words, and somehow, if I shut my eyes, it reminded me of good things, of summer and happiness and grass. It was the sort of music I could disappear into, so I let myself disappear. I could breathe. I almost fell asleep.

Afterward Lady Thorton seemed more relaxed too. "I do love concerts," she said.

Concert, piano, hotel, lift. Department store. Museum. I wished I had my dictionary.

"Has Maggie ever come here, and done all this?" I asked.

"Well, not these particular concerts," Lady Thorton said. "These are special, because of the war."

"I mean—stores and Claridge's and all the bright buildings."

Lady Thorton laughed. "Of course! It was a completely different world, before the war. Margaret and I used to come up for weekends. I took her to pantomimes, the zoo, all sorts of things. We had grand adventures." Lady Thorton's whole face smiled, remembering. Even her eyes looked happy.

We walked back to the hospital through streets damaged by bombs. Some buildings had been partially repaired; others lay in broken, twisted heaps. We both stopped to stare at a pile of rubble sandwiched between two stores open for business as usual. "I suppose there's been no time to clear things," Lady Thorton said.

At the hospital. Inside the door. Up the steps and down a long hall. White walls bisected by a dark wooden rail. A wooden door. A room full of beds.

Unfamiliar faces until we reached the very end, the last bed on the left, and there was Susan.

I ran the last two steps but stopped before I touched her. Was I allowed to touch her? She was sleeping, her head and shoulders lifted high on a pile of white-cased pillows.

Lady Thorton said, "Susan. Ada's here."

Her eyelids fluttered. They slowly opened.

Susan smiled.

A noise came out of me that was half a laugh and half a cry.

"You can sit down," Lady Thorton said. "You won't hurt her."

Very carefully, I sat on the edge of Susan's bed. I moved myself a tiny bit closer, then let my head and shoulders lean forward until I was just touching her side. I would have hugged her, the way Jamie did, but I didn't want to make it harder for her to breathe.

"I had to bring her," Lady Thorton said. "She was fretting herself sick."

Susan lightly touched my hair. "Of course," she whispered.

I needed to take care of Susan. She was sick. I was strong. I was her ward. But Lady Thorton was already unpacking the things of Susan's that she'd brought. Lady Thorton combed Susan's hair for her, and filled her water pitcher, while I just lay beside Susan, letting her stroke my hair.

"I'm not going to die," Susan said.

Lady Thorton and I both froze.

"Don't worry," Susan said. "They say I haven't turned the corner yet, but I think I have. I'm not going to die on you, Ada."

"Becky," I said.

"Yes. I know." She spoke slowly, with pauses in between each word while she breathed. "But now they have a new kind of medicine. Sulfa. Didn't have it when Becky was sick."

"It's a wonderful drug," Lady Thorton said, in the hearty voice she used to encourage the WVS.

"It's working," Susan whispered. "Ada. I won't die."

I didn't entirely believe her, but I believed her a little bit.

Chapter 55

When it was time to leave I kissed Susan's cheek. It was still too hot, from fever. When we walked away I felt like I was abandoning her. I felt like I was being abandoned.

"She's getting good care," Lady Thorton said. She grabbed my hand to make me walk faster.

"I should be taking care of her," I said.

"Don't be ridic—" Lady Thorton started. Then, to my surprise, her voice softened. "We would both do all we could," she said, "but we are not trained doctors or nurses. She needed to be in hospital."

We walked several blocks in silence. "After all," Lady Thorton said, "Susan herself couldn't repair your foot. You needed a surgeon for that."

The next morning Lady Thorton took me to the zoo. It was huge, spread out like a farm with lots of buildings, and every building housed different kinds of animals. There were sandbag huts and bomb damage and a Red Cross building, but most of the zoo was like London, carrying on despite the war.

"Here's the monkey house," Lady Thorton said.

Monkeys had faces almost like people. They swung on ropes and screeched. Some were little, but others called chimpanzees were bigger than I was. I stared and stared. Jamie would have loved them.

Zebras looked like striped ponies. Lions looked like huge versions of Bovril. Ostriches looked like nothing I'd ever seen. It was hard to believe they were actually birds.

Penguins. They were birds too. Elephants. Camels. Giraffes. A hippopotamus. I'd never imagined animals could look like this. "I wish Jamie were here," I said. He would be ecstatic.

"We'll find a time to bring him," Lady Thorton said. "I hadn't realized the zoo was open during the war until I inquired at the hotel."

The Reptile House was closed. "Had to put the poisonous snakes down," one of the keepers told us. "In case there was a bombing and they escaped. Moved the rest of them to the country."

"Pity," Lady Thorton said, "I particularly wanted to show Ada the dragon."

Dragon? "You said dragons were imaginary!"

"Certainly," Lady Thorton said. "The ones in stories are. But there's a largish type of lizard called a Komodo dragon. Margaret always found him fascinating."

You simply could not trust anything anyone ever said.

"He doesn't fly," Lady Thorton said. "Nor breathe fire. He's not that interesting."

"What about angels?" I said.

Lady Thorton raised her eyebrows. "What about them?"

"Are they here too?" If the zoo could have dragons, why not?

Lady Thorton said, "Not that I've noticed." I would have questioned her further, but suddenly she smiled. "Oh, the duck pond," she said. "We should have brought bread for the ducks. When Margaret was small it was her favorite thing." She pointed to the edge of a small pond surrounding a few tiny islands. "I remember her standing just there, in her little russet coat, surrounded by ducks, and laughing." Lady Thorton's voice was softer than usual. "She had curly hair when she was small. Curly hair and the most adorable little hat."

347

Adorable? I'd never heard Lady Thorton use such a word.

"We loved the zoo," Lady Thorton said.

Susan didn't get better, but she didn't get worse. Every day Lady Thorton and I woke, went to the hospital for news about Susan, walked around the middle of London, then went back to the hospital for visiting hours. Lady Thorton walked me past Buckingham Palace, where the king lived. It had been bombed, but not badly. She showed me the Tower of London, and the Houses of Parliament, and Westminster Abbey, which was like a church but with all the tombstones inside. She showed me a whole heap of buildings that were important to her but not to me. I didn't find any of them as interesting as the zoo. Plus, Susan wasn't better yet. It was so hard to pay attention to anything besides Susan.

One day, Lady Thorton and I struggled through heaps of rubble and half-closed battered streets to get to an enormous church called St. Paul's. It stood mostly unharmed amid blocks of destruction. Lady Thorton let out a long breath when she saw it. "A miracle," she said. "What would London do, without St. Paul's?"

I didn't mind looking at buildings—we had to do something before visiting hours—but they didn't hold my attention. I found myself mostly noticing small things, like the holes in concrete curbs where iron park railings had been torn out to be made into bullets and guns. Or a silver barrage balloon with one cable loose that bobbed and dipped in the wind. Or a wren on a street sign. When I wrote to Jamie on the fancy hotel stationery I told him about little things, not big ones.

On our fifth day in London Lady Thorton walked me down a curved street with grand white buildings lining both sides. "This is where I grew up," she said, pointing to a doorway. "Third floor, fourth window from the end, watched over by a nanny and then a governess."

I looked up at the window. The house was all fancy, but the window—"You were locked up?" I said. "You only had the one window?"

"Oh." Lady Thorton shook her head. "I got taken out on proper walks, twice a day. I usually saw my parents for an hour after tea."

Not entirely locked up, then. Not quite the same. Still—

"Sometimes I went to parties and children's teas, but I didn't have any real friends, not until I was nearly grown," Lady Thorton said. "It's partly why I insisted Margaret go to boarding school. I never wanted her to be lonely like I was."

I stared at the window. Third floor, like mine.

Lady Thorton and I had things in common after all.

Susan's fever broke. When we came into her room that afternoon she could lift her head from her pillows. She leaned forward, and she smiled with her whole face, and she put her arms around me. I put my arms around her, and I clung to her, and I cried.

I cried like I might never stop. All the tears I hadn't cried for a whole week came out in one long flood. Tears and snot drenched Susan's nightgown. I didn't care. Neither did Susan.

"I love you," I whispered. I buried my head against Susan's shoulder. "I'm sorry. I'm so sorry I didn't tell you before."

"Don't be sorry," she whispered back. "I know you love me. You know I love you too."

On our way out of the hospital, Lady Thorton took my hand and pulled me to a stop. "Now that she's better, we'll be leaving London soon," she said. "It'll take her a few more weeks to recover completely, but you and I have work at home."

I nodded. I missed Jamie and Butter and Fred.

"So I have a favor to ask you. I've shown you my London. Will you show me yours?"

I looked up at her, puzzled.

"Will you show me where you grew up?" Lady Thorton asked. "Will you show me where you lived?"

I didn't want to. I never wanted to go back there myself, let alone with Lady Thorton. But she'd brought me to Susan; I couldn't say no.

Chapter 56

Lady Thorton had the name written on a piece of paper. My first address, from the records kept with the WVS. A place called Elsa Street. I'd never known the name.

"Elsa Street?" said one of the elegantly dressed men behind the hotel counter. "Never heard of it. Is that in Mayfair?"

"I highly doubt it." Lady Thorton drew herself up and looked at him down the side of her nose. "I believe it's in the East End."

The man harrumphed and sighed and finally got out a large book of maps and searched until he had his finger on a small piece of London. Elsa Street.

"Very good," Lady Thorton said. "What's the best way to get there? It looks far for walking."

The man gulped. "Madam, you can't walk there," he said.

"Do we take the train? That would be an enjoyable adventure."

"Trains don't run there, madam," the man said.

Lady Thorton grew even more imperious. "What do you mean, 'trains don't run there'? We are talking about the city of London, not the back of beyond."

"Madam." The man pushed the map toward her. "The central line was expanding to Bethnal Green, but they stopped, on account of the war. There's no trains near there."

"Then we'll take a taxi," Lady Thorton said.

The doorman found her a cab. The cabdriver looked horrified. "Elsa Street?" he said. "You don't really—"

"I am quite tired," Lady Thorton said pleasantly, "of being told what I do and do not want." She turned to me as the cab pulled away. "You lived there, Ada. Did you feel it was unsafe?"

She had no understanding, still.

"Were you ever unsafe?" Lady Thorton persisted.

"I was never safe," I said. After a long moment, during which she stared at me, I said, "I think that was mostly Mam, not Elsa Street."

"Was Jamie unsafe?" she asked. "Poor, yes, under-fed, yes—but *unsafe*? As a child?"

I didn't know. How could I know?

"In daylight," Lady Thorton added, as though that made a difference.

We drove past the burned shell of a department store that had caught fire in the Blitz. Later, past the wrecked buildings surrounding St. Paul's. Then into new neighborhoods, not nearly as heavily damaged, but beginning to resemble the old view out my window: narrow streets, buildings jammed together in tight rows. No grass, no bushes, no trees.

"We're back on Oxford Street," the cabdriver said.

"My goodness," said Lady Thorton.

The driver pulled up beside a gray stone church with a square tower. "St. Mary's?" I asked. Jamie used to speak of St. Mary's. I'd never actually seen it.

"St. Dunstan and All Saints," he said. "Back of the yard, that's White Horse Street. Left to the corner was Elsa. I'll wait here."

As soon as we got out of the cab I understood why he hadn't driven us all the way there. Bombs had fallen everywhere around St. Dunstan's. What had been houses and shops facing the church was now nothing but broken bricks and boards. We walked slowly past the church. On the far side some houses still stood, partially damaged, but when we looked left—

—Elsa Street was gone.

There was no longer even a street, no longer a clear path between the piles of rubble that cascaded from both sides.

No noises. No dust. The wreckage had been scoured clean by rain and wind. It was empty of people or any other living things.

A makeshift flag flew from the top of one pile. Nothing else moved.

"Ada," Lady Thorton said, choking a little.

"There was a pub below our flat, where Mam worked nights," I said. "Out my window I could see a fishmonger's shop, and a pawn shop, and a bit of what was a grocery. We had a butcher shop too—once Jamie nicked a chop for me. He used to run down to the docks and watch the ships come in. And the school— the school we evacuated from, it wasn't far away." I searched, but couldn't begin to make sense of the destruction. Somewhere, there'd been a room where I was held prisoner. Somewhere, a lane filled with people I recognized, who sometimes stopped to wave at me. Maybe it had been here. It didn't exist anymore.

Lady Thorton had tears in her eyes.

Mam was dead. Elsa Street was gone. I really was never, ever going back.

I slid my hand into Lady Thorton's. "Thank you," I said.

"Oh, my dear," she said, her fingers tightening around mine. "This could have been what happened to you."

Chapter 57

I was alive. Susan was alive. Lady Thorton and I went home, leaving Susan in London to finish her recovery. I could picture her in my mind, sitting in her bed in hospital, reading the letters Jamie and I sent her. So it was okay. Hard, but okay.

I wrote to Ruth via her London address. The letter got to her somehow, wherever she was, and she wrote back. *I'm so glad about Susan. Send her my love.*

I told Ruth about Elsa Street. She wrote, *Now you have no home, like me.*

We have a home, I wrote back. *Jamie says our cave is big enough for everyone.*

At the Ellistons' Jamie slept in an old-fashioned bed cupboard built into the wall of the farmhouse kitchen. It was exactly like a small, cozy cave. I almost felt envious when I saw it.

"The Ellistons liked me," Jamie said. "They liked having a boy on the farm again."

A few weeks later Susan came home. Dr. Graham went to fetch her, to spare her the train ride. She was breathing fine but still very weak. Lady Thorton and I planned and cooked a gala celebration meal, with a roast chicken (Penelope), watercress salad, tinned fruit we'd been saving for a special occasion, and a boiled pudding using the remaining jar of last summer's blackberry jam. We invited everyone: Dr. Graham, Fred, the Ellistons, the Land Girls—everyone except Maggie, who was still stuck at school. One chicken for ten people didn't go far, but it tasted wonderful, and, anyhow, I roasted a mountain of potatoes to go with it.

I kept wanting to stare at Susan. Just stare at her. Put extra sugar in her tea, and watch her while she sipped it. Watch her while she breathed.

"Ada," Susan said, halfway through the evening, "stop hovering. I'm well."

"I'm not hovering." As though I knew what that meant.

"Hovering. Hanging around me in the manner of a hummingbird, or a housefly. You most certainly are. You can be easy now."

"I am easy."

"It was never your job to take care of me."

"It was," I said. "It should be."

"Archaic," she said, as though reading my mind. "Your definition of the word *ward* is archaic. No longer valid. It is once again my job to take care of you." She patted my hand. "When I couldn't do it, Lady Thorton did it for me."

My head snapped up. I looked at Lady Thorton, who gave me a quick smile on her way to the kitchen for more potatoes. "She did," I said, swallowing hard. I had been so anxious over Susan that I hadn't even realized it. I might have claimed I was taking care of myself.

I'd felt alone, but I hadn't been. It seemed so strange. I'd trusted Lady Thorton. Almost the way I trusted Susan.

Maybe she wasn't a terrible mother.

"I know," Susan said. "I didn't worry. I knew you and Jamie were in good hands."

Good hands. Lady Thorton's hands. Lady Thorton's good hands. Who would have thought?

Dear Maggie, I wrote, *Your mother looked happiest in London when she was talking about the things she used to do with you. She was glad to show me things, but* only because they reminded her of being there with you. I think she loves you more than you think.

Dear Ada, Maggie wrote, I am miserable. Tell my mother I must come home.

Chapter 58

Susan and I were scheduled to fire-watch, but of course Susan wasn't well enough to do it yet, so Lady Thorton volunteered in her place. We had a late shift, two a.m. until four. Lady Thorton set her alarm clock, and woke me.

It was a white, bright, moonlit night, the glare from the full moon reflecting on ground covered with snow. Since my summer watch with Maggie, I'd been fire-watching over and over again. Nothing ever happened. Each time I climbed the steeple, it grew just a little bit easier, but my fear never went entirely away. It helped me some to understand why I was afraid.

"Does being up here make you feel like you're back in London?" Lady Thorton asked. She stood on the parapet, binoculars trained to the sky.

"What?"

"The look on your face. It's the same look you had when we went to see your old street."

I stared at her. "A little," I said. "I don't want to be trapped."

Lady Thorton started to reply. Her mouth moved, but I couldn't hear the words. They were drowned by a sudden, unexpected, high-pitched wail. The village air raid sirens.

Bombs. Real bombs, coming toward us. The first in months.

Lady Thorton whipped around, straining her eyes to the sky. I did too. Off to the left, over the hills, we could see tiny shapes in the moonlit sky. Airplanes.

"Bombers," I shouted. Those were the big planes, the ones in the center. Smaller fighter planes surrounded them.

"Yes!" yelled Lady Thorton. "Pay attention!" We needed to know where the bombs hit. Where the fires might be.

The sirens kept going. I imagined Susan and Jamie running down the steps of the cottage, taking cover in our Anderson shelter. I imagined Fred and the Land Girls running to theirs.

Small dark shapes fell from the bombers' bellies, exploding when they hit the ground. Flames flickered and vanished, extinguished by the snow.

Thank heaven for the snow.

Spitfires from our airfield rose up to engage the

German planes. I heard the clatter of anti-aircraft guns, saw the bright streaks of their fire in the sky. And then, far above us and still quite far away, a Messerschmitt burst into flames.

It fell in a long burning arc. It roared straight past the steeple, missing us by feet, not miles, and crashed with a horrible squeal of twisted metal and a shattering of bricks and glass right onto the village main street.

We could feel the heat from the flames. We could smell the burning aviation fuel. Lady Thorton and I stood in the steeple, watching, until the sirens sounded all-clear, the rest of the German squadron was over the Channel, and we were certain nothing in the village except the Messerschmitt was on fire. Then we went down the stairs.

I wasn't trapped. My heart hammered but my footsteps never faltered.

On the street, Local Defence Volunteers worked with hand pumps to put out the blaze. Through sheer luck no houses had been destroyed. The newsagents' shop had taken a direct hit, but I knew the man who owned it didn't live inside.

The heat was so intense we couldn't get close. We stood with our backs pressed against the cemetery wall. Half the village watched, the only noise the crackle of the flames. As they began to subside, Lady Thorton stepped forward and ducked to look into the wreck. She straightened, her expression horror-struck. "I thought the pilot had bailed out," she said.

"Didn't he?"

"No."

Halfway home Lady Thorton leaned over and was sick in the road. She wiped her mouth with her handkerchief. Her hands trembled. "He was burned up," she said.

He'd been a German. A man, a pilot. The same as Jonathan once his uniform was gone.

Chapter 59

At home Lady Thorton sank onto her chair in the cold, blacked-out living room. "Aren't you going to bed?" I asked her. It was still hours before dawn.

"Do you think he suffered?" she asked.

I didn't know whether she meant Jonathan or the German pilot. I didn't know what to say. I'd burned my arm once, cooking. It had hurt a lot.

I put coal on the banked fire and stirred it up. "Will I make tea?"

Lady Thorton didn't answer. I repeated the question. She looked up. "No."

Susan wasn't in her bedroom. She and Jamie had fallen asleep in the Anderson shelter, cocooned in blankets together. When I opened the shelter door she untangled herself and held me tight. "You smell like petrol," she said. "How close were the airplanes? Was it dreadful?"

I said, "Lady Thorton has fallen to pieces."

Susan put Jamie back to bed. She stayed awake with Lady Thorton and me. She made tea, which Lady Thorton ignored. She covered Lady Thorton with a blanket and sat beside her in the cold morning darkness. "Go on to sleep, Ada," Susan said. "My turn."

I went up to my solitary bedroom and burrowed beneath the blankets. After a long time, I fell asleep. Hours later Jamie shook me awake. "Mum's sleeping on the couch," he said. "Lady Thorton's eyes are open but she won't talk. No matter what I say to her. She won't even look at me."

I said, "She saw a dead pilot in the village. In the German plane that went down."

Jamie's forehead creased. "So she can't talk because she's too sad?"

"That's right." I pushed the covers away. "Come. I need your help."

Lady Thorton was trapped. I knew what I had to do.

Chapter 60

Jamie had already fed Mrs. Rochester, Bovril, and the hens. I got dressed in my thickest socks and warmest sweater.

I took my special box from the bookshelf and dug out the shillings I'd saved. I stuffed them into my pocket. Downstairs, I made breakfast for Jamie and me. Susan was still asleep, and Lady Thorton was just as Jamie said: eyes open, immobile, suffering. I squeezed her hand hard and she jumped but looked away.

"She's scary," Jamie whispered.

I handed him a note I'd scrawled. I said, "When Susan wakes up, give her this. Only don't you wake her, wait till she gets up on her own."

Jamie read the note and looked up at me. "Why?" I was putting on my coat and hat. "Where are you going?"

"It's a secret," I said. "It's for the war." Jamie's eyes widened. "Don't worry," I told him. "It's perfectly safe."

"Like Ruth's job?"

"Yes," I said. I kissed him. "Do the barn chores for me, and help Susan as much as you can. And don't worry. I'll be gone a few days, but I'll come back."

In the village the charred wreck of the Messerschmitt still blocked the high street. I gave it a wide berth. I wasn't about to look inside.

I had the address, from Maggie's letters. I had the fare. I wondered if the stationmaster, who knew me, would ask questions, but he didn't.

I'd never ridden a train alone, let alone three trains with changes in between. It didn't matter. The trains were packed with soldiers, as always, and the soldiers kept going out of their way to be kind to me. They always found me a seat. Some gave me cups of tea. One pressed a piece of chocolate into my hand.

Invincible Ada. Inspiration to a dead airman. I leaned my head against the cold window glass and felt nothing but sorrow. I had no courage left. Out the window, the fields slid by empty and gray.

It was evening by the time I reached Maggie's school. The blackouts were already up, so no one could see me walk down the drive.

I knew there had to be rules and manners about boarding schools. I didn't know any of them. I didn't care. I told the girl who answered the door that I needed to see the head, and told the head I wanted Maggie.

When Maggie saw me, her face went milk-white. She stumbled and I thought for a moment she was going to faint. "She's okay!" I said. I grabbed Maggie by the shoulders and held her to me. She gasped and started to sob.

"She's not—my mother—you wouldn't have come—she's not—"

"She needs you. I've come to take you home."

Chapter 61

It was against the rules for Maggie to leave without the right kind of permission. I didn't care. I felt like Susan must have felt when she decided that, permission or not, I was going to have my surgery. "I've come to take Maggie home," I said. "You have to let me."

The head continued to protest. Maggie looked desolate. I should have written myself a letter that I could have pretended came from Lady Thorton. Too late for that now.

"If you speak to Maggie's mother on the telephone?" I said. "There's no phone at the cottage where we're living, but there is one at the stables."

Maggie's eyes widened. The head considered. "If I speak to her myself," she said.

"All right." The head showed me to a telephone, and I rang the Thortons' stables. I knew how, from when Susan was in hospital. "Grimes?" I said, when

Fred answered. "This is Ada Smith. I need you to fetch Lady Susan. The head of Miss Margaret's school is going to call you back in half an hour, and Lady Susan needs to be there to take the call."

"*Ada?*" said Fred. Maggie called him Grimes— she'd grown up doing so—but I never had. From the first day I'd known him, he was always Fred.

"Yes," I said firmly. "I'm at Miss Margaret's school. The headmistress is going to call back in half an hour, and she needs to speak to Lady Susan."

Fred said, "You went to fetch Maggie?"

"Yes."

I could hear him grinning down the phone line. "I'll fetch Lady Susan, then. Half an hour."

Lady Thorton's first name was Eleanor, but she wasn't ever called Lady Eleanor. Somehow that meant something different from Lady Thorton. I was counting on Maggie's head not knowing Lady Thorton's first name.

"Call them back in thirty minutes," I said to the head, hanging up the telephone. "Margaret and I will be spending the night here. We'll leave tomorrow morning. We'll need a ride to the train station so we can take her trunk." I reached for Maggie's hand. "Come. We'll start packing."

Maggie didn't say a word until we'd climbed three flights of stairs. Then she said, "Ada. That was marvelous."

"I don't know what we were thinking," I said. "I should have done this long ago."

While Maggie gathered her things, one of the other girls asked me, "Where do you go to school?"

"My mother teaches me at home."

The girl sighed. "Lucky," she said.

It was past suppertime, but a thickset woman came up to offer me something to eat. Maggie went down with me, back to the head's office, where there was a plate of sandwiches and the head herself poured us cups of tea. "Your mother said she was sorry to make us go to the trouble of phoning," she told Maggie. "She said she's been terribly upset. That's why she sent Ada."

"Yes," I said. I told them about the fire-watching, the steeple, the airplane, the pilot burned inside.

"You must have been terrified," the head said.

"I was," I said. "It didn't matter." Fear and what you did with it were two separate things.

On the last train, Maggie dozed. I watched the hills of Kent appear outside the train windows, rising up, then stretching down toward the sea, the way they'd been when I'd seen them for the first time. The way they'd always been, war or no war.

Susan was waiting at the station. She hugged me, hard and tight.

"Were you worried?" I asked her.

"No. Your note said to trust you, and I did." She looked at me searchingly. "But why didn't you explain?"

"I was afraid you'd try to stop me," I said, "and I knew I was right. Maggie didn't need to be safe as much as she needed her mother. Lady Thorton needed Maggie too."

Susan looked thoughtful. "I wouldn't have stopped you," she said.

In the living room, Lady Thorton leaned against Maggie and wept. It made Jamie nervous, so I took him into the kitchen and taught him how to make Lord Woolton pie while Susan made us all some tea. I let Jamie decide how many turnips to add. Jamie loved turnips. "Some things are very sad," I said to him, "but you were right. Our cave is big enough for everyone."

"Will Lady Thorton stop crying?" he asked.

"I don't know," I said. "She's always going to be sad about Jonathan." I rubbed his head. "It's okay to feel sad."

My own emotions were such a jumble. I'd known the right thing to do, and I'd done it. I'd helped take care of Lady Thorton the way she'd helped take care of me. I'd stood in the steeple while bombs and even an airplane had fallen past me out of the sky. I'd felt afraid, but I hadn't come undone.

My foot would never be all the way right, but I could walk and climb and run. My feelings might never be all the way right either, but they were healed enough. I lay in my bedroom that night, awake while Maggie snored from her bed, and I thought about everything I'd been fighting, everything I'd lost and won. Then I got up, put on my slippers, and went out the door.

Susan was still awake, in her bed, reading. When I came into the room she smiled. She held up the edge of her blankets, and I slid into the pocket of warmth beside her. I didn't say anything. I just breathed, and so did she.

Chapter 62

Lady Thorton never once argued with me about bringing Maggie home. She must have been aching for Maggie all along.

Lord Thorton came home for the weekend a few weeks later. He brought a big square tin of a new type of American meat. "Spam," Lord Thorton said. "Stands for 'spiced ham.' The grocer said it was like sausage."

Lady Thorton raised an eyebrow. "And what did it cost?"

Lord Thorton grinned. "Sixteen points."

Food that was rare or unusual was rationed on a point system now. Each person had sixteen points per month to spend on whatever they could find.

Lady Thorton shook her head at him and caught Susan's eye. "It's the lamb chops all over again."

"You've got lamb chops?" Lord Thorton asked.

"No, we do not," said Lady Thorton. "These children need to eat meat more often than that." She took the can of Spam and opened it, sliced the meat and fried the slices for our supper. It was delicious.

"We've been learning more about Hitler," Lord Thorton said while we ate. "About what he's doing in this war."

We all looked at him.

"You mean besides fighting the entire world?" asked Susan, her eyebrows raised.

Lord Thorton nodded. "It's not exactly open knowledge," he said. "Not top secret, of course, but nothing you'll see on the newsreels for a while." He paused. "I don't think I'd better share the details. But I can say that we're learning things about Hitler, and what he's doing in Europe, to captured civilians and even to his own countrymen, that make this war seem extremely necessary. More than necessary. Right."

"Do you mean like to Ruth's family?" I asked.

"Yes," Lord Thorton said. He paused again. "I'll never say Jonathan's death was worth it—I can't say that—but I can say that I know for sure that Jonathan died fighting for the side of right. I can say that no one on our side will have died in vain." He patted Maggie's hand. "That comforts me," he said.

Lady Thorton took a deep breath. "Perhaps."

"Not me," said Maggie.

"Not yet," said Lord Thorton. "It may someday."

That night Maggie asked me to tell her about my mother. Everything, every little thing, details I'd never told anyone, not even Susan. I told her my few faded memories of my father. I told her about Jamie growing up and the threat of him going to school. I told her how I'd taught myself to walk on my twisted, ruined ankle, smearing blood across the floor of our single, cramped room, then wiping it up with a rag.

"I'm going to be like you," Maggie said. "I'm going to let you teach me to be brave."

I snorted. "Oh, who's brave? Remember the day you fell off Oban, and he jumped into Susan's field? You were brave enough to ride him alone down the road, even though you hated him."

We both laughed, remembering. "You swore like a sailor," I said.

I could almost hear her grinning in the dark. "Sometimes I still do." Then, very quietly, she reeled off a string of swear words. She knew an awful lot of them.

I said, "You'd survive on a London lane."

"We'd both survive," Maggie said. "We're surviving now."

After a long pause, I laughed again. "We're doing better than that," I said. "I think we won."

Chapter 63

May 22, 1943

Over a year later

Jamie stuck his head into the kitchen. "Ready?" he asked.

I tucked the last of our sandwiches into a basket. I added the thermos of tea. "Ready," I said.

In the big room, Susan was putting on her hat. "I'm not sure about this," she said. "Is this trip truly necessary?"

I laughed. For Jamie's ninth birthday we'd gone to London Zoo, all of us, including Lady Thorton and Maggie. That trip had probably not been Truly Necessary, but it had been fantastic. Jamie loved the animals every bit as much as I thought he would.

Now it was six months later. I'd turned fourteen the week before, and while Jamie and Maggie had decorated the table with flowers like usual, and I breakfasted on a piece of bacon and an egg, I hadn't gotten any presents, because I had told Susan I knew exactly what I wanted. It was this day, and I was in charge of it.

"Yes, Mum," I said, "this trip is necessary."

We had waited for a Saturday so we wouldn't miss school. The village children had started returning the year before. The village school reopened in the fall, and Susan taught there part-time. She also tutored a new boy for his college entrance exams, but he boarded with the vicar, which was good because it meant we still had a spare room for when Ruth came home on leave.

We were still at war with Germany. We all still took shifts fire-watching in the steeple. Rationing was tighter than ever. A camp of American soldiers lived down the road, near our old bombed house. Jamie and his schoolmates liked to visit them, and Jamie could imitate their accent to perfection.

I'd finally gotten two letters from Stephen. They were short, but at least I knew he and his father were still alive.

At the train station, Jamie made Susan stand to one side while I bought the tickets. We didn't want her to know where we were going.

"I hope this isn't an overnight excursion," she said.

We just grinned at her. Outside the train windows, the hills rolled by, green with spring grass. I wondered whether Susan knew the route well enough to guess where we were going, but I don't think she did, because when the conductor announced the stop for Becky's hometown, Susan's face went white. Her smile faded. "I'm not sure—"

I tugged her arm. "Come on."

Jamie said, "We want to see her too."

Becky's village's church was bigger than the one in our village, but it was made of the same brown stone, with the same sort of wall around the cemetery. The headstones looked like the ones in our graveyard, marching down the grass in solemn, perfect rows.

"I don't know even where she is," Susan said. We walked slowly, reading the names, until we found her.

Rebecca Daphne Montgomery
April 11, 1909–September 5, 1936
Beloved Daughter. Beloved Friend.

Becky's stone looked like every other stone. There wasn't anything special about it. But underneath the dirt was Becky, or at least her earthly remains. Her soul, of course, was in heaven.

I'd decided to believe in heaven. I liked to think of Mam there, calm and happy at last. Fully and eternally capacitated, along with Jonathan, and Ruth's grandmother, and Stephen's family.

Now I opened the basket that held our sandwiches and took out the flowers I'd cut from the hedgerows that morning. They were bedraggled and limp, the sort of flowers you had to make do with, in war. I laid them at the base of Becky's stone. Jamie dug into his pocket, pulled out one of his tin soldiers, and stood it beside the flowers.

Susan dabbed her eyes.

"Do you want to say a prayer or something?" I asked. She nodded. We moved a little way away to give her privacy.

"Look," Jamie said, pointing to the stone beside Becky's. "It's got the same name."

Robert Nathaniel Montgomery
June 24, 1881–January 13, 1940

"Oh," said Susan, stepping back to our side, "that's Becky's father. I didn't know."

"He died in the war," I said.

"I doubt it had to do with the war," Susan said. "He was a choleric sort of man."

I was about to ask what that meant when a disbelieving voice behind us said, "*Susan?* Susan Smith? Is that really you?"

We turned to see a small, gray-haired woman holding a bouquet of roses. She stared at Susan.

Susan blushed. "Oh, I'm so sorry," she said. "Forgive me. Mrs. Montgomery. I—"

"I'd given up hope of seeing you," the woman said. "I thought you'd never come." She turned her bright eyes to Jamie, then me. "And who's this?"

"This is Ada, and Jamie, my"—I'd never seen Susan so ill at ease—"my children. From the war." She gestured toward the Robert Montgomery tombstone. "I'm very sorry—I didn't know. I would have sent a note."

The woman nodded. "I should have written you. After all, I did know your address."

Susan blushed harder. "Becky's house. Yes. We don't live there anymore—it was hit, I'm afraid. A total ruin."

Mrs. Montgomery made an exasperated noise. "This wretched war. I know I should have written. I suppose I was waiting for you to take the first step.

When you never came to visit I assumed you'd moved on."

"I didn't think you wanted me to visit," Susan said. "I didn't think I would be welcome."

Mrs. Montgomery drew in her breath. "Perhaps not by my husband, I'll admit. But you and I—we could always have sat in the garden, you know. We could have talked about her. I would have liked that."

I said, "We can do that now."

Jamie said, "We loved Becky too."

A small smile began to spread across the woman's wrinkled face. "Did you?" she said.

"Yes," I said. "We can go sit in your garden and talk about why."

"So we can," she said. "So we can."

She turned on her heel and began to walk away. We followed. "I just bought tea," she said, "and I've got a spoonful or two of sugar, and some biscuits I've been saving. And jam! I still have half a jar of jam. We'll make tea and sit in the garden." She extended a hand to Jamie. "How do you know Becky? You can't have known her, or I would have known about you."

"Susan tells us stories," Jamie said.

"Does she? I could tell you more."

I slipped back a step and took Susan's elbow. "You see?" I said.

Ahead of us Jamie asked, "Do you have other children?"

"No," Mrs. Montgomery said. "No. She was all I had."

"I see," Susan said to me. "I can't believe it, but I see."

Now Jamie was talking about himself. ". . . a cat named Bovril, and a pig named Mrs. Rochester, and some hens, Petunia, Pansy, and Peter—that's the rooster—and Ada, she's got a pony called Butter—"

Mrs. Montgomery swung around. "You still have Butter?" she said.

"I do," Susan said. "I sold the hunters, but I couldn't bear to part with Butter."

"Oh, Butter." Mrs. Montgomery beamed. "How I loved Butter! We raised him, you know, from a foal."

"I didn't know that—"

"I had so many ponies, once upon a time. I could tell you stories about Butter—"

"You can come visit him!" I said. "You could ride him."

"Oh, my dear—Ada, is it?—I haven't ridden in years."

"Butter would take care of you. He took care of me."

"That he would," she said, "but—"

"Please do come," said Susan. "We've plenty of room."

Becky's mother stopped walking. She studied Susan, and Jamie, and me. "I'll come," she said softly. "I will. It would be good to be among family again."

You can know things all you like, and someday you might believe them.

Author's Note

I never say so specifically, but Lord Thorton, Ruth's father, and Ruth herself were among the famous codebreakers of Bletchley Park, who cracked Nazi spy codes, including the "unbreakable" Enigma. Their work was top secret for years after the war, but is now widely known, and fascinating. You can learn more at bletchleypark.org.uk.

At the end of this story, Lord Thorton says that he has information that makes him feel that the war was entirely justified, that Hitler had to be stopped. Although Hitler's laws against Jews and other groups he deemed undesirable were well known from the start of the war, the full truth about the German death camps and the Holocaust only became public much later and more gradually. By July of 1942, however, the *London Daily Telegraph* could report that over one million Jewish people had already been killed by the Nazis, and, at government level, the full horror of the genocide was becoming known.

The Holocaust is a difficult and painful topic to research, but a very important one. Start with Yad Vashem (yadvashem.org), the World Holocaust Remembrance Center begun in 1953 for documentation, research, education, and commemoration of this global tragedy.

Kimberly Brubaker Bradley, a longtime Anglophile, first became interested in World War II evacuees when her mother read *Bedknobs and Broomsticks* out loud at bedtime. Her historical fiction has garnered great acclaim: *The War that Saved My Life* was a Newbery Honor Book, and won the Schneider Family Book Award, the Josette Frank Award, and an Odyssey Award; *Jefferson's Sons* was an ALA Notable Book and received four starred reviews; *Ruthie's Gift* was a *PW* Flying Start; and *For Freedom* was an IRA Teachers' Choice and Bank Street College Best Book of the Year. Ms. Bradley and her husband have two grown children and live on a fifty-two-acre horse farm in Bristol, Tennessee.

www.kimberlybrubakerbradley.com